DAKITI

ZIVA PAYVAN BOOK 1

EJ FISCH

Transcendence
Publishing

First edition: June 2014

If you would like to use material from the book, prior written permission must be obtained by contacting the publisher at transcendence.publishing@gmail.com.

The Transcendence Publishing name, imprint, and logo are trademarks of Transcendence Publishing.

ISBN-13: 978-0692230954
ISBN-10: 0692230955

DAKITI

· 1 ·
DAKITI MEDICAL RESEARCH CENTER
SARDONIS

"Hold still, now," the medical bot repeated in its monotone, mechanical voice. It leaned over him, nothing but a cold form against the blinding light above. He felt himself drifting out of consciousness again until the needle penetrated his skin just above his left elbow. He opened his mouth to scream as the burning sensation spread up his arm and into his shoulder, but no sound emerged. Maybe he had gone deaf...no, he'd obviously heard the bot speak. He gagged, spitting bile out over his chin. The restraints on his wrists and ankles seemed tighter than usual when he struggled against them.

"Hold still," the bot commanded again, clamping a metallic claw over his bicep. "Relax."

He gritted his teeth as the burning sensation migrated into his face and chest. With as many times as they'd done this to him, he thought it might no longer have an effect, yet it did. Everything around him was a blur, but this was perhaps the most awake he had been in all the times they'd brought him in here. How long had it been? Weeks? Months? *Years?* He couldn't recall ever being fully conscious. In fact, all he could remember was this room—this cold, pure white room and the strange beeping he could hear whenever they made him lie down on this table.

Somewhere around him, a door slid open, something that had never happened while he was there. A musty, salty scent filled the room—he was surprised he even remembered what salt smelled like. Desperate to see what was going on, he fluttered his eyelids and tried to sit up, but it was no use.

"How is he holding up?" a man asked in a strange accent.

Two shadows passed over him and blocked out the light. He struggled to see but his eyes glazed over and he felt his muscles relax. A desperate attempt to speak was thwarted when another needle jabbed into his throat. He gasped for air for a moment, and then the white room disappeared.

· 2 ·
HSP HEADQUARTERS
NORO, HAPHEZ

N oro, Haphez. People knew that name, perhaps because it was the planet's largest city and the site of Haphez's busiest spaceport. Maybe it was because it was named after the planet's sun and the star system in which it was located, or because everyone on this side of the galaxy knew of its notorious reputation. In any case, it was a sprawling city, home to over eight million people and stretching from the banks of the Tranyi River to the edge of the Tasmin Forest. Although it lacked the sparkling elegance of the Haphezian capital Haphor, a person still couldn't help but be intrigued by the city's towering structures and mysterious energies.

A thick fog had settled in on this particular morning, sending a chill through the air. A low hum could be heard far above as shuttles and aircars traveled about among the buildings, though the vehicles themselves were invisible in the haze. The sun was nothing more than a pale yellow disk that struggled to warm the earth through the dense cloud cover and the planet's thick atmosphere. The headquarters of the Haphezian Special Police loomed ahead, rising high above the fog and dwarfing the other buildings on the west side of Lakin Square. Parked cars filled the docking bays, and more hovered around the complex, waiting for a chance to settle in. It was the first day of a new service term, and operations agents from all seven of HSP's regional offices were reporting in to receive their new assignments. There was a certain tension in the air that seemed almost tangible.

The fog swirled around her heavy boots as she crossed the street, studying HSP's impressive campus as she walked. The Haphezian climate always took some getting used to after spending an entire service term doing contract work on the desert world of Aubin. She took a deep breath of crisp air and made her way up the long staircase to the front door of the headquarters' main building, acknowledging the guards as she slipped her identification key over the scanner and continued by. The holographic screen of her communicator lit up as the system processed her login information, displaying bold red text: WELCOME LIEUTENANT PAYVAN. REPORT IMMEDIATELY TO ASSIGNMENT TERMINAL.

She sighed and tilted her head. *Back to the same old grind.* Pocketing the communicator, she continued moving and fell anonymously into place among the rest of the agents heading upstairs.

· 3 ·
HSP HEADQUARTERS
NORO, HAPHEZ

A roska Tarbic took a deep breath and shifted his weight to his other leg for what seemed like the thousandth time. Despite the fact that he'd found the shortest available line for an assignment terminal, it still felt as though he'd been standing there for hours. He'd stood in line and received plenty of new assignments throughout his career, but never before had he done it alone, no doubt the reason time seemed to be dragging. It had been three months—a whole service term—since the explosion that had claimed the lives of his two teammates. He'd retained his title as lieutenant of the Alpha field operations team but had been assigned to the Solaris Control Unit, a special task force that tracked and monitored the local radical group responsible for planting the bomb that had killed Jole Imetsi and Tate Luver. As much as he enjoyed the position and the chance to avenge his friends' deaths, it was temporary at best, and there was no telling what the agency would do with him now.

The dull buzz of murmuring voices filled the commons where the assignment terminals had been set up. Everyone seemed more on edge than usual today, but maybe it only seemed that way because Aroska himself was on edge. He took a brief look around. There were the young agents who had just graduated from HSP's brutal training camp, eager to accept their first missions. He had to chuckle; some of them still sported bruises and bandages after their final combat test. Then there were the other lieutenants who stood patiently with their teammates, faces expressionless as they waited to see what challenges they would face next. Finally, there were the standalone agents, those like Aroska who had lost team members or had been holding temporary positions. Their faces were all devoid of any emotion, but each of them had a twinkle of anticipation in their eyes.

"What are you thinking about?"

The sound of Adin Woro's voice pulled Aroska from his thoughts. He turned and found the Beta team's lieutenant standing beside him, arms folded across his chest as he too surveyed the crowd.

"I suppose I'm trying not to think about *anything*," Aroska replied with a shrug.

"You plan on sticking around?"

"I put in a petition to continue my work with Solaris, but in the end, the decision isn't up to me." Aroska gestured ahead; only two people stood between him and the assignment terminal. "I guess we'll find out here in a minute."

Adin was quiet for a moment, no doubt sensing the emptiness Aroska felt without Tate and Jole there. The Alpha and Beta teams had been close, and Adin had always embraced Aroska's squad as if they were his own teammates. "I spoke with the director. He's agreed to let you stay on as a priority field ops reserve agent, regardless of what you find out today. I'd be happy to have you serving with us, and it's always nice to have someone you trust watching your back."

"I'd like that," Aroska said, feeling a bit better. "Have you already checked in?"

Adin forced a nervous chuckle. "Yes, we...we made Alpha team." He added a respectful dip of his head, aware it was a somewhat sensitive subject.

Aroska hoped his disappointment wasn't as apparent as it felt. He was by no means angry—the shuffling of personnel just meant his chances of ever leading a field ops team again had been reduced to nothing. If he'd been given a choice, however, he would have picked Adin's team as his replacement anyway.

"Hey man, that's really great," he said, shaking his friend's hand and masking his feelings with the most sincere smile he could muster.

"Congratulations, you deserve it."

"Thanks." Adin nodded toward the assignment terminal. "Looks like you're up."

Aroska swallowed and stepped forward, feeling the apprehension settle in like a cloud hovering above him. He swiped his identification key and lowered his eye to the optical scanner, then waited a moment for his information to process. After several uncomfortably long seconds, his profile appeared on the screen and his eyes went to work. PRIMARY DEPARTMENT: SOLARIS CONTROL UNIT. *Well, this is a good start.* The cloud of anxiety began to dissipate, and he released the breath he hadn't realized he'd been holding. ASSIGNMENT: SPECIAL OPERATIONS JOINT TASK FORCE. He lifted an eyebrow. *Interesting.* So rarely did the high-and-mighty special ops agents willingly accept a field investigator into their ranks. He could only imagine what the process of setting up this arrangement had been like. Regardless of how the spec ops team felt about him, this was an extraordinary opportunity and he found he couldn't fight away the smile spreading across his face.

REPORT TO SPECIAL OPERATIONS LIEUTENANT ZIVA PAYVAN FOR FURTHER INSTRUCTIONS.

Everything around him seemed to grind to a halt, and the only sounds to be heard were his own heartbeat and a dull ringing in his ears. He squeezed his eyes shut as an image of his younger brother, with dead eyes staring vacantly upward, tore through his memory. He could still hear the moist *thump* of the bullet striking Soren's head, smell the blood that splattered over their café table, feel the heat leeching from the young military engineer's body as he died in Aroska's arms. The same adrenaline that had surged through his veins as he looked wildly about for the shooter surged through him again now, and he took a step away from the terminal to keep from slamming his fists against it.

That had been two years ago. He'd heard the name plenty of times since then—*Ziva Payvan, Ziva Payvan, Ziva Payvan*—the name of Soren's killer. She'd been the Cleaner selected to carry out his death sentence, the death sentence he never should have been given. People said she was ruthless, brutal, that she'd get the job done no matter the cost. Supposedly, she was the best spec ops had to offer. But Aroska had never had the great privilege of meeting her. In fact, he'd never even *seen* her. He'd brought up her personnel file more times than he could remember and had wasted hours staring at the redacted paragraphs and blank space where her image should have been. Even as a field ops lieutenant, he was still outranked by the spec ops division's lowest-ranking intelligence officers, and his clearance level wasn't high enough to grant him access to their information. Half the people around him at the assignment terminals could be special ops and he wouldn't even know it. They were a secretive bunch; in the rest of HSP's eyes, they were merely anonymous agents. But regardless of his clearance level and how long it took to find her, Aroska had vowed that Ziva Payvan's life would end on the day he finally caught up to her.

Adin had worked with her once—she'd chosen the Beta squad to collaborate with her team thanks to certain intel they had. He'd been quick to praise her skill and marksmanship, at least until Aroska had shared the information about Soren's death and his plans for revenge. Adin had laughed at first, but he'd shut up after realizing the seriousness of the situation, refusing to reveal anything he knew about Payvan or her team.

"It's for your own good," he'd always said. "You're no match against her."

Aroska was vaguely aware of someone speaking to him, asking what was wrong, but the words were hardly more than an echo in the back of his mind. The pressure of Adin's hand on his arm was what finally brought him out of his trance.

"Oh *sheyss*," Adin muttered after getting a look at the screen. "Here, come on, let's move."

It was all Aroska could do to force his feet forward as his mind struggled to process exactly what was happening. Adin took him by the shoulders and led him away, shooting apologetic glances at the other agents who had been waiting behind them in line. They paused in the hallway that led to the elevator bank, waiting for some passersby to clear the vicinity before speaking.

"I don't even know what to say," Adin said. "If you—"

"Just stop," Aroska snapped, fending off another memory of cradling Soren's dead body. "Stop it. There's nothing you can say that'll fix this."

Adin lifted his hands in surrender and took a step back. "I know. I just wish there was something I could do to help."

"Why would they do this? What the hell were they thinking?"

"They were thinking you're the best agent the SCU's got," Adin said, crossing his arms. "They were thinking there's no possible way you could know Ziva killed Soren and that you'd be a great asset to whatever operation she's running. You think the director would purposely give you this assignment if he knew the circumstances? You can't think of yourself as a victim here."

Good old Adin, always knowing exactly what to say in any situation. That was why he was one of HSP's best negotiators. It was he who had talked Aroska into joining the Solaris Control Unit in the first place as a constructive way of dealing with the loss of Jole and Tate. Somehow, no matter how blunt he was, his words always managed to put Aroska's mind at ease.

"I've got to talk to someone about this," he said.

"Are you kidding?" Adin hissed, his dark gray eyes frantic. "The Cleaners' identities are always confidential. If anyone finds out you know, if anyone finds out you told *me*, our careers will be over!"

Aroska sighed. "What else am I supposed to do? I can't do this. I can't work with her. Did you know my father was accused of being a co-conspirator in that investigation against Soren? Someone tried to take him out even after I cleared his name. I'm almost positive it was Payvan again."

"Look," Adin said quietly, resting his hands on his hips. "I can't possibly imagine how you're feeling right now, but Ziva's the best this agency's got. I may have only worked with her once, but that was enough to give me a great deal of respect for her. Just try to put the past behind you and get through this mission. It will be over soon enough. Let it go."

"Let Soren's *death* go?" Aroska said, ready to storm away. "I cannot believe you just said that. I'm going to the director."

"You know that's not what I meant." Adin stepped around and cut him off. He was quiet for a moment before heaving a sigh. "Okay, if you really want to take this to Emeri, at least do it with a clear head. You'll be in deep enough *sheyss* when he finds out what you know. No need to add a temper tantrum and reckless behavior to your discharge paperwork." He winked.

Aroska nodded and took a deep breath, slowly letting it out through his nose. That was a good point, after all.

Adin clapped him on the shoulder and the two of them slowly continued toward the elevators. Most were crowded with people trying to get back to their respective squad floors after the excitement of receiving their new assignments. One of the cars at the end of the row was clear so they moved toward it, waiting patiently as it descended to their floor.

"Tell you what," Adin said as they stepped aside to let the elevator's occupants out. "You go talk to the director and then we'll go get something to eat. See if we can't ease your mind a bit."

Aroska almost didn't hear him, preoccupied by the lone woman who emerged from the elevator. She somehow seemed familiar, but he couldn't recall ever seeing her before. She was broad-shouldered and muscular, but despite her thick build there was a certain gracefulness in the way she moved. An HSP badge dangled from her hand, eliminating the possibility that she was a new recruit, and she wore a black field jacket that complemented her figure nicely. She was taller than most women Aroska knew, though he still had several centimeters on her, and looked athletic. But it wasn't her size, build, or clothing that caught his attention. It was her eyes. They were a deep crimson, and there was something strangely fascinating about them that he couldn't put his finger on. He'd seen plenty of red Haphezian eyes before, but these were different. They were fiery and intense, yet full of wisdom and curiosity at the same time.

For a moment she seemed startled by their presence, but she acknowledged them with a nod and turned down the corridor toward the commons and assignment terminals. Aroska watched her go until he realized he was staring, or until Adin pulled him into the elevator with a scolding grunt—he wasn't quite sure which came first.

"Something to eat—good idea," he said, struggling for a moment to remember what they'd even been talking about.

They continued the ride in silence, with Adin staring straight ahead and Aroska trying to decide why the strange woman had affected him in such away. He realized that, if only for a moment, he'd completely forgotten about the whole ordeal with Soren and Ziva Payvan, odd considering the subject had consumed him for much of the past two years. Adin had always teased him about having an eye for the ladies, and maybe that was part of it, but at the same time it felt like there was more to it than that.

He drew a breath, ready to ask if Adin had any idea who the woman was, but he hesitated when he noticed his friend's behavior. He was standing bolt upright, arms crossed in a defensive manner, one foot tapping against the floor. Aroska couldn't fathom what he could possibly be nervous about, especially after he'd been trying to make light of the situation only moments before. He found himself wondering if he was missing out on something important, and that familiar cloud of anxiety began to form again. "Who was that?" he finally asked.

"Don't you already have a girlfriend?" Adin muttered. His voice lacked the joking undertone the response might normally have warranted.

That didn't answer his question, but the elevator opened onto the director's private floor before he could ask for a more thorough explanation. Aroska stepped out, drawing quick glances from the executive aides at their stations. With a shrug, he turned back to Adin in the elevator. "Meet you in a few minutes," he said. "Wish me luck."

An overwhelming sense of déjà vu settled over him as he walked across the foyer toward the main office. For a brief moment, he was whisked back to two years earlier when he'd stormed out of the same elevator, clothes sweaty and bloodstained, ready to march into that office and demand an explanation for Soren's death. He hesitated outside the door just as he had then, still able to hear Emeri Arion's angry voice echoing through his memory.

To this day, Aroska still wasn't sure who the director had been on comm with that afternoon. He also wasn't sure what had possessed him to put his ear to the door and listen in on the muffled conversation, possibly the dumbest decision he'd ever made throughout his career. It had no doubt been due in part to his raging emotions and the fact that he was willing to go to any length for some answers. What he *did* know was that he'd gleaned several important pieces of information thanks to his eavesdropping.

"We have a situation," the director had been saying. "Ziva Payvan killed Soren Tarbic." There'd been a short pause, accompanied by the sound of footfalls as he'd paced back and forth across the room. "Yes, we received the data from Lieutenant Tarbic." More silence. "No, she wasn't. She shouldn't have even been there."

That had been enough for Aroska that day. He'd rushed away right then and there, fueled by this new knowledge he held, knowledge he'd only ever shared with Adin. Telling anyone else what he knew would cost him his job, and his job was the only way he'd ever catch up with Payvan and confront her. Today, however, he went ahead and knocked on the door, still driven by that same knowledge but finally ready to come clean.

A stifled voice bid him enter and he let himself in, allowing his eyes a moment to adjust to the office's dim lighting. The majority of the room's illumination came from the natural sunlight streaming in through the massive picture window on the far wall. Aroska had only been in the office on a couple of occasions, but he'd always been impressed by the view out that window; a person could see all the way across the city to where the sunlight glistened off the waters of the mighty Tranyi River. He imagined the director probably got a lot of thinking done while looking through that glass.

"Lieutenant, come in. What can I do for you?" Emeri Arion rose from his desk and beckoned for Aroska to come closer. He'd been the prime director of HSP—ranking even higher than the other directors at the agency's regional offices—since before Aroska had been employed there. He was generally well liked and respected, despite the fact that he was rather reclusive and rarely ventured beyond the walls of his office. Still, he knew all the operations agents by name and kept close tabs on all their major missions. As always, he was impeccably dressed in his

HSP dress blues, and the two turquoise stripes that ran through his graying hair were combed perfectly into place.

Aroska politely declined when Emeri offered him a chair. He felt numb again, unsure how the director would respond to what he was about to say. There was a good chance he could lose his job or even be imprisoned because of what he knew, but if he chose to stay quiet, the only way to successfully avoid working with Payvan would be to resign anyway.

Might as well get on with it, he thought. He crossed his arms and took a step back from the director's desk. "Ziva Payvan?"

A flicker of uncertainty flashed across Emeri's teal eyes. "So you received your assignment."

"She killed my brother."

If Emeri was shocked, he concealed it well. He remained completely silent for a long time, his mouth a straight line as he stared Aroska down. Finally, he cleared his throat and clasped his hands behind his back. "Lieutenant, you know as well as I do that the identity of the Cleaner assigned to carry out a death sentence is kept confidential. What makes you so sure it was Payvan?"

Aroska sighed and reluctantly explained how he had overheard the director's conversation on the day of Soren's murder, carefully avoiding the fact that he'd told Adin. Emeri stood with closed eyes, massaging his forehead for the duration of the story.

"Soren was innocent!" Aroska cried, recalling Adin's warning about losing his temper. "I submitted the evidence that proved it!"

"Evidence you weren't supposed to *have*," Emeri said, voice quiet but firm. "You were benched from the investigation because of your relationship with the convict. On top of that, his grace period was up. You missed the deadline. A Cleaner could have struck at any time."

"But HSP received my data before Soren was killed!"

"Yes we did, but—"

"So Payvan killed him even when she knew he was innocent! That *shouka* murdered my brother, and she tried to kill my father!"

"At ease, Tarbic," Emeri snapped. "You don't know as much as you think you do. She's the best operative HSP's got."

Aroska began to reply but was cut off when the office door burst open. The woman from the elevator stormed into the room, face contorted with frustration similar to what he himself was feeling. She bristled and stopped dead in her tracks when she saw him there, silently regarding him with those striking red eyes. Her presence made his stomach churn, but now it wasn't out of excitement as it had first been at the elevator. Thinking back on Adin's reaction and considering her current behavior, he was beginning to wonder if she was...*she isn't, is she?* The office fell totally silent as the two of them held eye contact.

"I'd appreciate it if you'd knock, Lieutenant," Emeri finally said, unimpressed.

Aroska's heart sank. *I should have known.* This powerful, attractive creature who had briefly distracted him from his troubles was also the ruthless monster responsible for the death of his brother. If not for the fact that he was paralyzed by rage, he would have lunged across the room and strangled her then and there, Emeri be damned.

Maintaining her rigid posture, Payvan began to move in a slow, wide circle around them, looking Aroska up and down as she went. She was certainly solid, with strong arms and long, powerful legs. She wore her jet-black hair pulled back into a tight braid, and she bore a long scar beside her left eye that Aroska somehow hadn't noticed earlier. She finally shifted her penetrating gaze to Emeri, who looked rather chagrined.

"Welcome home—I trust your missions were successful," he said, adding a sharp nod in Aroska's direction. *He knows.* "I'm sure you remember Lieutenant Tarbic."

"I do," she replied in a gravelly alto voice that sent chills down Aroska's spine. She turned toward him again, though she was still clearly addressing Emeri. "I must say he looked better through my rifle scope." She watched him through narrowed eyes and traced invisible crosshairs through the air with her fingers.

Aroska ignored her and turned back to the director, completely numb. The rage welling up inside him had tied a knot in his throat, rendering him speechless. He watched Emeri with wide eyes, unsure what the director could do to fix the situation but hoping he'd at least do *something.* The older man stared back, clearly at a loss. There must have been something truly special about Payvan if she could successfully shut down the veteran director of the planet's finest police force.

"Can I help you with something, Lieutenant?" he finally said. "Because if not, we're trying to carry on a conversation here."

Aroska was startled by the feeling of warm air on the back of his neck. He realized Payvan was now standing directly behind him, her mouth mere centimeters from his ear. The fact that he hadn't even noticed her move made his stomach flop. He tensed, ready to bring his elbow back against her face, but she caught his shoulder with a firm hand.

"I'd go take Adin up on that breakfast offer before things get *really* awkward," she whispered, digging her fingers into his collarbone and squeezing just hard enough to make him wince.

He tore away from her, not about to let the hands that had spilled his brother's blood touch him for longer than necessary. She kept her eyes locked with his, demanding his obedience without having to speak a word. A wave of nausea washed through him when he realized he was the first to break eye contact. He'd allowed her to take control of the situation, and she had gladly done so. *Fine, you win this round.* Blood boiling, he brushed past her and headed for the door. He could hear Emeri calling after him as he went, but he was done there, at least for the time being.

· 4 ·

Haphor–Noro Traffic Lane

Tasmin Forest, Haphez

The mid-morning breeze was already warm and carried with it a sweet scent Jayden Saiffe didn't recognize. He guessed it was coming from the bushes across the clearing from where their cars were parked, the ones with the bright pink blossoms bigger than his head. The local flora and fauna made the Haphezian jungle nearly as beautiful as the planet's cities, in some cases more so, considering the jungle didn't have the noise of traffic or the seedy underbelly.

Jayden finished stretching his back and leaned up against the car he'd been riding in, gazing off into the trees where his father and two of their guards stood studying a flock of colorful birds. Enrik Saiffe had halted their entire convoy upon spotting them—this was the second time in two hours that they had stopped to look at wildlife or scenery. Jayden appreciated the sights as much as anyone, but these stops were making the four-hour trip from Haphor to Noro even longer, and he was looking forward to getting the journey over with.

Several more security personnel milled about in the clearing, wandering to and fro among the three parked cars. One in particular, Captain of the Guard Gavin Bront, approached Jayden with an understanding twinkle in his eye. He was just as tired of the pit stops, but he did a better job of hiding his impatience. "How are you doing, sir?"

"Not as well as *he* is," Jayden sighed, gesturing off toward his father.

Bront chuckled. "The governor is an enthusiastic man. In the mere two weeks we've been here, he's come to love this planet. The opportunity for diplomacy means a lot to him."

Jayden lifted an eyebrow. "I just hope it's worth it. The Haphezians must be desperate to get their hands on the resources Tantal has to offer. Otherwise I can't imagine they'd ever want anything to do with a human colony."

"You don't think it will work out?"

"Don't get me wrong. Forming an alliance with these people is better than anything we could have hoped for. Military support in exchange for a few minerals is quite the deal. But I doubt the Haphezians have any real interest in babysitting a bunch of humans, especially when we're from a system in a completely different sector. When it comes down to it, I just hope they'll hold up their end of the bargain."

"Your caution is understandable, sir," Bront said. He hesitated and lowered his voice. "Do they know we've been friendly to the Resistance in the past?"

"They'd better not. *Nobody* is supposed to know about that." While that was true, Jayden had never exactly been sure what the Haphezians had against the Resistance in the first place. It was nothing but a band of freedom fighters from various worlds who opposed the Federation, the governing entity that unified many of the galaxy's civilized systems. As far as he knew, the real problem was the Nosti, a sect of Resistance fighters who had been introduced to a chemical called nostium that gave them telekinetic abilities. They were agile warriors who specialized in melee combat with kytaras, small but deadly double-bladed retractable swords. Jayden had never met a Nosti, and while he respected their skills, the ability to manipulate objects with the mind was just a bunch of hocus pocus as far as he was concerned. Still, it was no joking matter on Haphez. Ever since the Federation had retaliated against the Resistance and made the use of nostium illegal, the Haphezians had made it clear that the group was not welcome on the planet. They arrested and deported any known members, and Nosti were usually executed on the spot.

The best explanation Jayden could think of was that the Noro system was situated on the very edge of populated space—a Fringe System—and thus Haphez wasn't part of the Federation. Any sign of

Resistance presence on the planet would attract unwelcome Federation attention. The Haphezians didn't actually have anything to hide as far as he knew; they were just very private, protective of their culture and skeptical of outsiders.

The governor and his two guards were finally making their way back to the convoy, accompanied by the Haphezian man who had volunteered to guide them from Haphor to Noro. He was unarmed at Bront's request, but he towered over everyone and was burly enough that Jayden didn't doubt his ability to handle himself regardless of whether he had a weapon. He'd rolled up his jacket sleeves at some point during the journey, revealing an elaborate star tattoo on his forearm. Jayden still couldn't get over how commonplace body modifications were with the Haphezians; nearly everyone he'd met had some sort of tattoo or abnormal piercing, in addition to the dotted tattoos they all wore on their faces. *As if their colored eyes and hair stripes aren't strange enough*, he thought.

"With respect, I must insist we get moving," the guide said in Standard, his accent thick. He continued muttering to himself in Haphezian as he veered toward the lead car.

Enrik paid him no mind and continued to laugh along with his escorts. "Isn't this planet beautiful?" he said to no one in particular, clapping Jayden hard on the back. "You could live here for years and not even see half of what it has to offer."

"And we'll never get to see that other half if we don't make it to Noro in time for our meeting," Jayden reminded him, pointedly checking the time. "The Haphezians already think we're incom-petent. How will it look if we can't even keep a schedule?"

"Son, you worry too much," Enrik said with a sigh, putting his arm around the young man's shoulder. "No more stops, I promise."

Bront ushered them into the back of the car and then slid into the pilot's seat. The silence of the jungle was broken as the three vehicles roared to life and lifted from the ground, then took off in the direction of Noro.

· 5 ·
TARBIC RESIDENCE
NORO, HAPHEZ

Lieutenant Aroska Tarbic: a formidable young man—well, no, he was actually older than her. Tall, able-bodied, and, admittedly, not bad looking. When she'd first seen his name in her assignment description, Ziva hadn't quite known what to think. First of all, there had never been more than three agents on an ops team in the history of HSP. While this joint task force was only temporary, it still meant having a team of four for anywhere up to three months. She had handpicked her teammates after training and the three of them had held high positions in special ops for years, bonding into a single unstoppable unit. She wasn't sure what would happen when someone like Tarbic was thrown into the mix.

The biggest problem was the fact that he wanted her head on a platter. She'd always assumed he'd somehow found out she was responsible for his brother's death; the circumstances surrounding the shooting had set the special ops division abuzz for a while and it wouldn't have surprised her if information got leaked. She'd also received a notification that someone in field ops had tried—and failed—numerous times to access her profile, and she'd traced the attempts back to him. The field ops clearance level was inadequate for him to actually learn anything of course, but it had unnerved her all the same. She hadn't been sure exactly what he knew or how he knew it, but if he was seeking her out, it had to mean something.

Ziva watched as he took a bottle of liquor from the cooler and poured himself a glass, completely oblivious to her presence. She'd made herself at home on his sofa and had contented herself with reading through several of his data pads during the past hour. Tarbic had finally emerged from his bedroom just a moment earlier, hair rumpled, dressed in pajama pants. Twenty-six hours had passed since their encounter in Emeri Arion's office, but she doubted his attitude toward her had changed at all during that time. She'd stayed and pleaded with the director for a replacement Solaris expert—the reason she'd rushed into his office in the first place—but he'd stood fast in his decision despite the information that had come to light regarding Soren's death.

"Solaris is the real threat here," he'd said.

Tarbic tilted his head back and swallowed his drink, setting the empty glass down on the table with a *thud*. Brushing his shaggy black hair out of his face, he wiped his mouth and turned around, startled when he spotted her sitting in the shadows. His hand went immediately to his hip, reaching for a nonexistent pistol.

"It's a little early for that, isn't it?" she said, shooting him a quick glance over the top of the data pad.

Tarbic relaxed; unless it was her imagination, he almost looked relieved when he realized who she was. "What do you want?" he muttered.

"I think we should talk about our situation," she replied, putting the data pad away and crossing one leg over the other.

"Talk about our situation," he mimicked with a wry chuckle. He picked up a shirt that had been draped over the back of a chair and tugged it over his head. "I'm not stupid. You're not here to talk— you're just following orders."

Ziva smirked. "Very good," she praised, "but let's not be so harsh, shall we? Let's say the director gave me orders to come talk to you, and I complied. Care to hear me out?"

"Do I have a choice?"

She shrugged. "Sure, but if you have any desire to keep your job, I suggest you listen up."

Tarbic let out a reluctant sigh and crossed his arms, waiting.

She stood up and began to pace in front of him. "I talked to Emeri after you left yesterday. He's not happy that you know who I am, but considering the circumstances, he's decided to let bygones be bygones and keep you around. He's bent on keeping the logistics of this assignment the way they are, so don't bother whining about it. Trust me, if I could change anything, I would.

"But the mission is simple: we're hitting a Solaris stronghold and taking out one of their leaders, and you can provide us with the intel we need. Emeri tells me you're the best the SCU has to offer, and I settle for nothing but the best. I understand you've been in charge of the whole department for the past three months…since the death of your team."

He eyed her thoughtfully for a moment. "Was it you? I'll bet if I did a little research, I'd find that the day they died was the exact same day you left for your last assignment. Convenient."

Ziva stopped pacing. "What the hell are you talking about?" she demanded through clenched teeth. "Give me one good reason why *I* would want to kill *them*."

"They say you like to get inside people's heads, work them over, mentally torture them. I suppose it was you two years ago too, going after my father even after he'd been proven innocent."

"Oh, I'm disappointed," she said, clicking her tongue. "You of all people should know that if it was me, he'd be dead." She paused, taking a step forward to study his face. "You know, Soren looked just like you."

That did it. Tarbic's hand shot out—either to hit her or strangle her, it didn't matter which—but she deflected the blow and stepped back, ready for a full-scale fight. But none came. There was a brief period of silence as the two of them simply stared at each other, jaws set.

"If you say one more word about my brother," Tarbic growled through his teeth, thrusting a finger in her face, "so help me I will make sure you die a slow and painful death and feel every second of it. I'll be there to watch."

He went back to the kitchen and collapsed into one of the dining chairs, hanging his head in frustration. He was right, after all—she *did* like to get inside people's heads. That's what she'd spent the last several minutes doing. It was something she'd worked at since long before her HSP career had even begun, and she liked to think she'd become rather good at it. She watched Tarbic, wondering what he was thinking. His emotion could go both ways—it could motivate him and make him a better agent, or he would be distracted and drag the whole team down. The choice would be his.

"It's nothing personal," Ziva said, unable to suppress the icy edge in her voice. "I was only doing my job."

No response. *How about a different approach?* "You know I went through the initial selection program with Tate and Jole. They were my friends too."

Tarbic looked up, obviously startled by the information, though he was still turned away from her. "I never saw *you* at the memorial."

Ziva moved into the kitchen and stood across the table from him, arms crossed. "The fact that you can't see someone doesn't mean they're not there." She was tempted to make another comment about snipers and his brother but thought better of it. If they were indeed going to be working together, it would be best to start off on more amicable terms.

This time Tarbic made eye contact when he spoke to her. "And why am I supposed to believe any of this?"

"Because you do *not* kill people you went through elite training with," she snapped, slamming her palm against the tabletop. "And believe it or not, I don't kill *anyone* unless I have a good reason." She skirted around the table and seized a fistful of his shaggy hair before he could protest, tilting his head back to ensure she had his undivided attention. "Now you listen carefully. I need you for this mission, and you need me. I'm not your enemy here, but I damn well can be if that's the way you want to play this. Our battle is with Solaris, and when we fight, they win. Do you understand me?"

He composed himself more quickly than she'd expected and only hesitated for a split second before answering. "Yes."

"Good. Now, I'm giving you one chance to take this opportunity.

Are you as good as they say you are? Then prove it. Show up in the situation room for a briefing at twelve hundred hours. If you're not there, I'll have your badge." She released him, pausing long enough to fish a rusty pair of dog tags out of her pocket. Without another word, she dropped them on the table then turned and walked out the front door, leaving him speechless.

· 6 ·
HSP HEADQUARTERS
NORO, HAPHEZ

"**W**hat happened to you yesterday?" Adin Woro called, jogging up beside Aroska as he strode into HSP Headquarters. "I waited for hours. When you didn't show, I tried your communicator—must have tried ten times since then."

"I turned it off," Aroska replied bluntly, not breaking stride.

"Don't scare me like that. For a while there I was afraid she might have killed you."

Aroska threw his friend a cynical glance. "I'm fine. I've decided to go ahead and go through with this mission."

"Are you serious?" Adin exclaimed. "Honestly, I think that's great. Just don't turn around and do something stupid."

Aroska shrugged indignantly and picked up his pace, but Adin caught him by the jacket and pulled him into a vacant elevator. "Don't throw away your career," he warned. "You're no match against her."

It was the same thing he always said. "That's not it," Aroska muttered.

"Then talk to me here."

When he was sure the elevator door was shut, Aroska reached into his pocket and pulled the old military tags out. "Do you know what these are?" he asked, holding them up for Adin to see.

"Your brother's metal?" Adin said. "How did you find these? Weren't they—?"

"The only thing missing from Soren's body when he died," Aroska finished. "Payvan had them. I don't know how she got them, and maybe I don't want to. She left them on my dining room table this morning."

"She was at your house? Are you okay?"

"Not really."

Adin shook his head and handed the tags back to Aroska. "As crazy as it sounds, this might be her way of apologizing. What did you do to make her soften up?"

'Soften up' wasn't exactly the phrase Aroska would have used. "I haven't done a thing. I'd never met her—never even *seen* her—before yesterday. Why would she wait all this time to give them back? I'm telling you, she's just trying to mess with my head."

"You can't let her get to you." Adin sighed, putting an arm over Aroska's shoulder as the elevator reached its destination. The door slid open and they stepped out onto the squad floor. "You've experienced some horrible things, and words cannot express how sorry I am for everything that's happened to you. But the fact that you've persevered through it all says a lot. I know it won't be easy, but I'm sure you can get through this, too."

Aroska took one last look at Soren's tags before returning them to his pocket. "She killed my brother, Adin. He died in my arms."

Adin stopped walking and faced him, hands clamped firmly over his shoulders. "Ziva obviously knows what you've been through. She may not be very personable, and it's not right for her to manipulate you like this, but maybe she's testing you. It's possible she just wants to see if you can overcome this the way you've overcome everything else. Think of it this way: working with her team is an amazing opportunity for *you*. Ignore *her*. Focus on yourself and how you can do your job to the best of your ability. Promise me you'll try."

"I will," Aroska said, hoping this encounter hadn't made him late for his meeting. He brushed Adin's hands away and glanced toward the situation room. "I promise," he added in response to the man's doubtful look.

Adin smiled and patted him on the back before turning back toward the elevator. "Go get her."

Aroska nodded and broke away before he could be delayed any further. He wasn't as concerned with himself as he was for Payvan and what might happen to her if he got a chance to corner her somewhere. He kicked himself for not finishing her inside his own house earlier that morning. Adin was right—he couldn't let her get to his head like that. He couldn't let her win.

As he neared the conference room, he could hear her voice within. The situation was awkward on so many levels. The most obvious reason was the death of his brother. Secondly, having four people on an operations team was unheard of. Maybe that part wouldn't be so bad. It also seemed a little strange to be taking orders from someone younger than him. He wasn't quite sure how old Payvan was, but he had to have a couple of years on her if she'd started training with Jole and Tate.

Mustering up his confidence, Aroska stepped through the open doorway. The other two members of Payvan's team, Sergeant Skeet Duvo and Intelligence Officer Zinnarana Vax, were seated at the long conference table, and Ziva herself was perched on the edge of the table between them. Their conversation ceased abruptly when he entered, making him feel even more self-conscious. Ziva seemed almost annoyed by the interruption but took a look at the time and nodded his way.

"You made it," she said, eyebrows raised.

There was something about her now that didn't seem quite as hostile, though the mere sight of her still made Aroska burn with anger. "You weren't expecting me?"

She got up and motioned for him to take a seat, ignoring his comment. "You're actually just in time," she went on, activating the holographic map in the center of the table. "We've got a bit of a situation here."

Duvo and Vax each offered a friendly greeting and shook Aroska's hand. He'd heard their names before and even recognized them from around the agency campus, but he never would have pegged them for special ops. Vax was tiny by HSP standards and wore dark makeup that made her brilliant cerulean eyes stand out even more than they normally might. Most people called her Zinni, if he'd heard correctly.

Duvo was a brawny man, tall and thick-bodied. His bright orange hair stuck out in all directions, and Aroska wondered if he could possibly fit any more piercings in his ears.

"We received a tip that a Solaris group is massing in the forest about twenty klicks out of the city," Ziva said, directing his attention to the table.

Aroska leaned in and studied the detailed hologram, a three-dimensional map created by the many infrared probes that hovered in the Haphezian atmosphere. The group appeared to be gathered along the bypass that ran parallel to the Haphor-Noro traffic lane, the main transportation route between the spaceport city and the capital. "I've seen this kind of behavior before, just before Solaris ambushed a supply ship transporting weapons off-planet," he said. "They're setting up for an attack. Is anything coming through on the bypass we can't see?"

Zinni manipulated the map for a few seconds, her computer-savvy hands running gracefully over the delicate controls. "I'm picking up an approaching convoy, three vehicles. Estimated time until contact, twenty minutes."

"What kind of convoy?" Ziva asked.

"Passenger," Zinni replied instantly, checking the computer for further information. "Receiving a signal...these are Tantali codes, registered to...the governor's household." She looked up from the computer. "We're looking at Tantali royalty here."

"What?" Skeet said, leaning over her shoulder to get a look for himself. "I didn't think the governor of Tantal was due to arrive until tomorrow."

"Apparently he's here early," Ziva said, "and it certainly doesn't look like Solaris is there to welcome him."

Aroska hadn't heard anything about a visit by the governor of Tantal. "There's no telling what they're planning. These guys are relentless, and it never takes much provocation to fire them up."

At the moment, no one seemed to be paying attention to what he was saying. Ziva had opened a weapon cabinet on the wall and was checking the rifles. Zinni was still at the hologram controls, making calculations and looking for an angle of approach.

"How long until they hit?" Skeet asked, slinging one of the rifle straps over his shoulder.

"Eighteen minutes and counting," Zinni replied. "Our quickest route won't put us there for at least twenty."

Ziva tossed Aroska the last rifle. "Then we'd better get moving." She watched him for a couple of long seconds, almost glaring, almost sarcastic. There was still something fascinating about her eyes, but when he remembered they were the color of Soren's blood, he wanted to gouge them out.

"After you," he muttered.

· 7 ·
20 KILOMETERS WEST OF NORO
TASMIN FOREST, HAPHEZ

Ziva brought the armored car to an abrupt halt along the bypass, narrowly avoiding a collision with a patch of overgrown brush. She jumped out, listening to the sounds of the forest through one ear and Zinni's voice in the other.

"They're two hundred meters dead ahead," the intelligence officer said from her place in the control room at HSP. "I'm seeing about twenty hostiles. You'd better move. I've got an approaching shuttle, ETA ten seconds."

"Copy that, Zinni," Ziva said, motioning for Skeet and Aroska to follow as she began to run.

"Twenty hostiles, huh?" Skeet chuckled. "Sounds like a fair fight."

"Work to neutralize the threat," Ziva ordered. She could hear the hum of the approaching shuttle somewhere above and gunfire further ahead. "Use your judgment. Shoot to kill if necessary. Identify the attackers and do not harm the defenders."

"Got it," Skeet said. Aroska remained quiet but didn't break stride.

"Seventy-five meters and closing," Zinni reminded them. "There's a high concentration of hostiles on the south side of the clearing. Shuttle is touching down. I've got backup and medical on the way."

"Let's go, let's go!" Ziva called. "Skeet, take the right flank, I'll go left. Tarbic, go up the middle. Go in strong—we're outnumbered."

They split off, staying low with rifles raised. Ziva stepped off the road into the bushes, listening. The shuttle was either bringing reinforcements—bad—or was a means of escape for the Solaris attackers—also bad. She broke out of the foliage into the scene of the battle and paused for a split second to take it all in. The dark blue uniforms of the Tantali bodyguards were easy enough to pick out, and those wearing them were all of much smaller stature than the muscular Haphezian insurgents. Blue-white bolts of plasma zinged to and fro, and the stench of charred flesh filled the air.

Ziva turned and took down two hostiles coming at her from the right, somersaulting out of the way of a third. She rose to her feet, unsheathing her knife as she did so, and jammed the blade into the back of the man's neck as he passed. A sizzling green bolt burned through the air mere centimeters from her head and she dove behind one of the convoy's parked cars, firing on the Solaris attackers from cover. *Acquire and fire, acquire and fire, acquire and fire.* The motion was as smooth as it was fast. Her breathing remained slow and steady, her eyes unblinking as she squeezed off round after round, each of which sent a man to the ground.

A steady hum behind her told her the shuttle's boarding ramp was closing and she heard the thrusters kick in as the craft began to lift off. Judging by the number of insurgents who remained in the clearing, the ship had neither brought more nor taken any away. This was good. She recognized the little vessel as Haphezian military-class, probably stolen.

Maybe a third of the Solaris group had already been taken out by the Tantalis, though many of the humans were down as well. Two of them stood back-to-back in the center of the clearing, attempting to pick off their attackers as a unit. They were successful for a while, until the older of the two took a hit to the upper leg and fell to his knees.

Ziva bolted from behind the car with the intention of grabbing the younger Tantali, but he turned and fixed his sights on her, startled. She took aim with her own weapon, ready to neutralize him if needed, but Aroska appeared behind him and disarmed him, closing a massive arm around his throat.

"Don't shoot," she heard him say in accented Standard. "We're here to help."

Free of that distraction, Ziva swept the scene again and nailed two more insurgents. Skeet did the same on the other side of the clearing, and all was suddenly silent except for the distant hum of the shuttle as it disappeared into the sky. Ziva placed a finger on her earpiece and watched it go. "Zinni, see if you can get a reading on that ship. Solaris attackers are down. How far out is that medical team?"

"Two minutes," Zinni replied. "Are these people Tantali like we thought?"

"Definitely of the Tantali royal house," Ziva confirmed. She glanced over at the young man, who was tending to his friend while Skeet and Aroska cleared the area. "We'll keep you posted."

She took a couple of cautious steps toward him. His eyes widened when he saw her coming and he reached for the pistol he'd dropped when Aroska grabbed him. Ziva had her rifle back to her shoulder in a flash, her finger hovering over the trigger. "I don't want to shoot you, kid," she said in flawless Tantali, "but I will if I have to."

"Put the gun down!" Skeet ordered as he and Aroska came around behind him.

Breathing heavily, he did as he was told, though he didn't seem convinced of their intentions. He looked to be in his early twenties, had neatly-trimmed blonde hair, and was dressed like a prince. His bright blue eyes were intelligent yet terrified, but he still seemed ready to use his pistol—and use it well.

"Who are you people?" he stammered, his gaze flitting back and forth between the three of them as he sucked in shallow, raspy breaths and rubbed his chest.

Ziva lowered her rifle but motioned for Skeet and Aroska to keep theirs at the ready. "Lieutenant Payvan, Sergeant Duvo, and Lieutenant Tarbic, Haphezian Special Police," she replied. "And who might you be?"

"My name is Jayden Saiffe," he wheezed.

"Saiffe?" Skeet said. "As in Governor Enrik Saiffe?"

Jayden nodded. "He's my father. We're on a diplomatic tour of the planet, and we were on our way from Haphor to Noro when our convoy was attacked." He paused a moment and took a look around at the dead insurgents. "They took my father."

So that's what the shuttle had been for. "Solaris took him?" Ziva asked, looking around as well.

"Solaris," Jayden echoed as if he didn't understand.

"They're a local supremacist group that opposes forming alliances with other cultures," Aroska explained. "They're terrorists who specialize, if you will, in attacks on diplomacy."

"Any idea what Solaris would want with your father?" Ziva asked, cutting Aroska off before he could open his mouth again.

Jayden shook his head. "We stopped here in the clearing because we thought there was something wrong with one of the cars. I guess the man who was supposed to be guiding us was one of them. We were attacked as soon as we stopped, and that shuttle touched down in just a few seconds. They took him before we could do anything." He grimaced as if he were in pain and clutched his chest. "Please, I can't breathe."

"There's less oxygen in our atmosphere than what you're used to," Aroska said, taking Jayden by the shoulders. "You've just had a bit of excitement. Try to slow your breathing."

"Does your atmosphere stink, too?"

Ziva's eyebrows dropped into a scowl. "Excuse me?" But she didn't need her sensitive Haphezian nose to recognize the scent he had indicated. She looked around at the dead bodies surrounding her; they'd released their cha'sen, the chemical secreted by all Haphezians from a gland behind their ears. HSP trained its operatives how to control the release of cha'sen in combat situations, and Ziva realized she was subconsciously holding hers in at that very moment. To her people, it was simply a musty body odor, but many other races—particularly humans—had often described it as the stench of a decaying animal.

"You probably smell cha'sen," Aroska explained as Jayden gagged. "It's a chemical we produce in response to emotions like fear and anxiety. It all discharges at once when we die."

"Look kid," Skeet said, "we need to get you out of here. There's no way of knowing whether they left you on purpose or whether they left in a hurry when they saw us coming."

Ziva was about to agree when she heard more cars approaching form the direction of Noro. "HSP unit, stand down," a voice commanded over the comm channel in their earpieces. "This is medical dispatch. I repeat, stand down."

The three of them complied and moved aside to make way for the emergency vehicles as they flew into the clearing. Ushering Jayden along, they began to walk briskly back down the road to where their own car waited.

"What about the survivors?" the young man asked, looking back over his shoulder.

"The medical unit will transport them back to the city," Skeet explained, retrieving a small oxygen tank from one of the response vehicles and fitting the mask over Jayden's face. "Don't worry about it. They're in good hands."

"We're taking you into protective custody until we get all of this figured out," Ziva said.

They reached the car and she opened the door. Jayden paused, taking one last look toward the scene as if he still wasn't sure who he could trust. Heaving a sigh, he climbed in and shut the door.

"Let's go," Ziva said.

· 8 ·

EAST SUN
NORO SYSTEM

nrik Saiffe was jarred awake when the landing gear of the craft
he rode in struck metal. He blinked and rolled over, vaguely
aware that his hands were bound behind his back. He was on
the floor, surrounded by boots and a strange, salty scent. Rough hands
seized him and hauled him to his feet. The floor of the ship tilted under
him and he shook his head as his captors shoved him down the landing
ramp. Judging by what he could see through his swimming vision, they
were in what appeared to be the docking hangar of a large space cruiser.
The two Haphezians who held him forced him to his knees at the feet of
a man who waited at the bottom of the ramp.

"Welcome, Governor," the stranger said in a smooth accent. He
squatted down to eye level, examining the governor's face. "I trust your
trip was comfortable?"

"Who are you?" Enrik muttered. "Where am I?"

"Ah, how rude of me," the man replied, rising back to a standing
position and motioning for Enrik's captors to let him do the same. Aside
from the accent, he had leathery bluish-gray skin and eerie reptilian eyes.
A sleeveless shirt revealed toned, wiry arms, and it didn't appear that there
was a single hair on his body. *A Sardon.*

"My name is Dane Bothum. Welcome aboard my flagship, the *East
Sun.*"

Enrik's heart collapsed into his stomach. These people weren't
planning on letting him go, not if they were willing to share who and

where they were. He wondered if they'd hold him captive for the remainder of his life or merely kill him, and he wasn't entirely sure which sounded worse. He swallowed. "What do you want from me?"

Bothum waved the two Haphezians away and freed Enrik's hands, leading him out of the docking bay and into a narrow corridor. "I just have a few questions, which you will answer honestly and thoroughly. Then you may be on your way."

Enrik forced a disgusted chuckle, hoping he sounded more confident than he felt. "And how am I supposed to believe *that?*"

"Come now, Governor," Bothum replied with a smirk. "I think you'll find I'm a man of my word. I have no reason to kill you unless you give me one."

They reached a small, dark control room where several more Sardon techs monitored what appeared to be the ship's communications grid. Bothum led Enrik to the main control panel and motioned for him to place his palm against a small scanner. Keeping a wary eye on the Sardon, he reluctantly complied. The scanner read his prints and the Tantali royal database appeared up on the massive monitor above them.

"What is this?" Enrik exclaimed, yanking his hand away. "How did you get this? What do you want from me?"

"I said *I* would be the one asking the questions, Governor," Bothum said, selecting one of the database files. A prompt asking for another palm scan appeared. "It seems your office has recently intercepted a transmission regarding a research facility. You have to understand that I'd rather not have that information floating into the wrong hands, so if you wouldn't mind deleting it—"

"I don't know what you're talking about."

Bothum smiled gently and shook his head. "Now Governor, you're obviously an intelligent man. It's right there on the screen."

"I don't know what that is!" Enrik said, staring in confusion at the entry Bothum had indicated. "I don't remember seeing anything about a research facility."

"Then why don't you access the file and refresh your memory," Bothum snarled, flashing a set of yellow, incisor-like teeth that turned inward toward each other. He strode over and pressed Enrik's hand back onto the scanner.

The device read his handprint again, but this time the screen flashed red. *ACCESS DENIED. PROPER IDENTIFICATION REQUIRED.*

Enrik wasn't sure whether he should be relieved just yet. He and Bothum both stared at the screen, mystified.

"What does that mean?" Bothum cried, pushing Enrik's hand harder against the scanner.

"It means I'm not the one who authorized the interception of your precious transmission. And if I didn't intercept it, I can't delete it."

Bothum stepped in front of him, arms crossed. "Who else has authorization?"

Enrik immediately regretted saying anything. His racing mind was still trying desperately to think of a response when the door of the room opened.

"We have a problem," said a low female voice. Enrik turned to find the speaker but couldn't see the woman's face—she was nothing more than a silhouette against the light streaming in from the corridor. She was tall and spoke with a Haphezian accent. "HSP was tipped off about the ambush. I lost the rest of my men in the forest."

Bothum showed little interest in what she was saying. "Find out who else has access to the Tantali royal database," he growled. "Our dear governor seems somewhat reluctant to share this information."

All Enrik saw was Bothum's fist swoop through the air toward his head before everything went dark.

· 9 ·

HSP Headquarters

Noro, Haphez

The headquarters of the Haphezian Special Police was certainly a spectacle. Intricate architecture and a very professional atmosphere both intimidated Jayden and made him feel invincible. He was ushered across the special operations squad floor by Lieutenant Tarbic toward what the agents had called the "situation room." Aroska had by far been the kindest to him upon arriving at HSP, though he still made Jayden rather nervous. He was more slightly-built than some of the other Haphezian men, but just as tall. He wore his black hair slicked back into a tiny ponytail at the base of his skull and sported an impeccably-groomed goatee. The small patterns of dotted tattoos on his face were the same color as his strange amber eyes. Judging by what Jayden had seen so far, the man seemed to have some internal conflict with the other members of the team, or at least with Lieutenant Payvan.

They entered the situation room and found Payvan and Sergeant Duvo waiting with a smaller woman with radiant blue eyes whom Jayden didn't recognize. She stood upon seeing them and approached, hand extended.

"Jayden Saiffe, meet Intelligence Officer Zinnarana Vax," Aroska introduced.

"Call me Zinni," Officer Vax said, giving his hand a firm squeeze. "If I could get you to sit down, we can get started."

Jayden nodded and made his way toward the long table where the others waited. Skeet moved aside to give him some space. He was tall like Aroska, standing a bit over two meters, but he was thicker-bodied. His spiky orange hair seemed to lack the traditional Haphezian stripes, an abnormality he could have been banished for, unless Jayden was mistaken. Everyone else had colored stripes running through their hair that properly matched the color of their eyes and facial tattoos. The fact that they exiled people when this was not the case had always bewildered Jayden. At least the sergeant's eyes were the same color as the wild mane on his head, possibly the reason he'd never been sent away. He seemed less open than Aroska, but was still willing to help—at least more so than Lieutenant Payvan.

Ziva had barely spoken since the incident in the forest, except for barking occasional orders at those around her. She seemed rather uptight, but other than Aroska, no one seemed to mind. Jayden watched her as she loomed over Zinni, directing her through the holographic satellite recording of the clearing. She was big, nearly as tall as either of the men, and maintained a hardened facial expression. Jayden had asked Aroska about her, but the lieutenant had seemed reluctant to share his thoughts.

"The craft that landed in the clearing was using some sort of cloaking technology," Zinni said as she watched the hologram. "We can physically see the ship on the recording, but my scanner couldn't get a reading on its identification code or pick up any of its transmissions. I'm surprised our own comms were still functional."

Ziva crossed her arms and stared Jayden down for a moment, her striking red eyes unsympathetic. "Start from the beginning. I want to hear the whole story, every single detail. If I think you're leaving something out, you will have *one* last chance to get it right. Understand?"

Jayden swallowed and looked up at Aroska, who responded with a gentle nod. Ziva obviously wasn't joking around, nor did she seem like someone who would tolerate joking around. "Like I said, my father and I are...*were* on a diplomatic tour of the planet," he began. "We left Haphor early this morning and were scheduled to spend today and tomorrow here in Noro. The Haphezian man who was serving as our guide stopped in the clearing to check out what he said was a problem with the convoy's lead car. That's when Solaris attacked."

"Did this guy have any distinguishing markings, something abnormal?" Aroska asked.

Jayden paused thoughtfully for a moment. "He had a tattoo on his arm, something that looked like a star. I've seen a lot of tattoos since I've been here, but never anything like that."

"Sounds like he was definitely with Solaris then," Tarbic said. "That star is their trademark. They started using it about six months ago."

"You said they took your father," Skeet brought up.

"Yes," Jayden replied, fighting to control a fresh wave of anger. "Are you going to do something about it?"

"Keep going, kid," Ziva said.

He took a deep breath, bothered that no one seemed to care about anything but his story. "Everything was chaos after that. We were scrambling to react and lost at least half of our men in the first several seconds. I didn't even see that shuttle until it was right on top of us. I thought for a moment that it might be some help, but the next thing I knew, a couple of them had my father and were dragging him up the ramp. He was unconscious. That's when you people showed up." He glanced up at Ziva. "You're lucky Lieutenant Tarbic grabbed me when he did. I would have killed you."

For a moment, Jayden wasn't sure if she was going to hit him or laugh out loud at what he'd just said. "So, what does Solaris want with the governor?" she asked, pacing back and forth in front of the table.

Jayden wasn't sure whether to respond to what seemed like a rhetorical question. His answer came when she leaned across the table and slammed her palms down on the surface. Her tattoo-adorned upper arms bulged as she waited for a reply, and it immediately made him regret hesitating.

"Look, Jayden. You want us to find your father? You'd better keep talking. What would Solaris want with him?"

"Sorry," he said, rubbing his hands across his face and wondering if she was always this quick-tempered. "As you can imagine, I'm having a hard time trusting Haphezians right now."

"Well you should start," Skeet put in, moving around to stand beside Ziva. He crossed his arms, adding to the intimidating air that already radiated from his superior. "We're on your good side now, but you've got to help us if you want it to stay that way."

"I don't *know* why they're after him," Jayden exclaimed, leaping to his feet. All four of them immediately tensed and Aroska placed a firm, warning hand on his shoulder. He took a deep breath and sat back down. "You said Solaris is known for attacks on *diplomacy*. We were on a *diplomatic* tour. Does that answer your question?"

"It helps, but it doesn't give us the whole story," Aroska replied, perching on the edge of the table beside him. He turned slightly, addressing Zinni, Skeet, and Ziva. "Solaris has never attacked without a legitimate reason. They dig deep. They find the reasons for these diplomatic visits. They investigate alliance terms and exploit any weaknesses. There's always a specific motive. We're still missing something here."

An uncomfortable silence filled the room for a moment while Ziva and Aroska stared each other down. There was obviously something going on between them, and Jayden was suddenly very curious about their story.

"Then we need to find out what it is," Ziva said.

· 10 ·
DAKITI MEDICAL RESEARCH CENTER
SARDONIS

I t was the white room again, with the same bright light, same cold table, and the same restraints pinning him down. He was vaguely aware of the medical bot somewhere off to his left, but so far it hadn't spoken to him or touched him. There had been no visitors this time either, and no salty scent. The salty visitors had come on two occasions that he could remember, but all he'd ever been able to see were shadows. He was surprised he'd even been aware of their presence. It was almost like the drugs or whatever they'd been pumping him full of were no longer serving their purpose. The injections were still quite painful, but he found he was growing more conscious of his surroundings each time he was brought into this room. He tried to pick his head up and look around, though it seemed to weigh a ton. For a very brief second, after blinking several times, he saw a clear image of his naked torso, filthy pants, and even his bare feet at the end of the table. His vision became blurry again just as fast as it had cleared, fast enough to make him wonder if it had simply been his imagination.

The cold, gray shadow of the bot passed in front of the light and he could feel its metallic claw force his head back to the table. "Lie down," it commanded, securing his head with a strap.

He began to feel microscopic pinching sensations all over his chest and stomach and remembered seeing tiny sensors adhered to his body during the moment of clear vision. A loud, urgent pattern of beeps blared from an unseen machine somewhere in the room. The bot leaned over him again, disappeared, and then returned in a panicked manner. Before he could register what was going on, he felt the all-too-familiar needle impale his throat. The light above began to swirl in a slow circle as he gasped for a breath, and then he slipped out of consciousness.

· 11 ·
EAST SUN
FRINGE SPACE

Dane Bothum turned toward the door when he heard it open, hoping for some results. Instead, he found two of his soldiers watching him from the doorway. Annoyed, he motioned for them to come in and checked to see if the governor was still unconscious. "What is it?" he growled.

"Transmission for you, sir" one of them replied, handing him a comm.

He took it and waved the soldiers away. "Bothum here," he answered.

"I had to get back before I was missed," came the voice of his informant. "I'll return to you soon. It shouldn't be too long before they start to figure out what's going on down here."

"Did you get a name?"

"Two, actually," the woman replied. "The first person who had access to the Tantali database was Saiffe's personal assistant, and she was conveniently away on maternity leave at the time of the interception. The other is the governor's son, Jayden Saiffe."

Bothum straightened. "And what became of this Jayden Saiffe?"

"He was picked up after the attack. They're holding him at HSP Headquarters."

And the situation got complicated just as fast as it had turned for the better. "We need him."

"I'll send someone to get him out. We'll have him to you soon."

"For your sake, you'd better hope he hasn't told them anything," Bothum snapped. "Bring me that boy!"

"**F**ound anything on our Tantali visitors?" Aroska asked as he returned to the team's workstation after escorting Jayden to a private holding room.

Skeet and Zinni looked up from their work. Ziva was nowhere in sight. "I found something interesting in the agency's transmission logs," Zinni said. "The original transmission saying the governor would be here today *is* there, but it was overwritten. However, whoever did it either didn't know file history was enabled, or they didn't care." She paused, flashing a mischievous grin. "It was just a matter of restoring the original message."

"Good work," Aroska said. He paused a moment, bothered by the fact that he'd just sounded as if he were speaking to Tate and Jole. He suppressed the thought, burying it just as their remains had been buried under the rubble of the demolished building. "Where's Ziva?"

Zinni shrugged, either indicating that she didn't know or that it was none of his business. "Get this. The false transmission file—the one that said the Tantalis wouldn't be here until tomorrow—was created three seconds after the real one came through. That's when the edit took place. The switch happened like *that*." She snapped her fingers.

"They knew it was coming," Skeet concluded, "and they were waiting for it."

Aroska nodded thoughtfully, processing the information. "So someone inside HSP has been monitoring the Tantali Royal House, waiting for a transmission so they could replace it with a false one. They changed it quickly so nobody would know the truth—" he shot an approving glance at Zinni "—therefore enabling Solaris to set up an attack in the forest without us realizing what was really going on. It didn't really matter if someone found the original message as long as the false one bought them enough time to do their damage."

"We're lucky we got that tip when we did," Skeet said.

"Solaris is after the governor for a reason," Aroska continued, "and they've got someone good enough to hack into the agency's systems."

Zinni tapped furiously at her keyboard. "Either Jayden really doesn't know what's going on, or he's not telling us everything."

"Ziva will love that," Skeet scoffed.

Aroska looked across the squad floor. "Where is she?" he asked again. Upon thinking harder, he wasn't exactly sure why he cared, but somehow the idea of keeping tabs on her seemed appealing.

Skeet actually looked like he might answer, but a blaring alarm cut him off. A bright strobe flashed red from a unit on the wall.

"What the..." Zinni muttered, quickly transferring all of the data to a memory stick.

The three of them made their way out of the bullpen, falling into stride with the other agents as they filed toward the nearest exit. Most people remained quiet, but based on the looks in their eyes, the alarm had been unexpected.

"Maybe it's some sort of drill," someone murmured. "Aren't we usually notified about things like this?"

Aroska paused, held back by some inexplicable feeling in his gut. Had they not *just* confirmed that Solaris had access to some of HSP's systems? That meant they were certainly capable of remotely triggering the emergency alarm, but what would that accomplish? It would force everyone out of the building, keep them occupied as they searched for the source of the alarm. *Divert our attention away from what's really going on*, he thought. He stepped out of line and went up the stairs instead of down.

"We need to get Jayden," he said before Skeet or Zinni could even ask where he was going.

"He'll be evacuated with an escort," Zinni called. "We'll rendezvous with him outside!"

Aroska was grateful when he heard the two of them rushing up the steps behind him. "Skeet, you said it yourself. We don't know if Solaris is still after him or not. This could be nothing. Even if that's the case, I'd rather not leave him in someone else's hands." He hesitated before admitting, "Something just doesn't feel right."

He sprinted up the remaining stairs three at a time with Skeet and Zinni hot on his heels. Considering they both outranked him, he wondered if he was perhaps undermining their authority. But neither of them had explicitly told him to remain downstairs, and of all people, they were most likely to understand his thought process.

The three of them arrived at the holding area, a bank of secure, private rooms situated between the field ops and spec ops wings. The rooms were well-furnished and comfortable, designed for holding witnesses and visiting VIPs rather than criminals. All the doors were already open, no doubt unlocked by the warden when the alarm had sounded. Aroska went straight to the room where he had left Jayden, rendered momentarily speechless by the sight of the broken lighting panel and overturned chair within. The young man had been escorted out all right, but it appeared he hadn't gone willingly.

"Damn it," he muttered, glancing into each of the other rooms as he continued down the corridor.

"You were right about something being off here," Zinni said as she rushed forward to the warden's office space. "Oh *sheyss.*"

Aroska and Skeet leaned over the warden's desk to find Zinni crouched beside the man's body. A trickle of blood oozed from his temple, marking the spot where he'd been struck with something solid. His access key remained clipped to his belt, untouched.

Zinni pressed her fingers to his neck, checking for a pulse. "He's alive."

"Who the hell has Jayden, then?" Skeet demanded.

"You two go," Zinni said, waving them away. "I'll stay with him."

Skeet and Aroska took off down the hall at a brisk pace, dodging the occasional agent who was still trying to leave. "It takes Level 4 clearance to access anything on this floor," Skeet pointed out, looking wildly about as they moved. "Taking that and the shape of that room into consideration, I think it's safe to assume Solaris didn't break in remotely."

"If they still need him for some reason—and I'm beginning to think they do—they'll do anything to get him," Aroska said. "What's to say they didn't physically breach the building?"

"That's impossible. The whole complex has been on Code Orange lockdown since we brought Jayden in. Nobody's been able to get in or out without proper identification."

Aroska turned a corner and pulled up short. There was Ziva, standing alone, pistol aimed down one of the landing pad access corridors. Slowly, Aroska drew his own weapon and moved up behind her, followed by Skeet. "Then they were already here," he muttered.

Down the short entry hall, backing toward the door, was a large man with an HSP ID key clipped to his jacket. His right arm was clamped around Jayden's neck, and with his left hand he pressed a gun against the young man's side.

"Let him go!" Ziva ordered. "Drop your weapon!"

Rather than comply, the man began to drag Jayden closer to the door and opened fire on the three of them. The young human ducked as low as he could and wriggled out of the distracted Haphezian's grasp. The intruder immediately shifted his aim back toward the boy as he struggled to open the locked door.

"Jayden, down!" Aroska shouted, firing at the man before he could shoot. He crumpled to the ground as the sizzling bolt of white-hot plasma struck him in the chest, and in that instant the entire building fell eerily silent. Even the alarm had been deactivated.

Without a word, Ziva stepped forward to get a closer look at the dead man. She plucked his ID key from his jacket, tossed it to Skeet, and rolled his sleeve up. Aroska watched as she tore away his timepiece, revealing the Solaris tattoo underneath. It was lighter-colored than most, no doubt to help hide it, but it was there nonetheless.

"I've seen this guy around," Skeet said, giving Aroska a look before tossing the ID back to Ziva. "He's legitimate HSP. Still, someone of his rank wouldn't have had clearance to open the holding rooms. He had to have help from somebody else."

Ziva caught the tag but didn't seem to be paying attention to what he was saying. She stood up, her red eyes on fire. "What were you thinking?" she demanded of Aroska.

Perhaps killing the intruder hadn't been the smartest move, but did she not realize that in doing so he had saved Jayden's life? "I was protecting our witness," he replied bluntly, returning her hot stare with one of his own.

"And you also just killed our only link to Solaris," she snapped. "There were no survivors in the forest." She glowered at him for a few more seconds before storming away down the hall.

Skeet cleared his throat, shot Aroska an apologetic glance, and jogged after Ziva. Wondering briefly if he could ever do anything right in her eyes, Aroska watched them go and then turned to Jayden.

"You okay?"

The young man was shaking, but managed a nod.

· 13 ·
HSP HEADQUARTERS
NORO, HAPHEZ

"At ease, Lieutenant," Emeri Arion said before Ziva had even made it through the office door. "You're going to stand here and listen to what I have to say. Understand?"

Ziva sighed and came to a stop a meter or so in front of his desk, wondering why he had called her in. He clearly knew her well enough to know she was unhappy with the incident that had just occurred with Jayden, and he'd been smart enough to shut her up before she had a chance to protest. The young man was now under the watchful eyes of Skeet, Zinni, and Tarbic to prevent a recurrence of what had just happened. It was obvious that not even the walls of HSP could keep him safe, and he would have to be taken somewhere else.

"I know you well enough to know you're probably not thrilled with what just happened," Emeri began.

Ziva raised an eyebrow.

"Mr. Saiffe isn't going to give us any further information if he doesn't feel safe, and it's clear that he is no longer adequately protected here. Believe me, I'm launching a thorough internal investigation, but in the meantime I'm placing you and your team in charge of transferring him to more secure location. You will coordinate all investigation-related activities with Adin Woro and the Alpha field ops team while you keep Jayden in protective custody."

Ziva cleared her throat. "Sir, with all due respect, what the hell are you thinking? This isn't spec ops' job."

"Payvan, please be quiet and let me finish," the director commanded. "This has become your primary mission. The assignment you received yesterday will be postponed until further notice. You and your team will continue the investigation into Governor Saiffe's abduction from the field, all the while protecting his son. And when the time comes, your team will be responsible for recovering the governor, dead or alive. But until then, if I hear of anything—and I do mean *anything*—you've done to compromise Jayden's safety, you're off the case."

Ziva nodded. The idea of babysitting the young human was less than appealing, and so was finding the governor for that matter. She didn't know much about this potential alliance with Tantal, but in her opinion it wasn't worth the minerals—however valuable and useful they might be—the Haphezians would receive in exchange for protecting the small human colony. Even her original mission to take down the local Solaris captain would be better than this, although it too seemed like a waste of her talent. Not only were she and her teammates the best the special ops division had to offer, but she was one of a few contract assassins within spec ops who could be paid off the books to carry out tasks the agency and military couldn't be directly involved in. Only a few people—the ones she'd told—knew she was anything more than special ops. Emeri obviously knew, yet he was still willing to give her this menial assignment.

"We'll take Jayden to my place," she said. "He'll be safe there."

"Very well," Emeri agreed. "For security reasons, this information will go no further than this room. However, relocating will require you to work more closely with Lieutenant Tarbic, and as I understand, you two are having some problems. Believe me, I wouldn't have assigned him to your team if I'd known how much he knew about his brother's death. It's true that he's going to have to put the past behind him—at least temporarily—if this arrangement is going to work. But judging by what I saw in here yesterday, *you're* certainly not helping the situation."

It was all Ziva could to do keep from rolling her eyes.

"This is a massive agency, is it not?" Emeri continued. "I have more important things to do than break up fights between you two. You're the best we've got, and I will *not* have our best conducting themselves like juveniles. Now nod your head and show me you understand everything I just said."

Ziva didn't nod, but she did understand. He was right, after all; cooperation would require effort from both parties. It was just going to be a long evening. "Sir," she said, dipping her head and striding out of the room.

· 14 ·
HSP Headquarters
Noro, Haphez

Aroska emerged from the cafeteria stirring a glass of govino juice, the virgin version of the fruity drink derived from the fleshy seeds of the govino pods that were so plentiful on Haphez. He took a sip and winced, unable to help but think it tasted odd without the added alcohol he was used to. Rules were rules, though, and it was only logical—no drinking on the job.

He meandered out of the cafeteria, lost in thought as he made his way back to the elevator bank. He'd been right to shoot the Solaris intruder, hadn't he? Ziva was correct in that valuable information could have been gained from an interrogation, but wasn't keeping Jayden alive more important at this point? He convinced himself he didn't really care what Ziva thought and that he'd made a good decision.

Gentle hands suddenly took hold of his jacket, pulling him out of his thoughts and into a vacant office. He closed his eyes as a pair of soft lips found his, and for a moment he allowed himself to forget about the stress of dealing with Ziva and Jayden. The moment was exactly that, however, over just as fast as it had begun. The same stress he'd escaped from was what drew him back to the present, and he reluctantly pulled away.

"Not here, okay?" he said quietly.

Saun Zaid gazed up at him with her striking fuchsia eyes, forcing a disappointed smirk. "You're right, I'm sorry," she said, smoothing down his jacket. "Where have you been? I haven't seen you since yesterday."

"I was reassigned," Aroska answered, brushing some strands of loose hair from her face. She had gentle features, a radiant smile, and her black hair was streaked with vivid stripes that matched her eyes. Despite the fact that he outranked her, she'd taken him under her wing when he'd joined the Solaris Control Unit after losing Jole and Tate. The two of them had worked many cases together in the past three months and had become quite...*close*. Aroska still wasn't entirely sure what it was that they shared, but he liked it.

Saun took a nervous step back. "Reassigned? What does that mean?"

"I'll be back to the SCU in no time," Aroska reassured her. "I'm part of a temporary joint task force with a spec ops team."

"Are you serious?" Saun's eyes gleamed and she grinned wide. "That's fantastic! Who's your supervisor?"

Aroska hesitated. He'd never told her what he knew about Soren's death, so he doubted Ziva's name would have any real significance for her. Part of him was leery about sharing any information with anyone, but the other part trusted Saun just as much as Adin.

"Ziva Payvan," he replied.

Saun lifted her eyebrows. "Wow. Adin told me you'd been having a rough couple of days. I guess that explains it. Isn't she supposed to be some sort of hotshot *shouka* who won't take no for an answer and thinks she owns this place?"

The rumors that had trickled down through the agency's ranks over the years made Ziva sound like some fictional bully. Aroska often wished he could still be as sheltered as everyone else, oblivious to the woman's true identity and nature. "She's definitely a hardass," he said.

"You can be one yourself sometimes, you know," Saun said, jabbing her index finger into his chest. "Maybe you need to show her who's boss."

If you only knew the half of it, Aroska thought. "Right—I'd rather not be flayed alive, thanks." He turned to leave.

"Okay, okay." Saun caught his arm and pulled him back. "Seriously, we love having you downstairs working on Solaris, but you've been given a chance to get your old life back. How many times have you told me you wanted to go back to ops if you had the opportunity? Why would you let one person ruin it for you?"

Because that one person has single-handedly destroyed my life.

Saun put her arm around his torso and began to walk him toward the elevator. "When we first met, you showed more drive and focus than any agent I'd ever seen. Why? You were passionate about your teammates, and you wanted closure. You're passionate about getting back into field ops aren't you? Let me see that same drive and focus now. What's holding you back?"

"Nothing," Aroska replied quickly. It was more or less a lie—while Ziva presented a huge obstacle in his life, nothing should have affected his ability to work hard and do his job.

They reached the elevator and Saun pressed the button for him. "Good. Now get up there and show her what you're made of. Maybe she just wants to know if you can handle the pressure. Maybe she's testing you."

Hadn't Adin said those exact words? "Thank you," Aroska said, giving her a quick peck on the forehead before slipping through the closing doors. "You're amazing."

"I try," she said with a wink.

He'd originally planned on using the elevator ride to ponder the situation with Jayden and the Tantalis, but after the conversation with Saun, his thoughts were so jumbled that he arrived at the squad floor before he'd even had a chance to process them. He knew she was only trying to help, and he was grateful for her support, but there was nothing she could say that would change what Ziva had done to Soren. Sighing, he swiped his temporary special ops access key over the scanner, granting himself permission to even leave the elevator car, and walked out onto the floor.

He caught sight of Ziva in seconds—after merely a day, he could pick her black and red-streaked hair out of any crowd. She stood across the vast work floor on the stairwell, looking out a massive window similar to the one in the director's office. Last he knew, she'd been on her way to talk to Emeri, most likely to discuss the security breach and Jayden's safety. That conversation was obviously over already, and he wondered what the verdict had been.

Aroska downed the rest of his juice and swept his gaze over the rest of the squad floor. Jayden sat with Skeet and Zinni in the team's bullpen, looking anxious as the two of them worked at their stations. Aroska shifted his attention back to Ziva, wondering why she wasn't with them. She hadn't budged from where she stood; maybe she was waiting for him to return.

Show her what you're made of. Maybe she's testing you.

Aroska set the empty glass down on a nearby desk and veered toward the stairwell rather than the bullpen. *To hell with it,* he thought. Now was as good a time as any to say what was on his mind. He still wasn't entirely sure what that was, but he was confident the adrenaline and sheer frustration would be enough to carry him through. If all else failed, he could always just ask what the plan was regarding Jayden's protection.

The stairs had seemed kilometers away, but after what felt like mere seconds he looked down and found himself standing on the first step. Ziva remained on the landing where the stairs made a hundred-eighty-degree turn, still looking out the window with her back to him.

He took a deep breath and continued up the remaining steps, moving up quietly beside her. The view out the massive window was spectacular, very similar to the one from Emeri's office. He could see most of the Noro skyline, and ships of all shapes and sizes moved to and fro above the busy streets far below. He stared out for a moment too, wondering what Ziva was looking at, but when he looked at her he realized her eyes were closed.

"What are you thinking about?" he asked, hoping to start out on a good note.

"Nothing," was the rough reply. Her eyes remained shut.

"Ziva, we need to talk."

"Do you want to know why, Tarbic?" she went on, almost as if he hadn't spoken. "Do you want to know why I'm thinking about nothing? It's because *nothing* is what we have. Do you know *why* we have nothing? It's because you eliminated our only source before he could be questioned."

The thought had occurred to him that, for the sake of team cohesion, she couldn't possibly always be this irritable and that most of her ire was directed toward him specifically. Regardless, he'd seen that response coming from a light-year away. "I told you, I was protecting our witness. That guy was about to kill Jayden."

Ziva crossed her arms and finally turned to face him. "Right. How am I supposed to know you didn't kill him to *prevent* him from being questioned? Maybe you're the inside man who provided him with the access key. After all, you're the Solaris expert."

Aroska hoped his mouth hadn't hung open as long as it felt like it had. "You think *I'm* the inside man?" he exclaimed. "*You're* the one who was gone for so long just before the incident."

She scoffed. "Just like I supposedly killed Tate and Jole. Pulling the emergency alarm isn't exactly my style, and in case you haven't noticed, I prefer something more subtle than blowing up buildings."

That was it. Without thinking—or caring—about how she might react, he seized her by the shoulders and slammed her as hard as he could against the window, pinning her there.

"Enough!" he growled, attracting the attention of those working nearby. "Enough. The reason we have nothing is because you treat me like *sheyss* and won't let me do my job."

The look on Ziva's face had expressed genuine shock and pain, but she recovered quickly. She caught his arm, digging her thumb into the pressure point above his elbow, then spun him around, pinning him against the glass in return. "You have no idea who you're dealing with." She hesitated a moment. "You know, I honestly thought you knew what you were doing, but *this*? This is too far."

She turned to walk away but Aroska grabbed her by the forearm and pulled her in close, their faces centimeters apart. "You want results?" he hissed, certain he had her attention. "Then let me get some. I have tried to be civil with you for the mission's sake, but if you won't make any effort to let me in, then I'll play dirty too. *That's* when we're going to accomplish nothing. You're good, I'll give you that. But I'm here for a reason too and you need to stop ignoring that. Are we clear?"

She didn't reply, didn't move, and the expression on her face didn't change, but Aroska felt the muscles in her forearm relax. She watched him for another several seconds as if waiting to see if he was finished, then she yanked her arm free and hurried down the stairs. "We're leaving," she barked toward the bullpen.

More satisfied than he'd expected to be, he turned around to find everyone on the squad floor staring in his direction, stunned. Nobody spoke; they only gawked and occasionally shot surprised looks at each other. As soon as he made a move to walk away, everyone immediately went back to their work, avoiding eye contact as he went to join up with the team. Skeet hung back while Zinni escorted Jayden to the elevator, slipping his arm around Aroska's shoulder as he came by.

"You trying to get yourself killed?" he said.

Despite the lighthearted nature of the words, his tone gave Aroska the impression he was serious. "It needed to be done," he replied, shrugging the man's arm away.

Skeet gave him some space but continued walking alongside him. "True, but do you really think that was the smartest way to do it?"

"Maybe not, Skeet!" Aroska retorted. "But it was effective."

This time the sergeant backed off significantly. "You think you two can tolerate each other until we get all of this figured out?"

Aroska sighed and took one last look back at the stairs. "We'll see."

· 15 ·
PAYVAN RESIDENCE
NORO, HAPHEZ

Whatever was cooking in the kitchen smelled incredible. Ziva's stomach rumbled as she watched Skeet and Aroska attempt to teach Jayden an old Haphezian card game. He seemed to be catching on, but his mind was obviously elsewhere. His sagging shoulders and dull eyes told her how exhausted he was. Upon leaving HSP in three armored cars, they'd split up and switched places throughout the city to ensure they weren't being followed. The trip to her house overlooking the Tranyi River had taken nearly two hours, a journey that would have normally taken twenty minutes. It had been a long day for everyone.

They'd settled Jayden into the spare room and he and Aroska had been introduced to Marshay Rubin and Ryon Kittner. The hefty housekeeper had been delighted to have company, regardless of the circumstances, and she'd immediately gone to prepare the evening meal, fussing over everyone like a mother bird taking care of her nest. Ryon had respectfully volunteered his services as well. Ziva was glad to have him. He had served under her father in the military before losing most of his left leg and being discharged at a young age. He currently acted as her personal trainer and was in charge of her house while she was away. Both he and Marshay lived on-site, and she liked to think of them as an aunt and uncle despite the fact that they were nowhere near related. They made a better family than any of her blood relatives ever had.

"No need to be so hard on him," Ryon said quietly, coming up beside her in the doorway of Jayden's room. He watched Aroska for a moment and then turned toward her like a father waiting for an explanation from his child. "Skeet tells me he gave you a run for your money today."

Ziva shook her head, brows knit together. "I'd say it was more like a wake-up call," she replied. She would have preferred that Ryon not get involved in this business but understood he was only trying to help. They were about the same height so they saw eye-to-eye. The man's features were worn and battle-scarred, despite the fact that he really wasn't that old, but his dark green eyes were gentle and kind. His prosthetic foot gave him a slight limp, but he got around fine and was still one of the most capable people she knew. He watched her patiently as he always did.

"Do you need to work it out?" he asked. "When we fight—"

"—the enemy wins," she finished, reciting the phrase he was constantly repeating. She'd never told him she borrowed it on occasion. "I know, I know."

"Work it out," Ryon said, voice firm. "Now come on. Smells like Marshay's about ready." He gave her a solid pat on the back and wandered out into the kitchen.

"Dinner!" the housekeeper called seconds later.

Skeet took up the cards and put them away. "Come on," he said to Jayden and Aroska. "If there's anything that can make you feel better after a day like this, it's Marshay's cooking."

Ziva stepped aside to let Skeet and Jayden out but put her arm across the doorway to block Aroska's exit. "You've really got a pair, Tarbic," she said once the others had cleared the area. "I was beginning to wonder."

He crossed his arms and leaned against the opposite side of the doorframe. "I'm glad you noticed."

"You know, I'd just come back from having the same conversation with the director, although he didn't try to put me through a window."

That prompted a hint of a smile. "And whose argument did you find more convincing?"

"What you did took guts," she replied. "Any more of that and I might start to think you've got what it takes after all."

"So you're saying that if I use your body as a battering ram, I'm not an incompetent fool?"

She lifted an eyebrow. "That's not exactly what I had in mind. What I *am* saying is you don't seem to have a problem with telling it like it is, and I think I like that. The former leader of Alpha field ops shouldn't be running around with his tail between his legs. However, if you touch me or my team again, I'll skin you alive and mount your hide on my wall over there. Understand?"

Aroska's stance didn't change, but something told her he was very relieved by the compliments. *Perfect.* "Does this mean you're going to listen to me now?" he asked.

"Maybe," Ziva replied, "but here's the thing. If there's going to be any form of 'mutual' respect, it's got to go both ways. You've got to get over Soren and listen to me too. Agreed?"

He tensed slightly, almost as if merely hearing her say his brother's name could set him off, but after a brief hesitation, he extended his hand and nodded. "Ziva."

She made a point of ignoring his handshake offer but still managed a nod in return. "Aroska."

With that out of the way, she turned and led him into the kitchen where the others were already seated and helping themselves to the various dishes set out on the table. There was an enormous amount of food for such a small group, but Ziva was hungry and she guessed everyone else was too.

Skeet had already begun eating as Ziva and Aroska took their seats at opposite ends of the table. "Marshay, the warco is amazing, as usual," he said past the wad in his mouth, his eyes closed in bliss.

"Don't thank me, dear," Marshay replied with a smile, her pearly white teeth contrasting greatly with her dark *emilan* complexion. "Ziva made that the other day. I had to break into the leftovers when I found out all of you people were coming into my house."

"In that case, Z," Skeet said, taking another bite, "it's delicious."

"What's warco?" Jayden asked, eyeing the lumpy brown pile someone had spooned onto his plate. The early stages of a grimace were visible on his face.

"It's a stew made from a mollusk that lives down in the river," Marshay replied as she helped him choose more food. She handed him a small spice container. "Try this on it."

Ziva opened her mouth to comment, but she paused when her ears picked up the slight vibration of someone approaching the house on the walkway outside. A muffled *thump* beyond the front door halted her train of thought completely. All the Haphezians in the room—everyone but Jayden—immediately turned their attention to the door. The young human had most likely not heard such insignificant sounds, but he seemed to recognize the urgency of the situation and cautiously hunkered lower in his chair.

The thump was followed by a bit of scuffling. Ziva, Skeet, and Zinni stood up, pistols drawn, and Aroska, who was seated the closest, moved quietly to the door. They listened for another couple of seconds while Ziva positioned herself between Jayden and the unknown. Aroska threw them all a warning glance and punched the controls to open the door.

The girl outside dropped the bundle she was carrying and had her own weapon drawn nearly as fast as Aroska had drawn his.

"Name and rank!" she demanded, fearlessly taking a step forward.

"Lieutenant Tarbic, stand down!" Ziva ordered, rushing forward to push Aroska's arm away. "Jada, he's okay. At ease."

Jada Jaroon watched Aroska for a few more uneasy seconds, then holstered her gun and gathered up the things she'd been carrying. She immediately humbled herself and offered a free hand. "Pleased to make your acquaintance, Lieutenant," she said.

"My apologies," Aroska replied, casting a wary glance at Ziva as he returned her handshake.

Marshay hurried over to relieve Jada of her load. "You gave us a bit of a scare, my dear."

The girl smiled sheepishly. "I tripped on the steps and dropped the clothes," she explained. "Not *everyone* sees as well as you guys do in the dark." She turned to Jayden, who had risen from his chair upon realizing things were under control. "I thought you could use something clean to wear, sir. But as you might imagine, it's a little hard to find things that fit someone your size around here."

"So much for a formal introduction," Ziva said. "Jada Jaroon, meet Lieutenant Aroska Tarbic and Jayden Saiffe of Tantal. Tarbic has come on as a fourth member of the team and, well, you already know some of Jayden's story. Thanks for bringing the clothes."

"'Name and rank'?" Aroska asked, amused.

Ziva slipped her arm around Jada's shoulders, towering over her. "I've always told her that if anyone she doesn't know ever shows up here, they're probably going to be either HSP or military and she should verify. If they can't answer and can't give an alternative explanation, she can shoot them in the head." She looked down at her adoptive sister. "Stay for dinner?"

"Don't doubt it," the girl answered.

· 16 ·
PAYVAN RESIDENCE
NORO, HAPHEZ

Jada Jaroon was definitely human; after two weeks on the planet, it seemed almost foreign to see someone without colored eyes and those strange, dotted facial tattoos. Jayden watched her interact with the others and wondered how in the world she had fallen in with this group. Haphezians and humans had always been somewhat at odds, the main reason it was taking so long for Tantal to successfully form an alliance with them. Haphezians considered themselves a dominant species, and while they *were*, they usually had a rather haughty attitude when it came to interacting with the galaxy's other races. In fact, Jayden wasn't entirely sure why they were helping him now.

Jada was pretty, with long brown hair that trailed down her back in the form of a braid. She was only seventeen, maybe eighteen years old, but she'd clearly figured out how to fit in here on Haphez. Jayden found it interesting how Ziva's personality had changed upon her arrival. The woman been reclusive and uptight throughout the day, but around Jada she was relaxed and, dare he say, welcoming. It made him feel much more comfortable.

"Don't let them forget to feed you," Jada was saying. Jayden realized she was addressing him. "They tend to forget when they only have to eat every other day. It took me a while to get used to it."

"Ah," Jayden chuckled. No wonder there was so much food. He swallowed a bite of the warco stew, unable to get around its slimy texture. He'd been content to eat the provisions the Tantalis had brought from home throughout the course of his visit; it didn't take much of the rich, highly caloric Haphezian food to give him a stomach ache. It was no wonder they only ate every two days—the things they *did* eat could easily fuel them for that long, and having two stomachs no doubt helped.

Obviously Jada had managed to adapt to this strange culture. He was about to go ahead and ask how the young woman was related to Ziva, but Aroska beat him to it.

"So, Jada," the lieutenant began, "how do you know Pay...*Ziva* and the others?"

The girl smiled wide and finished chewing her bite of food. "It's really a long story. I'm actually her sister—adopted sister. I was brought here at age three when human slave trafficking was still big." She looked at Ziva as if seeking permission to proceed with her story. With no negative response, she continued. "I was first brought into the house of the Haphezian Royal General, Njo Jaroon...Ziva's stepfather."

"Ziva's royalty?" Aroska asked.

"No," Ziva snapped, "and you're interrupting."

"Things improved fast," Jada went on, "and before long Njo and his wife, Ziva's mother, adopted me as one of their own children." She cracked another smile. "Believe me, there was a lot of controversy at first, but when you're the daughter of the Royal General, people learn to stop asking questions. So what's your story?" This was directed at Aroska. "Four agents on an ops team? You don't see that every day."

Jayden watched as Aroska also looked to Ziva for permission to answer. Perhaps this topic had something to do with why they didn't seem to be getting along.

"The other two members of my team, Jole Imetsi and Tate Luver, were killed in an explosion three months ago," Tarbic began. "We were responding to a bomb threat in one of the government offices when it happened. The device was like nothing we'd ever seen before, and we weren't sure how to handle it." He took a deep breath. "I should never have left the building. We called for backup and I went out to meet the responders. The device was triggered remotely while I was outside and the entire place was completely leveled. Everything within a fifteen-meter radius of the bomb was totally vaporized, absolutely nothing left.

Jada had been listening intently with her eyebrows furrowed. "I remember hearing about that. I'm so sorry. Did you ever find out who was responsible?"

Jayden was quite intrigued with the lieutenant's story as well, but even more intrigued by the accusatory glance the man shot at Ziva before continuing.

"No," he replied, sighing again. "They immediately suspected Solaris because of the location. That's one of the reasons I requested a position in HSP's Solaris Control Unit after that. Still, because the device was detonated while Tate and Jole were inside, I've always believed my team was specifically targeted." His eyes shifted toward Ziva again. "But the case is cold now. We still haven't figured out who was responsible."

"Powers of Nosti!" Jayden exclaimed. "That's terrible! How can—" He stopped cold when he realized everyone at the table was staring at him in shock. "Sorry," he said quietly. "I'll leave it alone. I'm sure it's a difficult subject."

"You're fine," Skeet said. "We just don't usually say things like that here."

"He means the 'Nosti'," Ryon explained. "We've banned Resistance presence here on Haphez ever since the Federation outlawed the use of nostium a couple of decades ago. Being a Nosti is punishable by death."

"Oh," Jayden replied sheepishly, playing along. He felt his cheeks redden and kicked himself for allowing his tongue to slip. Lots of people around the galaxy swore by the Nosti though, regardless of whether they had any affiliation with the Resistance. Maybe his new Haphezian friends wouldn't think anything of it. "You know, Nosti are starting to resurface all over the galaxy. I guess someone figured out how to replicate the nostium formula even after the Federation wiped out all the Resistance's scientists and facilities."

Skeet chuckled and shook his head. "Well, they're sure not resurfacing here, not if they want to keep their heads. Their crazy brain powers can't save them from us."

"I'd love to get my hands on one of those retractable swords they use," Aroska said. "What are they called—kytaras?"

Jada laughed. "How exactly do you plan on doing that?"

"Do they even use those things anymore?" Skeet snickered past another mouthful of food.

"I'm pretty sure they do, Skeet," Ziva snapped.

Jayden couldn't help but notice the way she ran her finger over her scar as she replied, almost as if reminding Skeet what had caused it. It seemed the topic of conversation was rather sensitive, but there was one more thing he had to know.

"Have any of you ever met a Nosti?"

One by one, everyone fell silent and directed their attention toward Ziva. She glared across the table at Jayden with stone cold features and slowly finished chewing her food. Part of him regretted asking, but the other part was overcome with curiosity.

"I killed one when I was nineteen," she said, deadpan. Her tone told him two things: she wasn't kidding, and the conversation was over.

Nobody spoke for what seemed like a long time, though it was realistically only a few seconds. Jayden lowered his gaze back to his plate and pushed his food around with his fork, still able to feel Ziva's blood-red eyes boring into him. The awkward silence was finally broken when Zinni cleared her throat.

"Sorry to break up the party," she said, speaking for the first time. She had her portable computer in her lap and had barely touched her food. "I've been going over comm logs and I just got a hit on a Solaris member our intruder recently made contact with. His name is Vinny Jaxton."

"Jaxton," Aroska said thoughtfully. "I know him. He's a junkie who works out of the Square."

"You think he'll talk?" Ziva asked.

"I *know* he will. We can go to him first thing tomorrow."

"Will finding him help you get my father back?" Jayden said.

Once again, the group fell silent, and he feared the answer would be "no." Or worse—they already knew something and weren't telling him.

"Hopefully," was Ziva's abrupt response. The way she said it told Jayden she didn't actually think so, or she didn't care.

He stood up, rattling the table and taking everyone by surprise. "If you're not interested in finding my father, then why bother helping me?"

"Jayden," Aroska said, placing a hand on his shoulder. His other hand rested on his holstered pistol. "Sit down. We'll find your dad."

Jayden sat, only after realizing the others were also tense and ready to draw their weapons. Were they really going to shoot him? Was he nothing more than an inconvenience who had stumbled into their lives at exactly the wrong time? If these people weren't going to help him, he knew someone who would.

"I'm sorry," he whispered, rubbing his face. "I'm just...tired." He looked up. Everyone was watching him, completely emotionless. *Fine.* "Excuse me," he sighed, throwing his utensils down onto his plate. He stood up and stormed away into his room, leaving them to sit in stunned silence.

· 17 ·
PAYVAN RESIDENCE
NORO, HAPHEZ

Ziva exited the guest room on feet so light not even her own sensitive ears could register her footsteps. It was the wee hours of the morning and Jayden was fast asleep, completely unaware of the tiny transmitter she'd just planted on him. Based on the skill he'd shown in the forest and the way he'd lashed out at her team throughout the day, she was no longer convinced he would just sit by and wait patiently as the search for Enrik Saiffe continued. Somehow she couldn't picture him getting up and running off, but if he ever tried to take matters into his own hands, she thought it best to keep tabs on him.

Marshay and Ryon had already disappeared into their own rooms for the night. Everyone else remained in the living room, with the exception of Jada, who had left after dinner to make the trip back to Haphor after spending all day in Noro. Ziva had already instructed them all to go home and get some rest, but there they remained. She bid them all a terse goodnight and retreated into the darkness of her bedroom, reveling for a moment in the stillness and quiet.

The conversation at dinner had gone in directions she'd never expected it to. While it certainly wasn't illegal to *talk* about the Resistance and the Nosti on Haphez, people just didn't do it. Ziva had to remind herself that, as a foreigner, Jayden simply didn't understand that. The way he'd continued to press the discussion was what bothered her. Despite the fact that it had caused quite a stir throughout the city, her battle with the Nosti as a teen was not something anyone ever spoke about. The only reason she'd even admitted to it was to shut Jayden up, and luckily he'd done exactly that.

She swallowed and leaned against the closed door with her head tilted back and her eyes shut. A series of memories she had no desire to relive flashed through her mind. She saw her seven-year-old self sneaking off the supply transport and running into the heart of downtown Noro before anyone spotted her. It had been over two years since her father's death in the Fringe War, but at the time the pain had still been very fresh. Even now, more than twenty years later, the memory was clear enough to make her shiver.

In her mind's eye, she could still see the towering buildings and lights all around her. Despite the fact that she'd grown up in the city, that had been the first time she'd ever been into the center of Noro. She didn't remember being afraid, just lost and confused. Surprisingly, nobody had paid any attention to the little girl wandering through the crowd with her backpack, alone.

She'd made it several blocks from the spaceport before the man hit her. More accurately, she'd hit him—her attention had been directed upward at a colorful advertisement and she'd walked right into him. A glass container of clear liquid had slipped from under his coat and shattered on the ground, spilling its contents. Her skin crawled as she remembered tripping on his foot and falling, and she could still feel the shards of broken glass slicing into her forearm as she hit the ground. She'd just assumed the jar contained water, at least until her arm began to tingle when it came in contact with the liquid. The blood seeping from the cut had bubbled into thick foam as the mysterious substance entered her bloodstream.

Ziva shook away the memory and stood upright, switching on her bedroom light. That had been right around the time the Federation had first taken action against the Resistance, so even at such a young age she'd been familiar with nostium and how it had recently been outlawed. The thought that she'd been exposed to it hadn't even crossed her mind until two days later when the man from the street found her in an alley and dragged her away.

Now was hardly the time to be thinking about the past though. Sighing, Ziva cast aside the empty container from Jayden's tracker and crossed the room to her bed. She felt a familiar surge of energy course through her body, one that began as a tingle in her head and traveled down her spine all the way to her toes. It was something she hadn't felt in a while and she sometimes wondered if she'd ever feel it again. Most of the time it made her nervous—considering she wasn't supposed to ever feel it at all—but right now she was almost relieved it was still there. Drawing a deep breath in through her nose, she whirled and reached toward the first object she laid eyes on: a small antique vase that rested on a shelf across the room.

The vase flew into her hand.

· 18 ·

9 YEARS AGO

NORO, HAPHEZ

The sound of footsteps coming up the rickety stairs drew Ziva's attention to the door of the apartment. She continued folding clothes and stuffing them into her backpack, waiting for the familiar sounds of the lock disengaging and the rusty old door squealing open on archaic hinges. When nothing happened, she paused and listened. The footsteps had stopped at the top of the staircase, and she could hear a hushed voice speaking outside.

Curious, she moved silently to the door and placed her eye to the spy hole. Gamon stood a couple of meters away with his back to the apartment, communicator to his ear. He'd been making too many calls like this lately, and frankly she didn't like it. She dreaded to think of what he did or who he talked to when he was out on his own. When she thought about it, she wasn't actually sure when the last time was that she'd fully trusted him.

She had no idea who he was speaking with, but she could hear his side of the conversation perfectly. "She's scheduled for a fresh round today," he said. That much she knew; it was the reason for his visit, after all. The bag he carried over his shoulder contained the nostium that would be introduced into her system for the first time in six years. Without it, her Nostia—the telekinetic abilities it gave her—would gradually start to wear off.

"I believe she's ready," Gamon said. "You can be the judge of that when you see her in action. If we can convert one Haphezian to our cause, we can assume more will follow."

Ziva's eyebrows slid together and she took a step back from the door. *What cause?* As far as she knew, Gamon had cut all ties with the Resistance when he'd come to hide on Haphez. He was one of only a few members who had even survived the Federation's attacks anyway. The nostium he had was all he'd managed to grab before the development center was destroyed and the other Nosti were wiped out, or so she'd thought. She'd always just assumed the two of them were on their own, but the things she was hearing were beginning to make her think otherwise.

The conversation seemed to be drawing to a close so she moved back to her bag and continued packing, feigning surprise when the door opened. Jak Gamon strode in, face contorted with some unknown emotion spawned by the transmission he'd just ended. He gently set his bag down and removed a glass container identical to the one he'd been carrying through the streets of Noro twelve years before.

"Oh, hey," Ziva said, searching for a happy medium between sounding too suspicious and too enthusiastic.

"Are you ready?" Gamon asked, pouring the nostium into a clear sack. He attached a thin tube and needle to it, creating a crude drip bag.

Ziva nodded and slowly moved toward him, eyeing the powerful substance as she went. It looked like any other batch of nostium—she doubted he'd be trying to poison her or some such thing, given that he and whoever he'd been talking to seemed to want her alive. She stood still as he attached the makeshift IV to her arm. At nineteen years old, she'd already reached her peak height, standing just shy of two meters. Gamon was reasonably tall for a human, but he still had to look up to make eye contact.

She sat down and rested her arm on the small dining table while Gamon hung the bag from a hook on the wall. She'd been thirteen the last time she'd received a nostium infusion, but it was a feeling she hadn't forgotten. The substance felt cold and it almost tickled as it traveled through her bloodstream. It reached her brain in moments and the familiar dizziness set in. Gamon had always assured her that the faintness was perfectly normal. It usually wore off a few minutes after the infusion was complete.

The two of them sat in silence for a few minutes. "Going somewhere?" Gamon finally asked, gesturing toward her backpack and the other items she'd set out on the sofa.

"I've decided to join HSP's Junior Guard after all," Ziva replied, shivering as a jolt of energy shot down her spine. "I'm going to live in the dorms with the other recruits."

Gamon froze. "What?"

"You heard me. It's high time I made a decision about what to do with the rest of my life. I've done well in my training at the academy and want to continue honing my skills."

"What about *our* training?"

"What's the point?" She stole a glance up at the bag. It was about half empty. "Functioning here as a Nosti will be impossible. I'd rather be developing abilities I can actually use."

Gamon stared at her for a moment, dumbfounded. He raked his hand back through his brown hair and gestured at the drip line. "Then what are we even doing here?"

Ziva wasn't exactly sure. Maybe part of her wasn't ready to give up this power just yet. Her excuse could be that the invitation to join the Junior Guard had been a last minute thing and she hadn't planned on leaving so soon. "I..." she began.

"You were seven years old when you ran into me in the street," Gamon said, stooping down in front of her. "You'd been exposed to nostium and you didn't even know it. I couldn't let you just walk away and find out for yourself. I was protecting you, just like I've protected you for the past twelve years, and just like I'm protecting you now."

"You could have just left me alone," she spat, fighting away the haze swirling through her head. "Things would have been a lot simpler and you'd have all of your precious nostium to yourself."

"You're wrong, Ziva. I saw the potential in you. I saw someone who was hurting, someone who needed a new purpose. You'd lost your father in the War, your mother married the Royal General, your half-brother and half-sister were born. You were all alone and had nowhere to go. Do you remember that?"

Ziva refused to look at him but managed a nod.

"Don't forget: you *agreed* to let me train you. You agreed to let me give you a purpose again. You knew the risks but you did it anyway. Being a Nosti was just as illegal back then as it is today. Why say yes then and no now? Why would you let all these years of training and secrecy go to waste?"

Possibly because I just don't trust you anymore, she thought. The training hadn't gone to waste though. She *had* been desperate for a new purpose, a renewed sense of control in her life, and learning the ways of the Nosti had given her exactly that. After losing her father and being rejected by her new family, the rebellion and independence felt good. It gave her a confidence she'd never had before. On top of that, the physical aspects of the training had given her an edge at the academy. The military and police used very different fighting techniques than the Nosti, but already having a fundamental understanding of melee and hand-to-hand combat had helped her catch on fast. She couldn't deny that she'd enjoyed it. She'd enjoyed every last bit of it.

Everything except Gamon himself, that was. The fact that he'd managed to go undetected for all of these years was honestly impressive. The only thing that had saved him was that the Federation had never bothered to hunt for Nosti on Haphez, as the Haphezian government had assured them Resistance presence on the planet would not be tolerated. He'd treated her as an object he owned rather than a person. He'd never been a father figure, not even a mentor. The most gracious thing he'd ever done was put her up in this shabby apartment. She knew he'd only done it to save his own skin, to make sure the two of them would never be associated with each other, but it had benefitted her just as much. She'd lived in solitude and had been free to go to school, meet new people, and make her own decisions, meeting Gamon at a secret location for appointed training sessions.

Despite the way he'd treated her, she'd allowed him to teach her, to give her nostium infusions every six years, to walk her through the process of designing her own kytara, but never had she considered using her skills for any cause but her own. Gamon stood there watching her, jaw set, clearly upset but trying hard not to show it. Based on the conversation she'd overheard, it sounded as though he had other plans for her.

"It's just time I choose my own path," Ziva said. That much was true.

Gamon took hold of her jaw and tilted her head upward, forcing her to look him in the eye. But when he spoke, his voice was full of desperation rather than anger. "You have no future here. Come with me to Forus. There's a new Resistance hideout there, and they're trying to develop a new nostium formula. As a Haphezian, you'd be an invaluable asset. Come put your talents to good use and help us make a difference. I've spent twelve years creating the perfect warrior—don't tell me it was all for nothing."

So he'd had an agenda after all. Ziva wondered if he'd had it since the day they'd met. Maybe it didn't really matter. "You didn't create me, Jak," she growled. "I don't belong to you, and I certainly don't belong to the Resistance. I'm not coming with you, and if you can't accept that, I might just have to spread the word that a Nosti has been hiding out here all these years."

"Is that a threat?"

"What do you think?"

Gamon glowered down at her for a moment before fishing his communicator out of his pocket. "Fine," he muttered, holding the device to his ear and striding out of the room. The door slammed behind him.

Ziva felt her pulse quicken and glanced up to the hook on the wall. The last of the bag's contents were currently sliding through the tube and into her veins. She waited a few more seconds before easing the thick needle out of her arm and throwing it aside. A thin stream of foamy blood began to ooze from the swollen injection site, but she paid it no mind as she tip toed to the door and once more lowered her eye to the spy hole. Her vision swam for a moment as her brain continued processing the chemicals that had just been introduced to it, but soon she saw a clear picture of Gamon standing at the top of the stairs just as he had been before.

"We've got a problem," she heard him say.

Well, he wasn't wrong, though Ziva guessed they each had their own definitions for what exactly the problem was. The Resistance had tried many times to recruit Haphezians into their ranks—she kicked herself for not realizing this had all just been another attempt to do that. She still had the upper hand in the situation though; she doubted Gamon would turn her in or try to kill her while there was still a possibility he could take her to Forus. She pictured herself being sedated and taken there against her will, then being brainwashed and forced to fight with the other Nosti. She shivered, though whether it was a result of nerves or the nostium, she didn't know. What she *did* know was that she wasn't going anywhere.

Ziva turned and surveyed the room. She'd packed everything of importance already and could easily just grab her backpack and go. She had a small pistol, but ranged weapons were typically useless against a skilled Nosti who could pull a gun from the shooter's grasp or even alter the path of the bullet or plasma bolt mid-flight. She wished desperately for her kytara, which was currently buried in a strongbox at the location in the forest where she met Gamon for training.

A sudden realization hit her like a smack in the face. If she walked out of this apartment—regardless of whether she went to turn Gamon in—the man could easily go to their secret meeting place and retrieve that strongbox. A kytara with her fingerprints on it would be damning evidence the authorities wouldn't question, and she had no way to prove that Gamon was just as guilty as she was. She could always sneak away and retrieve the strongbox first, but that would give Gamon the opportunity to rat her out and then slip away, never to be heard from again. Leaving him unattended simply wasn't an option, and she swallowed as she contemplated what needed to be done.

She'd killed a man once. It was an old homeless man, drunken into a dazed stupor, but she'd done it all the same. He'd witnessed her use Nostia to move a large piece of scrap metal as she'd searched a secluded alleyway for materials with which to build her kytara. It had been a foolish, careless move on her part, using her abilities anywhere even remotely near a public place. Part of her guessed he was probably too wasted to remember what he'd seen, but another part knew she couldn't take any chances. There'd been a certain necessity about it, a sense of self-preservation that had helped her convince herself she'd done the right thing. That same feeling fueled her now as she went to her bag and pulled out her gun.

Ziva crept back to the door and placed her ear to it, unable to hear Gamon outside any longer. After several seconds of silence, she risked another look through the spy hole and shuddered when she saw the empty stairwell.

The squeak of a floorboard was the only warning she had before something dark passed in front of the hole and the door flew inward, striking her hard in the face. She shook her head and threw her weight against the door in return, hearing the satisfying sound of a body hitting the floor. She flung the door open and took aim but ducked out of the way to avoid Gamon's communicator as it flew toward her head. The familiar metallic sound of a kytara engaging echoed through the stairwell, and his nasty serrated blade suddenly filled her vision.

She turned her head away, but the tip of the sword still managed to find her face. Searing pain shot through her left cheek and temple, and she found herself blinded by the blood that streamed from the gash. She wanted to scream, but the only sound that came out was a choked gasp.

Ziva took several staggering steps back into the room and opened fire in Gamon's general direction, using her mind to hurl any nearby objects toward the door. The fog in her head had nearly dissipated, but enough remained to make her stumble and the gun slipped from her grasp. She squeezed her bloody eye shut and caught herself on the dining table, dropping to the floor and rolling out of the way before Gamon could pull the contents of the kitchen shelf down on top of her. Rising up on one knee, she seized the hem of the filthy curtain covering the room's main window and tore it down, taking up the metal curtain rod with both hands.

Gamon's blade whistled through the air behind her and she spun to meet it, blocking his blow with the rod and sweeping his arm away. He whirled and came at her again, bringing his kytara down against her makeshift weapon with a two-handed grip. Ziva could feel the rod give a bit; she dove to one side and brought it up hard against the backs of his knees, sending him to the floor as well.

The kytara clattered to the ground a short distance away and Ziva reached for it, but Gamon had an invisible grip on it first and called it back to his own hand. She threw herself at him, swatting the weapon away just before it met his fingers. She slammed her elbow down against his nose and mouth, satisfied by the sound of cartilage and teeth breaking, and reached for the kytara. The sound of a switchblade filled her ears, and she knew Gamon had drawn another weapon.

In that instant, her hand closed around the sword's grip and she swung it around behind her, slicing through Gamon's wrist and severing the hand that was about to plunge a knife into her femoral artery. She wrenched her body around and lifted the kytara above her head, reveling in the horrified look in his eyes just before she thrust it into his chest.

The blade pierced his heart and it was over.

· 19 ·
PAYVAN RESIDENCE
NORO, HAPHEZ

Ziva awoke for the fourth time from a fitful sleep and blinked several times, letting her eyes adjust to the darkness of the bedroom. Staying up until all hours with the day's events on her mind was definitely a contributing factor, but it was also outrageously hot in the room and every little sound made her jumpy. But Jayden, Solaris, and the heat weren't what had awakened her this time.

She wasn't sure how she had even heard it. Even now, she could barely hear anything over the sound of her own breathing, much less while sleeping. It was just one of those things....

There! There it was again, barely audible. It was the sound of something sharp scraping against a smooth surface somewhere in the house. There was a certain consistency to it, a gentle, arching movement that ruled out the possibility that it was a twig or branch scratching a window. Ryon kept all the shrubs and tree branches trimmed anyway, partly to protect the glass and also so nobody would become paranoid every time a breeze came up. No, this was definitely not a branch. Ziva had used enough glass cutters in her life to know what one sounded like.

She sat up, struggling to get her feet untangled from the bed covers, and took her pistol from the nightstand. She moved quietly to the door and slid it open far enough to poke her head out. The hallway and living room were dark and silent, and she slipped through the narrow opening, listening. The scraping had stopped.

Ziva paused for a moment to observe the two shadows standing in the living room, silhouetted against the dim moonlight streaming in from outside. It was Aroska and Ryon, both standing motionless and armed with pistols as well. They looked wide awake and also appeared to be listening. She glanced at the sofa where Aroska had been using the cushions and a blanket and she scowled at him. "*What are you still doing here?*" she mouthed, though she doubted he could see her clearly.

Rather than reply, he waved his hand under his nose, motioning for her to smell the air. Sure enough, she picked up the scent he had indicated, a strange, damp, salty smell. It seemed vaguely familiar. She gripped her pistol tighter and glided noiselessly over to the two men. She was about to ask how long they'd had been listening when a *thump* and a muffled groan came from Jayden's room.

The three of them burst forward to the bedroom door, weapons trained on it. Ziva flattened herself against the wall while Aroska waited with his hand poised over the controls and Ryon crouched to take the low angle. She took a deep breath and nodded, signaling for Aroska to hit the button.

The door slid open and Ziva swung around, pistol aimed into the darkness. The salty smell rushed into her nostrils and her mind made the connection just as Ryon activated the lights: *Sardon*. The soldier was attempting to drag an unconscious Jayden out through a large hole cut in the bedroom window. A syringe lay on the floor beside the glass cutter.

"Drop the kid!" Ziva commanded, taking several steps forward.

The Sardon was either ignoring her completely or he hadn't understood. He continued dragging Jayden, no longer bothering to be stealthy. With his free hand he began groping for the gun that rested in the holster on his hip.

Ziva squeezed off a shot, but the plasma bolt that hit him squarely in the chest wasn't hers. Her shot had struck just above his left knee, exactly as she'd intended; this time she wasn't going to let the intruder get away before gaining some information. The fatal shot, though, had come from behind her, from Aroska's weapon.

"Hold your fire!" she ordered, knocking his gun down. She rushed forward and pulled the Sardon away from Jayden, rolling him over onto his back. He clutched his chest, gasping for air, and blood dribbled from his mouth.

"What do you want?" she shouted, shaking him, patting his face, trying to get him to focus. "Why are you here?"

The soldier's reptilian eyes glazed over and he grabbed her arm, mumbling something incoherent.

She looked down to where his fingers were closed around her wrist and noticed the black Solaris star against his leathery gray skin. There was a smaller star just above it, different than what she had seen on the insurgents from the forest and the man at HSP.

"*Cach kem bola?*" she repeated in Sardon, shaking him again.

"*Tro...trosashina,*" he wheezed.

"Transmission? What transmission?"

He looked up at her longingly, as if he might actually tell her if he could. His fingers slid off of her arm as his head rolled limply to one side.

"Come on, come on!" she shouted, shaking him again. When he didn't respond, she checked for a pulse, and, finding none, stood up to face Ryon and Aroska. "Gone," she said.

They had pulled Jayden back up onto the bed and were covering him with a blanket. "He'll be fine," Aroska announced, tossing her the syringe. "Axonyte. He'll just be out of it for a while."

"What were you thinking?" Ziva demanded, barely paying attention to what he'd just said. "That's the second Solaris operative you've taken down before we've had a chance to question him!"

"So you'd rather they just kill Jayden?" Aroska retorted.

"Think about it, Tarbic. The inside man at HSP was leading him out of the building. This one was using Axonyte, a sedative. They don't want him dead. There's something else going on." She looked down at the dead Sardon. "Something involving a transmission."

· 20 ·
Tranyi River District
Noro, Haphez

I f one looked closely enough at the horizon, it might have looked like the sky was beginning to brighten with the first light of dawn. Of course, sometimes when you had been waiting long enough for something, the mind would begin to play tricks on you, and you would think you saw something that wasn't really there. So maybe the sun would be rising soon, maybe it wouldn't. He couldn't tell for sure, but he *did* know that his partner had been gone for nearly two hours. Peering through his spotting scope, he swept the area again and still saw no sign of anyone approaching. Even with an ally who could remotely disable Payvan's security system, breaking into the house had been a slow process. But two hours was just too long, no matter how slowly someone moved.

Suddenly, several lights came on inside the house, and yellow floodlights illuminated the yard outside. He shrunk back into the shadows, refraining from cursing out loud. That was it—the mission was a no-go.

"It's off," he hissed into his communicator. "He's gone. Mission failure."

· 21 ·
East Sun
Fringe space

Dane Bothum swore and hurled his comm unit across the room. This was twice now that Jayden Saiffe had slipped through his fingers.

"You're completely sure?" he growled at the translucent hologram standing on the communication pad across the room.

"Positive. One of the soldiers I sent just confirmed it."

"You've lost too many of my men today."

The hologram scoffed. "Those were *my* men in the forest. I had no idea HSP was going to show up."

"It was also your responsibility to make sure they didn't."

"The tip was from an anonymous civilian, out of my hands."

"And yet your man was able to alter the transmission logs to trick HSP into thinking the governor wasn't due to arrive until later today. Was a simple civilian tip so much more difficult to deal with?"

"Look, as far as we know, the kid hasn't told them anything about what he found. Otherwise, they'd be there knocking down your doors."

"It doesn't make any sense," Bothum mused. "Why hasn't he told them?" He took a moment to look at the hologram. "We have to get him before he *does*."

"Sir, with all due respect, I may have a better idea. I promised you Lieutenant Tarbic three months ago, and I'm sorry I couldn't deliver. He is currently working with one Ziva Payvan, who would serve as a very fine specimen for your program. Rather than go *to* Jayden Saiffe, we'll bring him to us. Use the father to bait the son. Tarbic and Payvan are on protection detail for Saiffe—if he comes, we'll get them too."

Bothum ran his thumb across his brow, intrigued by the offer. He'd heard rumors about Ziva Payvan—indeed, she could be perfect. Capturing her would more than make up for the shortfall three months earlier. "You're sure HSP doesn't know where we are?"

"I said as far as I know. I'm coming back to you this afternoon. They've got the Alpha field ops team working here and they're closing in faster than I expected."

"I suppose your cover was never going to last forever," Bothum agreed. "This had better work, Saun."

· 22 ·

9 Years Ago

Noro, Haphez

When Ziva awakened a bit later, it took her a moment to realize why her left eye seemed to be stuck shut. The overpowering scent of blood assaulted her nostrils and memories of what had happened came flooding back. She didn't remember passing out, but she wasn't surprised that she had. Using Nostia took its toll on both the mind and body, and when combined with the stress of Gamon's betrayal, the encounter had exhausted her. She'd gladly take the academy's brutal training camp over this any day.

She carefully wiped the back of her hand across her face and found that the blood was still warm and sticky; she hadn't been out for long, maybe a couple of minutes. The gash beside her eye stung like crazy when she probed it with her fingers, and she could feel the way the serrated blade had shredded her skin. It was going to leave a mark.

Someone would no doubt be along shortly to see what all the commotion was about. HSP had probably been dispatched to the building after the shots had been fired. She hauled herself to her feet and swept her gaze around the room, taking in the damage. Gamon remained on the floor with his own kytara still embedded in his chest. He was a Nosti who had attempted to kidnap her and recruit her into the Resistance. Yes, that's what had happened. He'd stalked her and followed her to the apartment, and then he'd attacked when she'd threatened to go to the police. There was a measure of truth to it all, which would make the story all the more plausible.

Her focus was drawn to the nostium jar and the drip bag on the dining table. She threw them into the kitchen sink with a wad of paper and lit them on fire, opening the window to allow the fumes to escape the room. The thin plastic tube and bag melted away quickly. The glass jar itself didn't burn, but the fire consumed the nostium residue and the shattered container contributed nicely to the rest of the mess in the room when she threw it on the floor. She pocketed the needle and rinsed any remnants down the drain, extinguishing the flames. The final step was Gamon's communicator; she retrieved it and tore out the memory chip, erasing any evidence that he had ever contacted her. She wiped all of her fingerprints from it and then chucked it at the wall, destroying the delicate screen.

The hum of engines outside signaled the arrival of law enforcement. The building's front doors burst open and the sound of hurried footsteps echoed through the spiraling stairwell. Ziva dropped back down to the floor, ready to play the part of the injured victim, but the swollen injection site on her arm caught her attention. While nostium was undetectable in the blood stream, any sign of an injection would raise questions she didn't want to answer. After a brief search for a solution, she did the first thing that came to mind. Gritting her teeth, she ran her arm across the end of the kytara that wasn't impaling Gamon's body, opening up a second gash over the hole left by the needle. She then collapsed onto her back and closed her eyes, and that was how the officers found her when they entered with weapons raised.

Ziva didn't remember much about the next two days. The first hours were spent in the med center receiving treatment for her face and arm. Then she found herself caught up in a whirlwind of HSP red tape and the relentless news reporters who had learned about her battle with Gamon. They no doubt wanted to make sure everyone knew about the young woman who had somehow killed a Nosti by herself. The agency took her under its wing, releasing her name but declining all interviews and photo opportunities. She remained safely anonymous, tucked away in the dorms at HSP's training center.

She lay quietly on her bed on the third day, staring up at the ceiling and wishing she could catch some shut-eye during her allotted down time. Her roommate, a short girl with stunning blue eyes, napped on the bunk against the opposite wall. Ziva recognized her from school and basic training. The girl had a long, cumbersome name, but everyone had always just called her Zinni. She seemed nice enough; in any case, she hadn't bothered Ziva with questions about Gamon or her injuries, and that was much appreciated.

A knock drew her attention to the room's open door and she found a training officer standing there.

"Payvan, someone here to see you," he said.

Intrigued, she got up and followed him down the hall, wondering if her mother had by chance come to visit after hearing about the battle. It was probably just wishful thinking, and it really wasn't even wishful—it was just thinking. She honestly had no desire to see her mother, not now anyway. Namani Payvan-Jaroon had changed after losing her husband in the Fringe War, after marrying the Royal General, after giving birth to Ziva's twin half-siblings. The woman was the primary reason Ziva had run away from Haphor and returned to Noro as a child. She had never been exactly sure what had caused the change. It was some combination of depression, denial, and no doubt persuasion from Njo, the bastard that he was. He'd despised Ziva from the beginning, so she'd loathed him in return.

She felt her face flush with anger and she shook her head. Getting worked up over the past was pointless. She followed the officer into the cafeteria, where several high-level agents were gathered around a man wearing a formal HSP uniform. She immediately recognized him as Director Emeri Arion.

"You must be Payvan," he said, reaching out to shake her hand as she approached. "I'd address you as 'Novice' like all the other recruits, but that title hardly seems appropriate after what you've done."

She wasn't entirely sure how she was supposed to respond, so she simply nodded and shook his hand in return.

"Ziva, I came here to make you a proposition. I'm sure you're familiar with the agency's operations divisions. Only the best agents become part of our ops teams." He consulted a data pad one of the agents passed to him. "The academy has given you some impressive marks already. You've broken some records that I didn't think could ever be broken, and you somehow managed to best a rogue Nosti without any formal training. Your background data and psych profile are exactly what I'm looking for. I want to turn you into a special ops agent."

Ziva blinked. "Sir?"

"You'll still undergo the same training regimen as everyone else, of course. We can fine-tune the skills you already have and build on them. It will be up to you to work hard and pass all the tests, but if you're willing to do that, I'll pull you out of the Junior Guard and move you straight into the ops training program. What do you think?"

It was the first time she had smiled in a long time. "I'd like that very much, sir."

· 23 ·
PAYVAN RESIDENCE
NORO, HAPHEZ

Ziva's foot twitched when she felt someone's fingers brush against it. Her eyelids fluttered open and she sat bolt upright when she saw morning light pouring in through the window. She was on the living room sofa, and she vaguely remembered sitting down to keep an eye on the front door while Aroska and Ryon sat with an unconscious Jayden. The idea that she'd accidentally dozed off made her sick.

"Morning, beautiful," Skeet said with a grin, tickling her foot again. He extended a glass of govino juice.

"Oh shut up." She pulled her legs down from where they'd rested on the center table and downed the contents of the glass. "How long have I been out?" she gasped.

"About an hour," Skeet replied. "Tarbic didn't want to bother you."

"Skeet, there could be a Solaris army surrounding this house as we speak. Please, by all means, bother me." She stood up and took a moment to brush some loose hair out of her face. "How long have you been here?"

"Twenty minutes or so," Skeet replied, stirring his own juice. "Aroska says you don't think Solaris wants Jayden dead. Tell me what you're thinking."

Ziva gave her sleepy mind another few seconds to wake up before mustering up an explanation. "Think about it. They've had three different opportunities. First of all, they could have just shot him in the forest along with the rest of the Tantali guards. Then, at HSP, our Solaris inside man had plenty of time to off him before we caught up to them. Instead, he created a diversion by pulling the emergency alarm and tried to lead him out of the building. Last night, that Sardon was obviously involved with Solaris, so why didn't he just kill Jayden while he was sleeping? He used Axonyte and was dragging him out of the house. They're trying to take him somewhere, somewhere away from us. They need him for something."

"Presumably related to this transmission the Sardon mentioned?"

She nodded. "Like you said yesterday, we're not sure if Solaris left Jayden in the forest when they saw us coming or if they just didn't know they needed him yet."

"What are you saying?" asked Aroska as he came in from outside.

"I'm saying we could be dealing with one of two scenarios. Case one: Solaris knew they needed Jayden but they were forced to abandon him in order to escape before we could capture any of them. Now they're trying again."

"Unlikely," Skeet said, shaking his head. "It wouldn't have been that hard to grab him. They took the governor easily enough."

"Which is why the second option makes more sense," Ziva went on. "Solaris captures Governor Saiffe, hoping he can provide them with information about this 'transmission,' but they realize later that they also require Jayden for whatever reason. That would explain why they just dumped him in the clearing—they didn't know he was the one they needed."

"I see what you mean," Aroska said. "They need him alive to do whatever the governor couldn't. Still, that guy at HSP was ready to shoot him yesterday before I took him down."

"Meaning they don't want Jayden telling us whatever it is that they want from him," Skeet concluded. "If they can't have him, no one can." He grew quiet for a moment. "You don't think Jayden was involved in the governor's abduction, do you? Maybe it's no coincidence he's still alive."

"I suppose it's something to take into consideration," Aroska admitted after several long seconds of silence. "But why would he have any reason to be in league with Solaris?"

"Either way, he's still hiding something from us," Ziva said. "I've got to go talk to him."

"He's still asleep," Skeet said, stopping her from rushing off. "He seems to be conscious now but we haven't been able to wake him up yet. Ryon is with him now."

"Maybe we'll learn something from Vinny Jaxton," Aroska suggested. "I'm leaving to find him now."

"Then I'm coming with you," Ziva said, slipping on her boots and taking a jacket from the hook by the door. She fastened her supply belt and holster and turned to Skeet. "You got things handled here?"

He nodded. "Go. Zinni will be here soon, and we'll contact you if anything comes up."

Ziva pulled on her jacket and made sure her pistol was fully charged. "I would still love to know how the hell Solaris found us," she said as she and Aroska went out the door. "And they somehow breached my security. This is an HSP-grade system...." She stopped there, her mind making the connection just as the words left her mouth. If someone had managed to alter the agency's transmission logs, trigger an emergency drill, and access the holding rooms, they probably wouldn't have had a problem remotely disabling her system. She swore under her breath; it was time for an upgrade.

It was another clean, crisp morning and a thin layer of fog crept across the grass as they made their way to the car. "I wish you'd be a little more patient with the kid," Aroska said, getting into the pilot's seat.

"He's not telling us everything," Ziva shot back. "Solaris keeps coming back because they want whatever he's hiding. All of this is his fault."

"He's alone and terrified. The people who are supposed to be protecting him shouldn't make him more afraid."

"I'd appreciate it if you'd stop telling me how to do my job."

Aroska maneuvered the vehicle across the massive yard and into the outskirts of Noro. "And what exactly is your job? Who are you, Ziva Payvan? You seem to know all there is to know about me, but I know next to nothing about you. Half of HSP is afraid of you, and the other half worships you, but nobody even knows who you are. What's so special about you?"

"That is both confidential and none of your business," Ziva replied.

He scoffed. "Well, as far as I'm concerned, you're just one more arrogant *shouka* who couldn't care less about anyone but herself."

Ziva took a moment to stare out the window at the passing scenery. "You're not wrong there," she sighed. *I don't care because I can't care, not in this business.*

Aroska's knuckles were white as he gripped the steering controls. "You're unbelievable," he muttered.

They completed their journey in awkward silence. A ten-minute flight brought them to Lakin Square, which accounted for the greater part of downtown Noro and stretched from the spaceport and HSP Headquarters to the projects on the east side. They veered the craft toward the latter, home to cheap housing and various shops, though the majority of the buildings were run down and abandoned. Aroska stopped the car a short distance from a shop that had certainly seen better days but still displayed an open sign in the window.

Ziva reached for the door handle, but Aroska's hand on her shoulder held her back. "Stay here," he ordered. "I'll go in first. We don't want to scare him off."

He got out and went inside, leaving her alone. She climbed out as well and leaned against the car. Suddenly so many questions—how was she supposed to answer? *"The greatest killer in the history of HSP."* People usually didn't take kindly to that. In fact, only a select few even knew: Emeri and some of the agency's captains, Skeet and Zinni, and then Marshay and Ryon were aware to an extent. The only thing everyone else knew was that she was the lieutenant of the Alpha special ops team who went off-world for one service term per year, not the part about being one of HSP's contract assassins. If Aroska really wanted the two of them to get along—which they needed to, at least for now—he didn't need to know.

Taking a deep breath of morning air, Ziva took a moment to look around what little of the huge square she could see. There were quite a few people wandering to and fro, some obviously drunk or high.

Although the city of Noro already had a reputation for being rough, this area exceeded the norm. The people here were dirty and fearful, and the crime rate soared. The streets were dark and narrow, and most of the buildings were old and scarred with bullet holes and plasma scoring.

Aroska emerged from the shop, disappointed. "He's not here," he announced, approaching the car, "but his stuff is inside and this is his bike parked out here."

"You know where to find him then?" Ziva asked, crossing her arms.

Aroska nodded and pulled a small sack from his pocket, displaying the bundle of short brown objects it contained: govino sticks. While the juice of the same name was derived from the fruity seeds inside the govino pods, the outer shells contained a hallucinogenic compound and were often crushed, rolled, and smoked recreationally. Ziva had smoked a stick on a couple of occasions but didn't like the way it made her head feel foggy.

"Jaxton is one of the SCU's CIs," he explained. "I didn't want to advertise that in front of everyone last night. He's a *very* heavy smoker—ergo it's not very hard to bribe him for information. These junkies will do anything for a fix. If I know Jaxton, he'll be nearby having a smoke. You take a look around out here, and I'll check out back." He showed her a photo of the man on his data pad. "We'll meet back here in five."

He disappeared down the alley beside the shop, leaving Ziva alone again. She turned back toward the square and began wandering toward a more crowded area down the street. Several benches were situated around a rusty old fountain that was blanketed in fungus and barely dribbling. A man who appeared to be Jaxton sat on one of the benches with his back turned, smoking a govino stick just as Aroska had predicted.

Ziva approached slowly and came around to perch on the back of the bench. A quick glance told her she'd been correct about his identity, but he was either too stoned to realize she was there or he just didn't care. He looked like an average inner-city junkie, with filthy clothes, greasy hair, and dark circles around his eyes. His hands rested in his lap, one of which held his half-smoked govino stick, and he stared vacantly ahead at the fountain.

Unsure whether to begin without Aroska, Ziva took a deep breath and cleared her throat, fixing her gaze on the trickling water.

For a moment Jaxton didn't move, and she wondered if he'd picked up on such a subtle gesture. But after several seconds of awkward silence, he brought the govino stick to his lips and shot her a glance. "Cash?" he asked, exhaling the smoke through his nose.

"Sure."

He was quiet for another few seconds. "What are you interested in?" he drawled.

"Information," she replied, revealing the HSP credentials under her jacket.

For appearing to be so out of it, Jaxton certainly reacted quickly. He dropped the stick and scrambled to his feet to run, but Ziva seized the back of his coat before he made it more than two steps. He only struggled for a moment before she wrenched his arm behind him and led him back to the shop, where she pinned him to the wall with her pistol to his chest.

"Please," he whimpered. "I'm only holding it for a friend. None of it is mine! I swear!"

"I'm not here about drugs, you idiot," Ziva snarled, moving the barrel of the gun up to his forehead. "I want—"

"Hey, hey, hey! Ziva, Ziva!" Aroska stepped into the shop, keeping his own pistol trained on her for a couple of seconds longer than she would have liked. "Let him go."

Ziva glanced from one man to the other and then holstered her weapon, huffing a sigh as she stepped aside. This was Aroska's turf after all, and although she felt more confident in her own interrogation techniques, it couldn't hurt to let him run the show.

"Jaxton?" Aroska said, extending a hand in an attempt to calm the man. "We're just here to ask a few questions."

Jaxton hadn't taken his eyes off Ziva since Aroska had entered. "Is she okay?" he asked, finally turning away.

"She's with me," Aroska replied, sliding his gun back into its holster. "In fact, if Lieutenant Payvan wants any information from you, I expect you to fully cooperate. Can you do that?"

The man still seemed unsure, but nodded anyway. "What do you people want?"

"I need some information about Solaris," Aroska replied. "What have they been up to lately?"

Jaxton moved around to the other side of the shop's counter and took a seat on a tall stool. "Not much," he answered. "You of all people would know if something was going on. What do you want to know?"

"We want to know what connections they have with Sardonis," Ziva said. She took hold of his arm and rolled his sleeve back to reveal the Solaris star, the same one the insurgents in the forest bore. "I came across a Sardon last night with this tattoo, only there was an extra mark here. What do Sardons have to do with Solaris?"

At the mention of the word "Sardon," Jaxton's pulse had quickened—she could feel it in his wrist.

He was hesitant to reply, but swallowed. "The other mark is to differentiate—" he began as beads of perspiration appeared on his forehead. His breathing became quick and uneven. "I can't say..." he said, attempting to stand up.

Ziva clamped down on his arm and held him there. "Differentiate between what?"

He tried to pry her hand away, but he was shaking so badly it was no use. "Please," he murmured, running his tongue over his dry lips. "I...I need another smoke."

"Jaxton?" Aroska pressed.

"They'll kill me if they find out I told you."

Ziva glanced at Aroska, who immediately went to shut and lock the door. He made a quick sweep of the rest of the shop, ensuring the environment was secure.

"Who?" Ziva asked as soon as he returned.

"I can't tell you," Jaxton sputtered. "Please, they have complete control over me. They *will* kill me."

"We'll make sure that doesn't happen," Aroska said. "Is there any way they'd know we're here right now?"

Jaxton shook his head. "I don't know. I...don't think so."

"Then talk to us."

Ziva slid her hand from Jaxton's arm and leaned forward in anticipation. "Who are 'they'?"

Still shaking, Jaxton raked his fingers through his hair and took a deep breath. "The second star you saw on the Sardon is to differentiate between us and them," he explained, glancing around as if he was unsure whether or not to go on. "It's a second Solaris cell based on Sardonis, controlled by a man named Dane Bothum."

"Do you know where this Bothum is located?" Ziva asked.

"He uses Dakiti as a primary headquarters."

"The Sardon medical facility?"

"That's right."

Ziva nodded to herself, thinking things over. "Are you aware that Solaris abducted Governor Enrik Saiffe of Tantal yesterday?"

"Yes," Jaxton replied, "and I also heard there were no Solaris survivors after HSP showed up. Can I assume you were there?"

Aroska didn't answer. "Jaxton, who is the Solaris agent working inside HSP?" he asked.

"I don't know what you're talking about."

His shifting eyes gave away the lie. "I'm pretty sure you do," Ziva said, removing her pistol and holding it where he could see it.

Aroska held a warning hand out to her and pulled out the bag of govino sticks. To Ziva's surprise, he lit one of the sticks for himself and pointedly took a long drag from it, looking the junkie in the eye as he did so. Jaxton immediately grabbed for the sack, but Aroska kept it just out of his reach. "Who?" he repeated, watching the man through the cloud of smoke he exhaled.

"You don't want to know," Jaxton answered.

"Don't do this to me, Jaxton."

"One stick. Let me think things over, and then I might tell you. Just one."

Aroska looked to Ziva for a moment and then sighed, tossing the man a single stick. "Fine. You've got two minutes."

Jaxton gratefully took up the govino stick and let himself out the front door. He leaned up against the large window, staying in sight.

"Will he run?" Ziva asked.

"If he does, he's too wasted to make it very far," Aroska replied, pocketing the remainder of the sticks and taking one last drag from his own before snuffing it out on the counter.

"Then how do you know the information he's giving us is even credible?"

"I don't, but at least he's giving us something."

Ziva looked toward Jaxton at the exact moment the sizzling plasma bolt struck him in the head. She dove to the floor, dragging Aroska with her. "Someone obviously doesn't want him giving us *anything*," she muttered, straining to see out the window. There was a streak of blood where his head had struck the glass on impact, and she could see part of his limp body where it had collapsed on the walkway outside. The shot had come from a distance, but there was no way to tell whether the shooter was aware of their presence inside.

"*Sheyss*," Aroska swore, pulling himself into a sitting position against the wall. "Can you see anything?"

She shook her head but looked out again anyway. There was a line of sickly trees that obscured her view of the shops across the street, and beyond that were the tall buildings of the city. The shot could have come from just about anywhere.

"Is there a back door?" she whispered, though there was no real need to be quiet.

"This way," he replied. Crouching low, he led her around the counter and through a storage room where a door led into the alley behind the building. Everything was quiet. The shooter was probably long gone—anyone with a brain stem would be out of there before surveillance probes could catch them on cams.

The two of them crept along the outside wall, moving back around toward the front. So far nobody else had approached the building or stopped to examine the body. Their vehicle waited directly down the alley, also untouched.

"Come on," Ziva said. "Stay low." She sprinted for the car and turned to find Aroska, who had stopped to rifle through Jaxton's coat pockets.

"Give me a second," he said, aware she was waiting. His hand emerged with what appeared to be a communicator, and he hurried to join her in the car.

Ziva pulled the vehicle away and took off as fast as she could. "This certainly complicates things," she muttered, taking a look at Aroska. "Find something?"

"Maybe," he replied, plugging the communicator into the car's portable computer. "Let's see who he's been talking to."

The device's contact history came up on the small screen and Ziva did her best to read through the numbers as she steered through the city traffic. "That looks like an HSP code," she pointed out, motioning toward a frequently-used number. "Is it traceable?"

"Won't be able to get any chatter," Aroska replied, "but I've already pinpointed a location. We need to get to Headquarters right now."

· 24 ·
HSP HEADQUARTERS
NORO, HAPHEZ

Aroska held the portable computer from the car as he and Ziva came out of the elevator onto the field ops squad floor. "We're right on top of it," he said as his gaze fell on a garbage receptacle just to his left. Handing the computer to Ziva, he took hold of it and spilled its contents onto the floor. She joined him and together they dug through the scraps of discarded food, paper, and plastic.

"What's going on?" Adin exclaimed, rushing over from his desk.

"We're looking for this," Ziva replied, recovering a small white communicator from the pile of trash. She stood up, as did Aroska. "Someone was using it to contact one of Lieutenant Tarbic's CIs."

Adin took it from her and looked it over. "This is one of the encrypted comm units all the captains use." He handed it back to Aroska. "You're saying the mole was using it to get in touch with your contact?"

"Yes," Ziva replied, snatching the communicator and handing it back to Adin before Aroska could get a word in edgewise. "And he happens to be dead now, shot in the head right before we could question him. Whoever has been talking to him wanted to make sure he didn't tell us anything. They probably dumped the communicator here recently, maybe when they realized Jaxton had company." She warily swept her eyes over the squad floor but saw nothing of interest, and the area was clear of any surveillance cams that might have caught sight of the mole. "See if you can pull any information from it," she said to Adin. "If it's encrypted, we won't be able to listen in on any transmissions, but see if you can bring up any of the other recent contact codes."

"Sure, sure," Adin said.

"Have you made any progress toward finding Governor Saiffe?"

The man shook his head. "We've had surveillance on all of Solaris's known bases since yesterday, and we sent strike teams into each of them early this morning. There's been no sign of him. It would help if we could find the shuttle he was taken in, but as long as they've got someone in here who can cover their tracks, we're screwed."

Aroska's gaze ventured toward the workstations of the Solaris Control Unit across the massive floor. It looked like the agents were starting to mobilize. "I'll be right back," he said.

He jogged toward them and caught sight of Saun Zaid as she made her way out of the bullpen with a field pack slung over her shoulder. "Saun!" he called, hurrying to catch up.

She whirled, startled, and didn't seem terribly relieved to see it was him. "What are you doing here?" she said, stifling a cough.

"What's going on?"

"Most of the SCU is being dispatched into the field. The director wants us out there as close to Solaris as we can get so we can look for anything that might help us find the governor."

"How long will you be gone?"

Some of the tension in her body released when he reached out to stroke her arm. "Could be hours, could be days," she answered, "whenever we find something."

"Saun, Jaxton is dead."

Her fuchsia eyes widened. "What?"

Aroska looked back across the floor to where Ziva and Adin were hovering over one of the Alpha team's workstations. "He was shot, probably by Solaris to keep him from talking. He was about to give us the name of the Solaris agent working inside HSP."

"You still think there's someone?"

Aroska nodded. A sudden and terrible thought hit him as he watched her, but he dismissed it as absurd and shook his head. "The guy we found yesterday couldn't have been acting alone."

Saun raised her eyebrows and took a step closer to him, all signs of her jumpy behavior gone. She glanced over at Ziva and Adin. "So, how's it going with the *kef shouka*?"

He sputtered in response to the coarse language and stifled a chuckle, hoping no one else had heard her. "We're still driving each other crazy, but I'm getting by."

"Did you take my advice?"

"I did. I was afraid she was going to take my head off, but I think I made an impression."

Saun punched him playfully in the arm and sidled closer. "You're pretty good at that."

"So I've heard," he said with a wink. Then he sighed. "I'm just trying to ignore her and focus on what I need to do to complete the mission. I can't wait until this is all over."

"It will be soon," Saun assured him, leaning up to plant a quick kiss on his cheek. "You'd better get back to work. I have to go."

"Let me know if you find something," he said.

"I will," she replied, walking toward the stairs to join the others. "Goodbye, Aroska."

Something in her tone disturbed him, but he shook it off as he had before and watched her go. If anyone could find something of use, it was Saun—he may have been the highest-ranking agent in the SCU, but she was the veteran expert.

"Tarbic!" Ziva's voice boomed across the floor. "Let's go!"

Ah yes. He chuckled to himself as he made his way back toward her; while vulgar, Saun's description of her was certainly accurate. "You ready?" Aroska asked as he approached.

She said nothing, her mouth a straight line.

He shook his head and followed her into the elevator.

· 25 ·
PAYVAN RESIDENCE
NORO, HAPHEZ

Z iva sighed and leaned back against the seat's headrest. The scrambled communicator had been handed over to Adin, and according to Aroska, most of the SCU had been deployed into the field. So far, the director hadn't found out about the little mishap with the Sardon the night before, either. Everything seemed to be running smoothly for once, something she'd learned to never take for granted. Now she could devote all her energy to questioning Jayden about this mysterious transmission.

Her communicator beeped and she looked down at the incoming identification code, recognizing it immediately as Skeet's. Perhaps she had thought too soon. "Yeah, Skeet."

"We've got a problem here."

They came into sight of her house at the exact moment the words left his mouth. Five armored cars were scattered across the yard and a couple of strange men in uniform stood near the front door.

"What the hell?" Aroska muttered, speeding up.

"I'll say," Ziva replied to Skeet. Her hand went to her holster. "We're almost there."

She was somewhat relieved when she recognized three of the armored cars from the Tantali convoy in the forest—at least it wasn't more Sardons or HSP. However, the guards outside didn't seem so happy to see them.

Aroska pulled the car up and they leaped out, pistols drawn. The two Tantalis reacted quickly with their own weapons, and two more came out of the house.

"What is this?" Ziva demanded as they advanced toward the front door.

"Drop your weapons!" one of the guards ordered.

Ziva holstered her gun and held her hands up but didn't break stride. "What's going on here?" she asked again.

The guards didn't stand down but seemed unnerved by her lack of hesitation. Skeet appeared in the doorway and held out his hand. "Easy, boys," he said. "They're with us."

Ziva and Aroska proceeded into the house, receiving nervous looks from the soldiers. Zinni, Ryon, and Marshay were all seated in the living room with about ten Tantalis surrounding them. Five more stood in the kitchen with Jayden. Some of them were rather disheveled and sported various bandages and braces, probably survivors from the ambush in the forest.

"Don't look at *me*," Skeet muttered, stepping aside.

Ziva shot an accusatory glare at Jayden. "What have you done?" she asked, arms crossed.

One of the guards bore a captain's insignia on his jacket. He approached her, hand extended. "Lieutenant Payvan, Gavin Bront, Captain of the Tantali Royal Guard."

She ignored his handshake offer and stared him down, jaw set. She recognized him as the man who had been fighting back-to-back with Jayden before being shot in the leg. "What the hell are you people doing in my house?"

"We received a message from Mr. Saiffe last night," Bront replied, keeping his tone professional. "He requested assistance, claiming you weren't putting an adequate amount of effort toward finding the governor."

Ziva closed her eyes in frustration and took several steps toward Jayden. "Do you even *know* how many precautions we took to make sure Solaris couldn't find you here? You led them straight to you!"

Jayden stood his ground but glanced to his comrades for support. "I don't understand."

"If you called your people, whoever's working inside HSP could have picked up your chatter and monitored it," Aroska put in, trying to be less abrasive.

Ziva stepped even closer to the young man, placing herself between him and his guards. "What do you know about a transmission regarding Sardons?"

"What?"

"You heard me. That's why they're after you. What do you know that they don't want you to tell us?"

Jayden looked to the captain, who attempted to step in front of Ziva. She cut him off without giving him a second glance, placing a solid hand on his chest.

"Lieutenant Payvan, please," Bront said. "Mr. Saiffe has been through a lot since yesterday. He's in our jurisdiction now, and if you don't mind, we're taking him home. After all, our governor is still missing, and his son is the next person with the authority to succeed him and lead our people."

"Hang on a minute!" Skeet exclaimed, moving toward them and drawing a tense reaction from the guards. "As long as Jayden has anything to do with Solaris, he's in *our* jurisdiction."

"I'll handle this, Skeet!" Ziva snapped. She shifted her focus to each of the guards individually, addressing them as a whole. "You're not going anywhere until I find out what I need to know."

Bront wasn't convinced. "Lieutenant, if this delay affects the wellbeing of the governor or his son in any way, the Tantali government will hold you responsible."

She paid no attention to the man and kept her focus on Jayden. "Then *you'd* better start talking."

The young man straightened his shoulders and looked her straight in the eye. "It doesn't concern you," he replied. "I don't know what you want to know."

Ziva felt her face flush. "I'm not so sure I like your attitude," she said flatly, drawing her pistol and pressing it to his forehead.

Every guard in the room instantly had his rifle trained on her, but her team and Marshay and Ryon had their own weapons and held their ground.

"You think I'm afraid to shoot you, Jayden?"

He shook his head, though it had been a rather rhetorical question. With a quick wave of his hand, the Tantalis reluctantly put down their rifles and waited.

"Talk to us, kid," Aroska said.

"It was two weeks ago, just before we came here," Jayden finally began, his eyes fixed on Ziva's pistol. "I intercepted a transmission in my father's office. It came from Sardonis and was headed for a ship passing through our system. At first, I didn't think anything of it, but then something was said about The Dakiti Center. They were talking like there was something more than just medical research going on."

"Like what?"

"Military stuff, the building of an army. They were calling it 'Shelora Boeta' and I wasn't sure what it meant."

Ziva put her gun down and turned to Aroska, who nodded. "Solaris Beta," they said in unison. At that moment, all the pieces fell together in Ziva's mind. This was the second Solaris group Jaxton had spoken of, the one based on Sardonis and controlled by this Dane Bothum. "Did you pick up any names?" she asked Jayden.

"The message was being sent to a man they were calling Bothum. It sounded like he's heading up the operation." He hesitated a moment. "They have my father at Dakiti, don't they? They took him there because they thought he knew about the transmission. But I'm the one they really want."

"Now sir," Bront said, "we don't want to jump to conclusions."

"It's the best lead we have so far. It's better than anything *these* people have found."

Ziva set her jaw and stared him down through narrowed eyes. He did have a point; if the governor wasn't at any of the local Solaris compounds, he could very well be at Dakiti. Jayden's description of the transmission confirmed everything Jaxton had told them, though it sounded like Bothum was up to something more than just running a second Solaris cell. The fact that the Sardons felt the need to meddle in Haphezian diplomacy was cause for concern. Even if they didn't find Enrik Saiffe, investigating the facility might still be high on HSP's priority list.

She sighed. A ludicrous idea had just come to mind and she silently debated with herself for several seconds over what should be done. She thought about the tracker she had placed on Jayden the night before. *It could work.* At this point, she was angry enough with the young man that she was willing to go with it.

"Sergeant Duvo!" Ziva addressed Skeet without taking her eyes off of Jayden and Bront. "See to it that these men have enough fuel and supplies to get safely home to Tantal."

"Ziva...?"

"That's an order, Skeet."

Bront watched her for a moment as if looking for sincerity in her request. "Stand down," he ordered his guards, who had been standing in a strict formation around Ziva's people in the living room.

She broke off from the group and veered for the front door, but Skeet caught her arm.

"Z," he said, such an obnoxious, questioning tone in his voice. Did he not trust her to have control over the situation?

"Just do it," she replied, feigning defeat for the sake of the Tantalis. She pulled her arm away and headed outside, ignoring the two guards who still stood on the front steps. A massive sarmi tree stood about twenty meters from the house, rising up near the edge of the sheer drop-off down to the Tranyi River. It had been there for as long as she could remember. She had spent many hours in that tree as a small child, climbing up into a crook between two branches and leaping down into her father's arms. She'd been pleasantly surprised to find it still standing when she'd purchased this property back as an adult. The day before he left to fight in the Fringe War, Kalim Payvan had carved the native Haphezian symbol meaning "eternal" into the tree's mighty trunk. That was the last time she had ever seen her father, but there the carving remained after all these years.

Ziva paused for a moment in the shade of the tree, eyes closed, feeling the cool air from the river on her face. She wasn't one for sentiment, and in that sense she sometimes wondered what she was doing living in the house she'd been born in. But being there brought about a certain peace, a certain calmness, and right now that was exactly what she needed. She needed time to think, to settle down. Ryon always encouraged her to spend some time under the tree. Said it was therapeutic. She agreed; this was always the first place she came upon returning from a high-stakes mission. The sweet scent of the tree and the fresh air helped her unwind, and she'd often found that it was a good place to get some thinking done.

Squinting against the mid-morning sunlight that glinted off the massive river below, Ziva lowered herself into the depression she'd worn in the ground from lying there so often. She lay down flat on her back, knees up, eyes closed, hands on her forehead. Taking a deep breath of earthy air, she let herself forget about the whole affair with Jayden for just a brief moment. She would have rather kept him in her custody, if for no other reason than to maintain a sense of control, but at the same time she was relieved to have him out of her hair. The only problem with her plan was that these overzealous humans would be no match against the agile, quick-witted Sardons if they made any attempt to go find Governor Saiffe. They would rush to Sardonis too hastily, hoping sheer numbers would win the battle, and get themselves either imprisoned or killed. And who knew what this Dane Bothum was concocting behind the scenes at Dakiti? There was no way to know if they would find the governor or if any of them would even survive, but it was a risk she was willing to subject them to.

Her sensitive Haphezian nose could smell Aroska coming just before her ears picked up the soft crunching of his boots in the grass. What did he think he was doing out here, and why had Skeet and Zinni allowed him to follow her? She let her frustration out in the form of a sigh and held completely still. Maybe he'd actually stop and realize what a novel idea it would be to respect her privacy.

He didn't stop. Ziva rolled her eyes behind their closed lids and ran her tongue across her lips. "Damn it, Tarbic, what are you doing?" she demanded, too tired to bother raising her voice.

Aroska made a noise that sounded like a stifled chuckle. "I think I've got you figured out, Ziva Payvan," he replied.

"I told you to leave it alone," she scoffed, opening one eye and tilting her head just enough that she could see him. He stood a couple of meters away, hands tucked into the pockets of his jacket, admiring the impressive tree. He directed his gaze back down toward her when he realized she was looking at him.

"Fine," he said with a shrug. "Eternal?" He gestured toward the carving.

Ziva pulled herself into a sitting position and stared out across the river. "Leave that alone too."

"All right." He came up and leaned against the trunk of the tree, almost directly behind her. She was glad she didn't have to look at him—otherwise she might have strangled him just for the hell of it. "So why the change of heart?"

Ziva looked over to where the Tantalis were exiting the house and starting up their cars. "It wasn't."

"Oh?"

She shook her head and looked back to the river, wondering briefly if Aroska was still interested in killing her. Maybe she shouldn't have her back to him. She could still sense some anger and hostility directed her way, but there no longer seemed to be any desire to put a bullet through the back of her head. Ever since she'd caught him in the doorway the previous night, his attitude had been one of cautious tolerance...and maybe even curiosity.

"No. I have a plan."

"That plan wouldn't happen to involve leaving Jayden to his own devices and then using him to bait Bothum, would it?"

"You forgot the part where we bag Bothum and get both Jayden and the governor out."

Aroska scoffed. "And here I thought you didn't care. You think they've really got the governor at Dakiti?"

"Jayden was right. The agency has checked the rest of the Solaris bases here, all of which have turned out to be dead ends. It makes sense that they'd take him there. But even if he *is* there, he may be dead already. We're grasping at straws here, but it's the best chance we've got." Then she sighed and added under her breath, "And if we don't get the governor, we can at least nail these Solaris scumbags."

"What makes you so sure the Tantalis would go to Dakiti instead of home to Tantal?"

"Even if they do go home, they'll be on their way to Sardonis with reinforcements within a day or so. They'll go to Dakiti, most likely get captured, and Jayden will lead us straight to Bothum."

"And if he dies in the process?"

That's not my problem. "We'll just have to catch up to him before that happens."

"You're crazy," Aroska said. "Do you know that?"

Ziva turned her head, addressing him without looking. "I've learned to take it as a compliment."

"Fine," Aroska said, exhaling through his nose with a hiss. "How exactly do you plan on catching up to him?"

Ziva explained how she'd placed the tiny tracking device on Jayden the night before. "With the way he was acting at dinner, I was afraid he'd bolt. Figured it might come in handy, and I guess it has. Now we'll know exactly where he is in that facility."

"And if he doesn't go to Sardonis? I can't imagine Bront would let him accompany them on a rescue mission."

"He'll go," she replied, watching a colorful bird glide gracefully across the river. She gave no further explanation, but based on what she'd seen, Jayden was resilient enough that he would want to be part of any attempt to get his father back.

Aroska sighed, unimpressed. He stepped around in front of her, offering his hand to help her up. "Then I guess we'd better get started planning this crazy operation," he said, his face expressionless.

Ziva wanted to ignore his hand, but finally took it. Aroska pulled her to her feet but didn't let go once she was there. Instead, he flipped her hand over and ran his thumb over the calluses that had formed after years of handling her favorite sniper rifle. Maybe he *did* have her figured out. Unconcerned, she shifted her eyes from her hand to meet his questioning stare. Perhaps it was better that he knew about the things she did outside of special ops—he'd be less inclined to bother her.

Aroska no longer seemed quite so eager to make eye contact, letting his gaze flit around. He let go of her hand and took a slight step backward. She could sense the anger welling up inside him, anger about Soren's death.

"Sniper?" he finally asked, his voice dry.

Frustrated, Ziva planted her fist into his gut and used the brief moment of immobility to push him back against the tree trunk. "Contract assassin," she corrected, taking up fistfuls of his jacket. "*Black Agent*. Why do you have to keep pushing it?"

Aroska closed his eyes, swallowing against the pain of the blow. She let go of him before he could answer and placed her hands on top of her head. Any progress she'd made toward calming her nerves had officially gone down the drain.

Once again looking out over the water, she mentally took herself back through the motions of lying down in her hollow and feeling the breeze on her skin. She straightened her thoughts out into a single-file line, slowing the rush of emotions and memories that flooded her mind. This wasn't healthy. She needed her time alone before she snapped.

"I'm sorry I even asked," Aroska muttered, his voice cutting through the silence like a knife and causing her train of thought to derail again.

Ziva bit her lip. "Lieutenant, please go inside before I kill you," she said through her teeth. "I'm not going to ask you again."

· 26 ·
PAYVAN RESIDENCE
NORO, HAPHEZ

Skeet didn't bother looking up when Aroska came wandering back into the house. He remained in his place on the sofa beside Zinni, looking over the information on Dakiti she had already pulled up from the agency's files. The Tantalis had made a hasty exit without so much as a thank-you for the fact that Jayden was still alive, and Marshay and Ryon had disappeared again, minding their own business. The relative peacefulness in the house was a relief. He didn't mind having the kid out of the way, and he understood now that it was for good reason. Ziva would have never just given up an argument. Judging by the tone of her voice, she had a plan. Now he and Zinni were trying to stay one step ahead of her.

Realizing that Aroska had neither moved nor spoken since entering, Skeet stole a glance in his direction. The man stood just inside the doorway, staring vacantly ahead, his face contorted with anger and disbelief. The fact that this reaction had been incited by an encounter with Ziva piqued Skeet's curiosity. If Tarbic was going to keep pestering her, he was going to get what he deserved, and he probably just had.

"You okay?" he asked casually, the majority of his focus still on Zinni's computer.

"Skeet," Aroska said, desperation in his voice, "you've got to tell me about Ziva. I need to know about her *now*."

Skeet honestly hadn't seen that coming. He'd expected a barrage of questions, not a demand. He sighed, feeling quite put on the spot.

"I'm not going to get into this. If I tell you *anything*, she's going to find out. Don't ask me how, but she will, and she'll take pleasure in cutting me up into little pieces. There's a lot about her that's classified anyway."

"She's one of the assassins, Skeet. I know."

For several long, awkward seconds, the only sound that could be heard was the gentle hum of Zinni's computer. Skeet couldn't fathom what force in the galaxy would have compelled Ziva to share that information. Intimidation factor, perhaps? He had to admit this beef she had with Aroska had turned her—the most logical, methodical person he knew—into an irrational mess over the past couple of days, so it wasn't much of a stretch. He looked to Zinni for support, but she only stared at him with wide eyes and shrugged.

"How do you figure?"

"She told me."

"And somehow you're still alive."

Aroska snorted and shook his head, ignoring the smart remark. "I was starting to put the pieces together anyway."

"That's confidential information, Aroska," Zinni put in quietly.

"Don't worry, I don't plan on going around telling everyone," the man replied, fiddling with one of the decorative spindles on the back of a dining chair. "After she killed Soren—" he paused as if it was painful to even mention his brother and Ziva in the same sentence "—I tried and tried to find out more about her so I could, frankly, plan my revenge. Her HSP file is virtually nonexistent—redacted records, no photo. I just thought my clearance level was too low but..." Aroska turned to face them, sending them a glare that made Skeet feel like an idiot. "She's got the hands of a sniper. We all handle our fair share of weapons, but there's no mistaking those calluses."

Skeet sat forward and rubbed at his eyes for a moment before dragging his hands down his face. "Okay," he said, "maybe you deserve a little credit." He got up and went to the kitchen window, peering out to where Ziva lay under her sarmi tree. "She wasn't like that when you talked to her, was she?"

Aroska joined him at the window and forced a short chuckle. "She was at first, but not for long. As soon as I—"

Skeet's hands curled into fists. "No!" he cut in, appalled by the man's ignorance. "Number one Rule of Ziva: *never* bother her while she's under that tree. If you need something, you wait for her to come to you. If you absolutely can't wait, tell either me or Zinni and we'll go to her. It has taken us years to develop this level of trust. Don't think you can rise to that level overnight—you'll get yourself killed."

"All right, all right," Aroska muttered, humbled. He crossed his arms. "Are there any other 'rules' I should know about?"

Skeet turned away from the window. "Sorry, it's not your fault. You didn't know. I have to admit Ziva hasn't been very welcoming, and I apologize for that too. I realize you're not her biggest fan, but pressing her isn't the way to go. The harder you push, the more she's going to shut you out."

"Then help me out here." Aroska took another look out the window before turning away as well. "Understanding people is part of my job, and I can't do that job if I don't even understand the people I'm working with."

Skeet led him back to the living room and sat him down in a chair opposite the sofa. "Well," he began, returning to his place beside Zinni and trying to decide where to start, "always coordinate work-related activities with her. If you can't tell her what you're doing, you probably shouldn't be doing it. You especially don't want to lie to her. She hates being lied to more than just being kept in the dark. Somehow she always finds out, and you'll be in worse trouble than you would have been in the first place. Also, think for yourself. Never ask her if you should or shouldn't do something, or she'll dismiss you as incompetent." He waved toward Zinni. "For example, we're already finding out what we can about Dane Bothum and Dakiti so that when she walks through that door, we'll be able to tell her everything she wants to know."

"And if she doesn't ask?"

She always did. "Then we'll have that knowledge in case it's ever needed in the future."

Aroska seemed far too amused. "Where'd you come up with all of these rules?"

"You learn to make them up over the years," Zinni replied absent-mindedly.

"Ever wonder what it would be like if everyone's lives didn't revolve around her?"

Skeet's brows dropped into a scowl. "We *respect* her," he snapped, "and you should too."

Aroska was quiet for a moment, letting the words sink in. Skeet rubbed his face again and turned to Zinni, who was once again absorbed in her computer. He wished she would chime in again and back him up. He hated talking about Ziva behind her back just as much as she hated being talked about behind her back. Although forming attachments was risky in the special ops business, he'd come to think of her as a sister. He vividly remembered being impressed by her test scores during the year-long spec ops elite training program, and when she'd been chosen as a team leader, he'd desperately hoped to be selected for her squad. When she'd hand-picked both him and Zinni, he'd been ecstatic.

Skeet chuckled to himself at the memory. Despite the bond the three of them had formed, they all still had their secrets. Ziva had been the most reserved by far. Neither he nor Zinni had exactly had an ideal childhood—they'd both grown up as orphans in local children's homes. But Ziva was another story entirely. She'd told them a little about her past, about losing her father and being disowned by her family before running away to Noro as a little girl. Then there'd been that whole business with the Nosti that still had him baffled as well. She'd killed him with his own kytara, catching the eye of HSP. Skeet was sure Aroska had heard about that—the incident had dominated local news headlines for weeks. But considering the way Ziva had reacted to the conversation at dinner the previous night, he decided the subject would remain off limits for now.

He didn't blame her for the personality she'd developed. It was true that she could be abrasive and manipulative and distrusting, but that was how she'd survived and protected herself for so many years. It was part of what made her such a good operative now.

Everything seemed to have turned out okay in the long run. He and Zinni were Ziva's family now. She'd purchased her childhood home, hired Marshay and Ryon, and had gotten to know Jada. Best of all, they got to work together every day, proving their worth as the Alpha special ops team. They were living proof that people who had started out with nothing could still accomplish anything they wanted if they were willing to work hard.

"So what's with this tree?" Aroska finally asked.

"Ziva suffers from a mild case of post-traumatic stress disorder," Skeet answered, reminding himself that he should leave out details about her father. "Ryon helps her with some therapy, and he thinks spending time out there is good for her." *Except when you show up and start bothering her with questions.*

"You'll have to forgive me for being unsympathetic," Tarbic muttered. "You're telling me she actually feels *bad* about what she does?"

"I didn't say that," Skeet retorted. "She's been through a lot of horrible things, and she has to *do* a lot of horrible things. She copes by becoming a different person when she's in the field. It's almost like she's flipping a switch, turning part of herself off while simultaneously activating another part. Same thing happens when she's defending herself or one of us. She's relentless—fast, strong, smart, accurate, inventive. You just have to give her some space, let her do her thing, and know the old Ziva will be back when it's over."

"But the way she's been acting the past couple days—"

"That's nothing compared to what I'm telling you," Skeet said. He saw Zinni take a peek at the two of them over the top of her computer.

Aroska's brows were knit together as he thought. "Explain to me how she can be like that and still care about anyone. I saw the way she treated Jada last night, the way she treats you and Ryon and Marshay. How can she do what she does and still have a heart?"

"I don't fully understand it myself," Skeet replied, shaking his head. "Ziva is *very* independent, but there's a small circle of people she would do anything for. Just because she kills for a living doesn't mean she's not capable of compassion. If you think about it, a lot of the things she does are actually for the best in the long run. Kill one to save many. Affect one person's life negatively in order to affect someone else's positively."

"Yeah, well sometimes it's not just *one* person she's affecting negatively," Aroska scoffed, rising to his feet.

"Look, you're not the only one who's ever lost someone to her. It would be different if it was personal, if she killed out of hate or retaliation." Skeet hesitated—sometimes those were indeed the reasons. "But that's not the way it is. She pulls the trigger because someone tells her to. Anybody could have been assigned as the Cleaner who killed your brother—me, Zinni, maybe even Adin. The fact that Ziva's a professional killer has nothing to do with it. She was following orders and doing her job. Any of us would have done the same. You're taking this way too personally and she's just feeding off of it because she knows it makes you miserable."

"Soren was innocent and she shot him anyway!" Aroska exclaimed. "What's not to take personally?"

Now it was Skeet's turn to stand up. "You don't know the half of it! If you believe she killed him just for the hell of it, you're wrong. Think what you will about her, but she would *never* do something like that."

Surprisingly, Aroska made no argument. In fact, he said nothing at all. His mouth hung open slightly as if his next thought had fizzled before it made it to his tongue. He stared in silence for a moment, making Skeet wonder if he even knew what he was talking about.

Does he not know the whole story?

All three of them looked to the front door when it hissed open. Ziva entered, eyebrows furrowed, mouth a straight line. She strode across the room and disappeared into her bedroom, ignoring them as she went.

Skeet sat back down on the sofa and pulled Zinni's computer toward him so he could catch up. He'd shared enough with Aroska for now. "Just cut her some slack," he instructed. "And listen to her. She's always right. Even when you think she's completely wrong, she's right. Got it?"

"Yeah," Aroska sighed.

· 27 ·

EAST SUN

FRINGE SPACE

Saun had just docked with the *East Sun* when Aroska's message came through. She hesitated for a moment, but, seeing no immediate sign of Bothum, went ahead and opened the transmission.

"Aroska, I'm busy," she said, instantly regretting the bite in her tone.

"Where are you?"

"I'm in the field. I told you that." She walked down the boarding ramp of her shuttle and headed across the docking hangar.

"Listen. Have you heard of a man named Dane Bothum?"

Saun winced. "No. Who is he?"

"He's a Sardon who's running a second Solaris cell out of Dakiti on Sardonis. He's the one responsible for this whole mess with the Tantalis."

"You said Dakiti?" So they were on to Dakiti. This meant her men either hadn't reached Jaxton soon enough or the Saiffe boy had spilled his guts—or perhaps it had been a combination of the two. How long had it been since she'd spoken to Aroska at HSP...an hour?

He grunted in the affirmative. "I thought I should let you know. I think we're planning on going out there, but we're not on board with HSP yet. I thought you and the rest of the SCU might want to look into it. See if anyone else knows anything. Maybe we can coordinate something."

"Right," she said, catching a glimpse of Bothum down one of the flagship's corridors. She picked up her pace. "I'll let everyone know. I'll contact you if we learn anything."

Bothum turned at the sound of her voice and retraced his steps, waiting patiently for her to finish the conversation.

"This is crazy stuff, Saun," Aroska said, "a lot bigger than we ever thought. Be careful."

He had no idea. "I know," she murmured. "I will. But right now I have to go. We're about to question one of the local Solaris leaders. I'll talk to you soon."

Saun ended the transmission abruptly so Aroska wouldn't hear her sudden coughing fit. She recovered after a moment and returned the communicator to her belt, looking up to meet Bothum's cold gaze.

"Tarbic?" he asked.

The way he said it made her feel sorry for Aroska. She nodded. "They know about Dakiti."

"Saiffe told them?"

"I imagine so."

"Good. He hasn't seen the whole picture. We still have the upper hand in this game."

This was true, and it made Saun feel better.

"So," Bothum went on, turning to stroll back down the hall, "can we expect to have the Haphezian fleet on our tail before long?"

Saun followed, still feeling congested. She coughed again. "I would be more worried about the Tantalis. There were survivors in the forest yesterday, and if the Saiffe boy told Payvan's team, I'm sure he told his own people."

"Tantalis do not concern me."

"Well then, no, no Haphezian fleet. Not yet, anyway. Aros...*Tarbic* said the team is planning something but the director isn't on board yet. We still have some time."

They worked their way up a level to the ship's bridge where perhaps two dozen Sardon crewmembers controlled the massive craft. Bothum barked something about the jump drive and they scrambled, chattering among themselves as they prepared to make the transition to faster-than-light speed.

"Do we know where Saiffe is now?" he asked, studying the readouts on the large holographic display at the front of the bridge.

"I'm sure wherever he is, Tarbic is with him," Saun replied, plugging her communicator into a vacant terminal. "I'll pull up a location from his last message."

The machine did its work, displaying a large translucent map with a flashing green dot marking Aroska's position. It was the same as the night before, the same location from which they had picked up Jayden's transmission to his Tantali friends. Saun scoffed. "They're still at the house."

"Fools," Bothum said. "They should have moved him. Bring him in."

"You're sure that's necessary if he's already told them?"

"I told you, he doesn't know the whole story. They have no idea what they're looking for."

Saun took up her communicator, entered a code, and braced herself for the FTL jump. "He's at the house," she said into the device.

· 28 ·
PAYVAN RESIDENCE
NORO, HAPHEZ

Z iva stayed in the solitude of her bedroom long enough to let her mind recover from being so rudely interrupted outside— twenty minutes, to be exact. She stood and studied her haggard reflection in the mirror beside her wardrobe. There hadn't been much time for rest in the past few days, and she hadn't realized how badly it was showing. Her team's independent service term on Aubin had consisted of several significant missions that had taken them to all corners of the galaxy. They'd been busy right up until the last minute and had had to rush to make it back in time for Assignment Day. Besides her hour of sleep this morning and the two, maybe three the night before, she had only slept about fifteen hours total in the last five days.

It didn't help that she'd had Jak Gamon and nostium on her mind since the previous evening. At the moment, she could still feel a bit of a tingle in the back of her head, but it had come and gone since she'd moved the vase. Even that simple task had been difficult; it had taken her full concentration and left her with a pounding headache. The nostium infusion Gamon had given her the day she killed him was the last one she'd ever received, so it had been nine years—a whole Phase and a half— since she'd been exposed to it. Her Nostia was failing, and in another year or two it would be gone completely.

She wasn't entirely sure why she cared, since she really had no reason to use it and legally couldn't unless she wanted the death sentence. It was just something that had been a part of her for most of her memorable life, and she imagined she'd somehow feel empty without it. She directed her attention toward a spare rifle scope that sat on the wardrobe shelf and focused intently on it, willing it to rise from the shelf's surface and hover in the air. When nothing happened, she swept her hand upward in a lifting motion. The scope quivered for a moment, stood up on one end, and then fell back down with a *crack*.

Ziva shook her head and turned away from the mirror. There was work to be done, and going in after Jayden and Governor Saiffe—assuming he was at Dakiti—would be no easy matter. Bringing the rest of HSP on board would be the first problem. What was she supposed to tell the director?

Excuse me, sir. I'd like to take a force out to investigate Solaris activity at Dakiti and possibly rescue the Tantali governor.

And what will become of Jayden while you're on this escapade?

Well, sir, we don't have custody of him anymore. He's refusing our assistance and is unwilling to communicate.

It would be easy enough to lie, but it would take a little time to come up with a plausible story that could be backed up. The real issue would be if Jayden and Bront had already gone to HSP to tattle on her for the night before.

Which they more than likely had.

Sheyss.

She needed facts. Where had the Tantalis gone since leaving the house? What would her team be up against at Dakiti? Skeet and Zinni would probably have the answers. They'd been busy with the computer when she had come inside.

Ziva opened the door of her bedroom, ready to go out and join the others, but the look she saw on Ryon's face stopped her dead in her tracks. He stood outside the door of his own room at the opposite end of the hallway, partially hidden in shadow. He gripped a pistol in his right hand.

As soon as she saw him, she proceeded cautiously toward him, as he toward her. "What's going on?" she asked in a low voice. Her hand came to rest on the butt of her own gun as if it had a mind of its own. She looked into the living room at Skeet, Zinni, and Aroska, who had caught on and were watching intently.

"We've got company," he replied at the same volume, jerking his head toward his room. "Bedroom window."

She took a deep breath, motioned for the other three to stay down in the living room, and then caught up to Ryon. He had already entered the room and was crouching against the wall just to the left of the large window that looked out over the yard and the river.

"Down!" he whispered, leaning away from the glass.

Ziva dove to the floor behind the bed without question, catching a glimpse of the Haphezian man just as he passed in front of the window. She waited a moment until she was sure he'd gone by and then crawled on her stomach toward Ryon, taking up her position on the opposite side of the window. She ventured a peek outside but pulled away just as a second man passed by and peered inside, placing a hand on the glass. He had the Solaris star on his arm.

As soon as he moved on, Ziva looked out again. Roughly fifty meters away, a third insurgent approached the house, holding a rifle low to the ground. There was no sign of a vehicle, but Ziva guessed there were probably more of them.

"Who invited these guys?" Ryon scoffed.

She shook her head. "There's no party here," she said, darting back across the room.

Marshay was just coming out of her room, eyes wide. "Ziva!" she hissed. "There's—"

Ziva pressed a finger to her lips, placing her other hand over the woman's mouth. "We know. Help me with the gun safe, will you?"

The housekeeper nodded and followed her to a closet in the center of the hallway. Ziva ran her fingers along the inside of the doorframe until she found the hidden switch. The closet's back wall slid away when she pulled it, revealing a narrow passage lined with a variety of weaponry. She stepped inside and examined the stash; it was a collection she had accumulated and restored throughout the past several years, some items taken from fallen enemies and some purchased new. There were other things besides guns—explosives, a grenade launcher, and a variety of survival equipment. Skeet and Zinni called it "HSP in a Closet." She selected several assault rifles, ensuring they were all adequately charged, and handed them to Marshay who in turn passed them out to everyone else.

"Three hostiles on our west side," Ziva announced, slinging the rifle strap over her shoulder as she gave Marshay a pistol of her own. "I'm sure there are more."

The three of them nodded and readied their own weapons before moving back out into the main room.

"Zinni, we need a head count."

The intelligence officer was already working with the living room's center table before the words were out of Ziva's mouth. She kept a cautious eye on the window as she activated the three-dimensional infrared image similar to the one in the HSP situation room. "I see eight of them total," she answered, "all within a fifty-meter radius."

Ziva switched off the lights and studied the hologram for a moment, noting that there were groups of insurgents covering both the front and back of the house.

"We've got to be quick and smart," she said, glancing warily toward the front door. At the moment, it wasn't an exit option. "They want us to come to them, and they'll be able to see us a long time before we see them."

"I'll provide a walkthrough," Zinni offered, switching on her ever-present earpiece.

Ziva shook her head, motioning for her to fall into position as she led the rest of the group toward the basement stairs. "No. Zinni, Skeet, Ryon, Tarbic, you're with me. Marshay, do *not* let them get inside this house."

The group made their way down to the house's lower level where a narrow hallway led out to the below-ground parking bay that housed Ziva's car and personal ship, the *Intrepid*. She opened the door and listened; the bay appeared to be clear and both craft remained untouched. The Solaris insurgents were covering the home's main exits, expecting them to come *out*, not *up*.

"Skeet and Aroska, you go left and take the back of the house. Zinni, cover the middle and then follow Ryon and I to the right. Sweep the perimeter first and then pinch in." She took one last look over her shoulder at each of them. "Keep your eyes open. Shoot to kill if you have to, but I want to know what these guys are doing here." This was directed at Aroska.

With that, she took off up the landing bay stairs with everyone else hot on her heels. It was one thing to infiltrate a building from the outside, but going outside *from* the building was a different matter entirely. She swept the area as far as she could see and veered to the right ahead of Ryon and Zinni, staying as close to the exterior wall of the house as she could. To her surprise, there was no sign of Solaris anywhere. Perhaps they had all gone around back, exploiting the weakness that remained in the broken guest room window. She wondered for a moment if someone else should have stayed inside with Marshay.

She paused at the corner of the house, listening and taking a moment to scan the area again. Still nothing. She could, however, hear scuffling a short distance away followed by footsteps somewhere above them. Someone was on the roof, probably waiting to pick them off if they tried to run to the cars.

Ryon and Zinni heard it too. All three flattened themselves against the house, rifles up. Ziva looked back the other direction. Skeet and Aroska had already disappeared around the other end. Slowly, cautiously, she turned back and stole a peek around the corner. She caught a whiff of cha'sen; the musty scent got stronger as they crept forward, but she still didn't see anyone. *Where are these guys?*

A low hum reached her ears a split second before an explosion rocked the ground and one of the cars in front of the house went up in flames. Ziva ducked as something black flew by overhead: a drone. A thin trail of smoke remained in the air from the missile it had just fired, and it had a mini gun mounted on its opposite wing.

"Go!" Ziva shouted. She sprinted forward, no longer concerned about making noise. She rounded the corner, rifle up, and took out the first insurgent she saw. Two others were on their way to the ground with new holes in their heads, compliments of Skeet and Aroska.

"They're on the roof!" she called, diving out of the way just as the drone passed by again and left a trail of bullet holes up the wall of her house. It was using solid ammunition instead of plasma—Solaris wanted to cause some damage.

Skeet and Zinni both leapt forward, quickly climbing the grappling cables the Solaris men had used to access the roof. Ziva turned to Ryon, placing a hand on his shoulder and listening as the drone made its turnaround somewhere beyond. "Go help Marshay," she instructed. "Make sure none of these guys get inside."

Ryon gave her an affirmative nod and hurried away around the opposite end of the house, avoiding the attack craft as it passed over again, mini gun blazing. It flew out over the river, banking to the right to prepare for another flyover.

"Where the hell did Solaris get a drone?" Ziva exclaimed.

"Probably the same place they got that military shuttle," Aroska said, brushing past her. "Let's take this thing down."

Ziva didn't need to be told. She took a quick step forward, cutting past him in return, and strode out into the open, taking up a position at the edge of the sheer drop-off down to the water. Aroska stopped a couple of meters behind her and to the left, rifle raised.

The drone was on its return path. Ziva took two shots, successfully striking the port side missile launcher on the second try. The automatic gun began firing a spray of bullets, the targeting computer damaged. Still it approached. She fired again, this time hitting the nose of the craft straight on. It spun out of control and dove downward, colliding with the cliff below her in a billowing fireball.

The ground under her feet crumbled from impact before she could move. She swiveled, ready to jump, but the piece of earth she stood on was muddy from the moist river air and her feet slipped out from under her. In a last-ditch effort, she threw her rifle up over the edge and reached out to grab whatever she could. Her hand found a piece of ground that disintegrated instantly when she touched it. She felt herself start to fall.

It all happened in slow motion. Ziva looked down as her hand slipped, estimating the drop to be nearly seventy meters. The realization that she was going to die hit her just as someone caught her hand.

Ziva looked down at her boots where they dangled in mid-air. Smoke and hot fumes drifted upward from the downed drone, making her eyes smart. She swung slowly back and forth, striking her shoulder on a piece of rock that jutted out of the cliff side. Her focus moved up to where Aroska had both of his hands closed around her arm. He was flat on his stomach, and her weight was pulling him over the edge centimeter by centimeter.

Desperate for an alternative handhold, Ziva clawed at the rock with little faith in its ability to support her. It came loose with the slightest touch, taking another chunk of dirt with it as it fell.

Aroska began looking wildly about for something to grab onto. An exposed root from the sarmi tree nearly reached him, and he let go of her with one hand to take hold of it. He grasped her wrist and she held his, but his arm was muddy and the grip wasn't going to last much longer.

Ziva couldn't recall her life ever being quite so completely in someone else's hands—*literally*. She looked up at Aroska, whose face was contorted as he strained to hold her up and keep himself steady. He was looking straight into her eyes. *No.* He was going to just drop her. She could sense it.

"Don't you dare even think about it!" she hollered. "If I fall, I'm taking you with me!"

She felt the muscles in his arm tighten as he mustered his strength for one last pull. He squeezed his eyes shut, but he was gaining ground and Ziva felt herself rise a short distance. She dug her feet into the side of the cliff and pushed, helping him as best she could.

Aroska heaved until her head broke the plane of the ground. She flailed for the sarmi root and he took hold of her other arm, helping her scramble over the edge.

Rolling as far away from the loose ground as possible, Ziva recovered her rifle, allowing her gaze to shift toward Aroska as the two of them took off for the house. *Why would you do that? Why not let me die?* While she was thankful to still be breathing, she couldn't fathom what force in the galaxy had prompted him to catch her. Perhaps it didn't really matter—there was hardly time for gratitude at the moment anyway.

No noise came from the roof as they approached. All that could be heard anywhere for that matter was the crackling of the flames that ate at the demolished car out front. The silence no doubt indicated that Skeet and Zinni had already dispatched the insurgents; they may have been outnumbered, but they never made mistakes.

Ziva slung her rifle over her shoulder and established a grip on one of the grappling cables, ready to hoist herself up, but the unmistakable *click* of a hammer being pulled back stopped her cold.

"Ziva," Aroska murmured.

She let go of the cable and held her hands out to each side as she slowly pivoted. One last insurgent appeared from around the side of the house and stood directly behind Aroska with a projectile pistol pressed against the back of his neck.

"Drop your weapon," the man growled.

Aroska watched her for a moment, then let go of the rifle he'd been holding in his right hand.

"Hand over the kid, Payvan, and we can all go home."

All of this is still about Jayden? "Would if I could," Ziva replied, "but he's not here."

The insurgent appeared confused for a moment, then his eyes widened. "That's impossible."

"Sorry to disappoint you."

By the time the shadow crossed over the man's face, it was too late. The sound of a rifle discharging echoed through the air. The plasma round passed within centimeters of Aroska's head and burned a hole through the insurgent's right temple. Ziva watched him collapse and then shifted her gaze to Tarbic, who had his hand over his ear and as though he didn't believe it was still attached. She turned her attention up toward Skeet, who stood on the edge of the roof with his rifle still aimed at the dead man.

"Slippery bastard thought he could get away," he said matter-of-factly.

Ziva stepped back to make room for Skeet and Zinni as they climbed down. "You guys okay?" she asked, scraping some of the mud from her shirt and glancing back toward the cliff. It seemed ironic that *she* was the one asking *them*.

"Fine," Skeet replied, exhaling with relief. "They said they were looking for Jayden."

"So I've heard," she said, poking the dead insurgent with the toe of her boot. "And they came with heavy artillery. They're getting desperate, and they're willing to kill him if they have to."

Zinni lifted an eyebrow. "So what do we do about the pile of dead bodies on your roof?"

"Toss them into the river. The pylae fish will be at them in no time. Now let's go get that fire put out. We've got work to do."

· 29 ·

PAYVAN RESIDENCE
NORO, HAPHEZ

T he three-dimensional image of the main Dakiti building stood a meter tall and turned in a lazy circle over the living room's center table. Most accurately, it was a massive, self-sufficient medical research facility about ninety kilometers west of Calova, the capital city of Sardonis. It was well known throughout the Fringe Systems as the med center that handled only the most extreme cases. During the Fringe War it had been a military installation used by the Sardons and the Biasi—a scaly reptilian race from a neighboring system— in their efforts against Haphez. The whole conflict had started when the Haphezians refused to trade their caura extract, a gel-like substance derived from the saliva of the ill-tempered caura lizards that resided in the jungle. The extract possessed phenomenal healing properties and was one of Haphez's primary exports, so the last thing they wanted was for someone to synthesize the formula and take control of the market.

After the Haphezian military had defeated both enemy civilizations, Sardonis had been ordered to destroy their base as one of their terms of surrender. Instead, they had negotiated and converted it into one of the most-high tech medical establishments in the galaxy. Besides serving as an exclusive hospital, Dakiti was known to conduct many biological experiments designed to help patients overcome chronic disorders and cure rare illnesses. Much of the research that took place there was classified.

Ziva studied the hologram intently, massaging her chin as she considered their infiltration options. The surveillance data Skeet and Zinni had pulled up showed the perimeter to be more heavily-guarded than usual, telling her something other than research was currently going on. She guessed the governor's presence might have something to do with it and was growing more confident in her theory that Solaris had taken him there. But then there was still the *reason* he was there, the reason the radical group didn't want Jayden and Vinny Jaxton talking. They were covering something up, and the thought of finding out what it was sent a tingle of excitement down her spine.

She minimized the hologram and got up from the sofa, heading to the dining table where Zinni was attempting to catch up to the Tantalis.

"Based on their current trajectory, they appear to be on their way home to Tantal," Zinni announced when Ziva peered over her shoulder at the computer. She manipulated the data on the translucent screen and retraced the route with her little finger. "You're sure he'll go to Dakiti?"

"Mmhmm," Ziva replied. "If he doesn't go voluntarily, Solaris will find him and be after him again before long. They're persistent."

Ryon and Skeet came inside from disposing of the insurgents just as Aroska emerged from the spare room in a clean change of clothes Skeet kept there. "What do we have?" all three asked simultaneously.

"Sorry," Ryon said with an apologetic chuckle, "old habits." He rushed away to clean up without another word.

Zinni relayed what she had just told Ziva and showed them the tracking system on the computer. "I'll be keeping a close eye on this thing this afternoon. We'll be the first to know if anything changes."

"Figured out how we're getting in?" Skeet asked Ziva.

"She's only had five minutes," Aroska scoffed.

Ziva cocked her head and scowled at him, re-activating the hologram with the remote in her hand. "Of course," she said to Skeet.

They all went back to the living room and sat around the center table, watching as she controlled the image. "There's a massive sewer system that runs under the entire complex," she explained, highlighting the route in red. "The drainage runs through to this outlet here—" she panned out to where it could be seen "—and into this river. There's an access hatch there." She switched to the infrared view, which showed the area to be crawling with soldiers.

"It's not usually so heavily guarded," she said in response to the vacant looks around her, flipping through a series of images taken at earlier times. "I'm beginning to think the governor *is* there, just like Jayden said, and as long as they have him, they're not letting anybody in. However, they won't be ready when someone gets *out* that way. This can be our exit route."

Everyone nodded as they studied the figure. "You know how much I love sewers," Skeet muttered.

"The exterior of the compound is thoroughly patrolled so going in on foot is out of the question," Ziva continued. "The sewers will be our back-up point of entry if all else fails. We'll have to come in from above."

Aroska maintained a calm and collected tone as he began to speak. Ziva guessed Skeet had finally talked some sense into him earlier that morning. "They're going to pick up anything we fly through there and shoot us out of the sky before we know what hit us. What exactly is your plan?"

He might as well have called her an idiot right there in front of everyone. "You're forgetting that Sardonis doesn't have nearly the caliber of defense systems we have," she said, playing with the remote. An image of a small, two-man stealth fighter appeared, suspended above the minimized version of Dakiti. "I give you the H-26 Scout. We'll fly at thirty klicks, out of radar range, and go for a high-altitude low-opening jump. We can have the onboard VIs hide the ships and then pick us up for extraction, and we'll have plenty of cockpit space for passengers on the trip home. HSP has all of the equipment we'll need."

Skeet laughed out loud. "You came up with all of that in five minutes? Ziva Payvan, you never cease to amaze me."

"We'll focus on details later," Ziva added, ignoring his outburst. "For now, start gathering supplies and we'll see what becomes of Mr. Saiffe."

· 30 ·
DAKITI MEDICAL RESEARCH CENTER
SARDONIS

S aun had feared the worst when Solaris hadn't contacted her after the second hit on Payvan's house, but now that she was hearing the news for herself, she nearly threw her communicator against the wall. Bothum stood silently beside her, scrutinizing her with his yellow eyes as she spoke to Aroska.

"So then I guess it's a good thing the Tantalis came for him when they did." She willed herself calm despite the fact that she could feel her face redden with anger. This was the third time her men had failed her.

"Except that leaves him even more vulnerable," Aroska said. "The Tantalis don't have any idea what they're getting into."

Well, that was a plus. Jayden was now separated from his Haphezian protectors, so even if they *did* set out on an excursion to Dakiti, they would never find the truth until it was too late. Bothum would get Tarbic and Payvan, and she would get her life.

"At least Solaris won't know what became of him," Saun said, signaling for Bothum to pay attention to the conversation.

"They shouldn't. Ziva placed a tracking device on him so we'll know if they try to take him again."

A tracking device! If it was an HSP device or anything remotely similar, she would be able to find and monitor the signal as well. "So," she said casually, "are things still working out okay with her? I can't imagine she'd take kindly to her house being attacked." She stopped herself just before adding "again"—if she understood correctly, no one else knew about the attempted kidnapping the previous night.

"Things are...*confusing*," Aroska replied, sounding rather uncomfortable about discussing the topic. "I don't know what to think. I found out some things about her, Saun, things I can't tell you. Hell, I shouldn't even be talking to you *now*."

Saun grew quiet and looked down, away from Bothum, unsure what to say.

She heard Aroska sigh. "I've still got to wrap my head around some things. I want so badly to hate her for what she did to Soren, but I'm starting to think I'm missing part of the story. I don't know. She's a manipulative, heartless *shouka*, but it's hard to keep from admiring her talent and tenacity."

Saun took several steps away from Bothum. "Things have changed that much since we talked at HSP four hours ago?" she said, forcing a short chuckle.

"Enough that I saved her life."

There was total silence for several long seconds.

"Her life was literally dangling from my hands. I thought about just dropping her, but when I looked into her eyes, I couldn't do it. Then of course she threatened me." Here he laughed a little too. "One minute I want to kill her, the next I want to know more about her. I almost feel sorry for her. At this point, I'd pay money to see the woman smile. That's got to be quite a sight."

Saun felt an involuntary tingle of jealousy course through her for reasons she couldn't explain. She knew he was only joking, but he'd always told her how beautiful and comforting her own smile was. She had truly come to care about him after the incident with his team, despite the fact that it was never supposed to go that far. She often found herself wishing they could still be together when this was all over, but she always had to remind herself she had work to do and that if she did it correctly, he would most likely have to die. He and Payvan would both die, and she would get to live.

"Aroska Tarbic, pull it together!" she snapped, afraid she was starting to let her petty personal feelings get in the way. No, her anger was legitimate. He needed to have his head in the right place in order to do his job, and she needed him to do his job so she could do hers.

He said nothing. Saun coughed, feeling the burn in her lungs and a great urge to change the subject. "Aroska, I'm at Dakiti." That much was true. The *East Sun* had arrived in Sardon airspace about an hour earlier, and she and Bothum had been shuttled down to the research center.

That caught his attention. "What!"

"You said it would be worth checking out, so I did."

He swore. "Yes but I didn't tell you to *go* there! Are you alone? Damn it, you'll get yourself killed!"

That's what he said every time, word for word. It had always been a part of her charade, acting immediately on any tentative plans he ever came up with. He'd been forced to come and bail her out of something on several occasions in the mere three months they'd worked together, and she'd always hoped his coddling ways would work to her advantage when the time came. It appeared they would now.

"Relax," she said, stifling another cough. "I'm fine."

Aroska's voice was frantic. "How long have you been there? What have you found? Any sign of the governor?"

"I arrived about twenty minutes ago," Saun lied. "This place is huge, and they're definitely hiding something. Everything below ground level is completely restricted. They wouldn't even let me get close, even when I told them I was HSP, and now I think they've got eyes on me."

"Saun, be careful!" Aroska was almost shouting. He groaned and swore again. "This is all my fault."

Perfect. She had him hooked. "Aroska, stop it. I'll just find somewhere to...hold on a second." She held the communicator down to her side, but she could still hear him hollering even at that distance.

"This conversation needs to end now," Bothum said quietly as he observed the assembly area below the balcony on which the two of them stood.

Saun nodded. "Someone's coming," she hissed into the communicator, hoping Aroska would shut up for a few seconds. He did, and she held the device away from her mouth again just long enough to kill him with suspense.

"We need to start a trace on an HSP homing beacon," she whispered to Bothum before returning the communicator to her mouth. "Okay," she breathed, "I think they're gone." Then, in a normal voice, "As I was saying, I'll find somewhere to lay low for a while and then I'll get out. I told you, I'll be fi—"

She screamed in shock, startling Bothum, and tossed the communicator to the floor several meters away. "Aroska!" she shouted, drawing the attention of those down in the assembly area. She began reciting Dakiti's coordinates and strode over to where the device had fallen. "Level three!" she cried, giving it a shove with her foot. She followed it across the floor, shouting for help in Haphezian, and then brought her boot down hard on top of it. It shattered, emitting an ear-piercing squeal for a moment before going completely dead.

When Saun looked up, she found Bothum watching her approvingly. "Will that bring him in?" he asked.

"Yes," she wheezed.

· 31 ·
PAYVAN RESIDENCE
NORO, HAPHEZ

Aroska stood under the sarmi tree and listened to the silence of his communicator for what seemed like hours. If he hadn't just imagined the last few minutes of conversation, Saun was currently alone inside Dakiti and had just been captured. And it was his fault.

Once he broke out of his stupor, he quickly ended the dead transmission and entered the comm code of Mack Markel, another man in the SCU who had worked under him during the past three months.

"This is Markel."

"Mack, it's Aroska. When's the last time you saw Saun?"

He could hear Mack in the background asking around and was glad he hadn't started questioning him or trying to change the subject. "Nobody's seen her since we left Headquarters this morning," he replied after a few seconds. "Another SCU group returned to base about an hour ago. She could be with them."

"Did she say anything to you about Dakiti?"

"Dakiti? What—no. Nothing. Like I said, I haven't seen or spoken to her since we left. I just figured she was with another team."

"Mack, she's there!" Aroska exclaimed. "She's at Dakiti. We got a lead this morning and I made the mistake of telling her about it. *Sheyss*, I shouldn't have even been talking to her. I thought you guys might be able to help—"

"Tarbic, settle down," Mack said. "How do you know this?"

"I was just talking to her. She told me she was there and that she thought she was being followed. Then she was taken."

Mack exhaled sharply. "Okay, listen. We'll pack up and head back to HSP. You figure things out on your end and let me know what you need me to do."

Aroska was already running back to the house. "Got it." He cut off the transmission just as he reached the front door and burst inside. "We've got a problem."

Skeet and Zinni whirled from their nearby positions. Skeet waved his hand for silence and moved toward him. "I hope your problem is the same as ours or that means we've got *two* problems."

It was then that Aroska noticed the life-size hologram of Emeri Arion standing on the center table in the living room. Ziva stood on the communication pad beside the table and shifted her attention from Aroska back to the director.

"Answer me, Payvan," Emeri ordered. "Did you or did you not willingly give up custody of Jayden Saiffe without the consent of this agency?"

"I did," Ziva replied, "but it—"

"I specifically told you that if he was put in any danger, you would be taken off the case. Not only did you give up custody, you almost allowed him to be killed by Solaris last night. The Tantali captain called earlier and told me *all about that.*"

"Solaris isn't trying to kill him. They only came because whoever they've got working inside HSP was able to monitor and track a transmission Jayden sent out to his colleagues."

"And you had no knowledge of this transmission?"

Ziva hesitated. "No. We did not."

"And whose fault is that?"

"He was in private quarters! We had no way of knowing. I only let him go this morning because he could potentially lead us to the governor and the Sardon Solaris leader. We're tracking him now."

Emeri wasn't impressed. "Payvan, that's outrageous. We have no way of knowing if the governor is even still alive. Your mission was to protect Jayden, not send him straight into the core of Solaris."

"We're going to get him out."

"Not if you're off the case."

"Sir!" Ziva exclaimed. "You take me off and Jayden will die in the time it takes to brief and mobilize another team."

"Then perhaps that is the price of failure," Emeri said, eyes cold. "Your orders were to ensure the safety and maintain custody of Jayden Saiffe while searching for the governor and you failed. Was multitasking too difficult for you?"

"Sir—"

"Lieutenant Payvan, as of this moment, you are relieved of your command on this case. Full responsibility will be transferred to Adin Woro's Alpha field ops team." With that, the hologram flickered and disappeared, leaving the living room and its occupants in stunned silence.

For a moment, Aroska forgot all about his conversations with Saun and Markel. He wasn't thrilled with the approach Ziva had been taking on this mission all along, but he was confident in her abilities to follow through. He *needed* her to follow through—if she didn't, Saun and Jayden would both die, and the Solaris cell at Dakiti would only grow.

"What was that last part?" he said, taking a step forward. "I didn't quite catch it."

Ziva turned around and watched him quizzically.

Skeet stepped toward her as well. "Neither did I," he said, taking the comm remote out of her hand and re-activating the image of Dakiti. "The director has never stopped Ziva Payvan before, and he's not going to now."

Everyone began to gather around the table, but an alert tone from Zinni's computer stopped them dead in their tracks. "*Sheyss,*" the intelligence officer muttered after taking a quick glance at the screen. "Jayden's already on the move. It looks like they rendezvoused with a Tantali transport halfway between here and their home system. They just entered the primary FTL lane to Sardonis."

Ziva nodded thoughtfully, unfazed by these sudden and inconvenient developments. She turned to Aroska, brows furrowed, chin resting in one hand. "Now, what's *your* problem?"

Aroska felt a nauseating wave of guilt hit him like a slap in the face. "One of our own has just been captured at Dakiti," he said quickly.

Everything stopped. "And you know this how?" Ziva asked, eyes narrowed and head tilted as she moved her hands down to rest on her hips.

It was the moment of truth. Aroska didn't even care how she would react. "She's a Solaris Control analyst I've worked with, Saun Zaid. I was just in contact with her, and she was taken. It's my fault she's even there—I told her it was our best lead."

For a moment Ziva only stared at him, dumbfounded, unmoving. "You've been in contact with someone outside the circle?" she exclaimed. "That's a blatant violation of protocol."

"You're one to talk about 'protocol'," Aroska snapped. "She's as knowledgeable about Solaris as I am, if not more so."

"Bloody hell, Tarbic, use your head!" Ziva turned in a slow circle, muttering under her breath in what sounded like another language. She turned back and locked eyes with him. "For all we know, *she* could be the Solaris informant."

"No Ziva, not Saun. I trust that woman with my life. Maybe that's too hard for you to grasp."

Ziva scoffed. "Are you saying I'm not trusting?"

"That's exactly what I'm saying."

She shook her head and advanced toward him. "You don't even know—"

Skeet caught her and stepped between them. "Hey!" he exclaimed. "Now is not the time for this. Back off, both of you."

The room was so quiet for the next minute or so that it almost seemed loud in Aroska's head as he tried to sort his thoughts. He stared at the Dakiti hologram rotating on the table, picturing Saun inside of it. Ziva's accusation about her involvement with Solaris made him want to vomit. He of all people would certainly know if she was working as a double agent...at least he hoped he would.

He looked back to Ziva, who now sat in a chair staring vacantly at the image as well. Skeet had said it himself earlier that morning—she was capable of compassion. Aroska was determined to make her prove it.

"We've got to get her out of there."

She said nothing as she watched the hologram, her face scrunched in a thoughtful manner.

"You have a plan?" Skeet asked. "I see that look in your eyes."

Ziva stood up. "Nothing's changed. We'll fly in with the H-26s and drop in from above. We'll have passenger room to get them all out—Zaid, Jayden, and the governor."

"You want to steal stealth fighters from HSP?" Skeet said, raising an eyebrow. "At this point we can't exactly waltz in and just take them."

"*Borrow forcefully*, Skeet," Ziva corrected. "We never steal. And no, we can't just waltz in. That's why Adin's team is going to do it for us."

Skeet chuckled. "Have you talked to *them* about this?"

"Give me five minutes," she replied, "and we'll need another man to bring the fourth fighter. Any ideas?" This she directed at Aroska.

He nodded. "Mack Markel. He's offered his assistance already. I'll make sure he's on board with Adin."

"You're sure he's not our inside man?"

His only response was a brief glare; he was done arguing. "So, we're going to go through with this mission without consent or backup from HSP." It was more of a statement than a question. He was perfectly aware of what needed to be done, but it didn't stop him from thinking the idea was completely ludicrous.

Ziva remained deadpan. "Basically."

"This is insane," he murmured, rubbing his eyes.

Zinni had been glued to her computer for the duration of the conversation. "It's a two-hour FTL trip from here to Sardonis," she announced. "If we leave within four hours, we can still make it there to jump under the cover of darkness. We've got plenty of time to get everything set with Adin's team, then the only matter is getting there."

Ziva nodded. "Then let's get going."

· 32 ·
HSP Headquarters
Noro, Haphez

din stepped into HSP's massive fighter hangar and gazed out across the vast expanse of docked ships. The overhead lights were off, casting the huge floor in shadows. He quietly descended the short flight of stairs that led to the shuttle used to deliver pilots to their appropriate craft. He paused for a moment at the bottom, thinking the situation through again. This was crazy. Ziva, Aroska, they were all crazy, but he trusted their judgment and was ready to do his part to help.

His intelligence agent, Colin Zier, moved down to stand beside him. "Scouts are in Section G," he said, studying a holographic map of the floor layout.

Adin powered up the shuttle, opting to leave the lights off, and motioned for Sergeant Mari Rebek and Mack Markel to follow. He kept reminding himself they didn't have to sneak, as they were now in charge of this investigation. In his mind, however, Ziva would always be in charge, no matter what the director said. It had taken long enough to get the opportunity to come down to the hangar, and now that they were so close he hoped he wouldn't have to stop and explain to anyone where they were going with the stealth fighters. Such a delay would be most unwelcome.

The little shuttle platform glided across the floor in silence. The plan was to fuel the ships and fly them out to Ziva's house, where her team would then be deployed to Sardonis. She hadn't given him any further details when she'd contacted him—plausible deniability, she'd said—but it didn't take a genius to realize they would be completely on their own once they reached Dakiti. Adin had instructed Ziva to contact him if they needed anything else, even if that meant he would lose his so-called deniability.

Colin pulled the shuttle up to the end of a long row of H-26 Scouts. All of the ones registered to HSP sported a dark gray finish, but they looked black and eerie in the darkness of the hangar.

Adin jumped off the platform and connected the thick tube that pumped fuel from the reservoir under the hangar floor. "We have to move fast," he said to the others. "Ziva wants to get out of here ASAP and this is going to take a few minutes."

Colin, Mari, and Mack hurried to their respective ships and hooked up their own fuel lines. They were making more noise than Adin would have liked, but he once again reminded himself they had every right to be down here. He climbed up into the cockpit and readied the controls for takeoff. These slick ships were as easy to handle as they were stealthy. They were equipped with state-of-the-art cloaking systems, infrared scanners, long-range targeting computers, and, perhaps most importantly, they had FTL capabilities. For a very brief moment, he wished he had a little more time to play with such an exceptional piece of equipment, but when he thought about the task at hand, he knew what he had to do.

Adin looked down the row and saw that the others had disconnected their fuel lines and were climbing into the cockpits. He started up his engine and descended the ladder, ready to shut off the fuel. Before he could do so, however, he heard the *click* of a weapon behind him and turned to find one of the field ops captains watching him, rifle lowered but ready to use.

"Lieutenant, would you mind telling me where you're going?" Trey Rhenza asked, looking smug in his unsoiled uniform.

Adin casually finished disconnecting the fuel line and faced Rhenza, arms crossed. "We're heading out to investigate a Solaris cell in Seran," he said. "There may be a lead on Governor Saiffe."

Rhenza smirked and looked down the row at the three agents who watched anxiously through the cockpit windows. "Markel?" he asked, nodding toward the second ship.

"Why not? He's a Solaris expert." That much was true.

"Tell me something, Woro. Are you and your team committing treason by assisting Lieutenant Payvan despite her removal from this investigation?"

Adin shook his head and leaned back against the ship. "That's ridiculous. Certainly the director has better things to do than make false accusations and send his dogs out to spy." He turned away, ready to climb into the ship.

"The director knows Payvan well enough to realize she's not going to just roll over." Rhenza raised his rifle. "You're not going anywhere."

Adin hung his head. He didn't have time for this—they were running late as it was. This was an unexpected turn of events, a problem that would need to be solved before they could carry on. "Look, Trey," he said as he raised his hands in surrender and turned around.

"That's *Captain* to you," Rhenza snapped, stepping forward.

Taking advantage of the captain's brief distraction, Adin seized the barrel of his rifle and gave it a quick shove backward, striking Rhenza in the jaw with the butt end. The man let go and staggered back, knocked off balance. Adin kicked him hard in the groin, sending him to the floor, and brought the rifle down against the back of his head as he fell.

He stood for a moment, slowing his breathing and listening for anyone else approaching. Satisfied that nobody had been alerted by the commotion, Adin dropped to the floor and fished through Rhenza's uniform, removing his communicator and handcuffs. The communicator he threw as hard as he could across the hangar, and the cuffs he slapped over the captain's wrist before dragging his unconscious body over and securing him to the H-26's access ladder. He quickly coiled up the fuel line and climbed into the ship, receiving shocked looks from his team.

"You okay, boss?" Mari snickered.

Adin ignored her and remotely opened the huge overhead door

above them. He guessed it wouldn't take long for someone to find Rhenza, and he didn't want to be anywhere nearby when the man woke up. "Let's get out of here," he said, piloting the Scout up and through the opening. They took off into the evening sky where the sun was just disappearing behind the distant mountains.

· 33 ·
PAYVAN RESIDENCE
NORO, HAPHEZ

Aroska stepped into the lightweight jumpsuit and watched as Ziva, Skeet, and Zinni did the same. He slipped the life support system over his shoulders and strapped his rifle securely to his back. This whole mission seemed suicidal to him, but it seemed to be a regular routine for Ziva and the other special ops agents. While it was true that both field operations and special operations required much of the same training, they required very different *amounts*. He tried to remind himself that Emeri would have never allowed him to work with spec ops if he didn't think he could handle the missions, but then he remembered that this mission wasn't even supposed to be taking place. Though he would never admit it, he was scared out of his mind.

Adin handed him his flight helmet, which he put on, leaving the visor up. "You doing okay?" he asked, nodding his head in Ziva's direction.

Why do people have to keep asking? Aroska picked up his supply belt, checked it for all its contents, and put it on. "Better. Not great, but better."

"You can't let her get to you now. Focus on what you have to do."

"Damn it, Adin, I know!" Aroska hoped he wasn't shaking. "I may be new at this but I'm not incompetent."

"Adin!" Ziva called, mercifully drawing the man's attention away. She strode over to them, sporting her flight suit like a professional. "Did you ever pull any more information from that scrambled communicator?"

"Nothing of importance," he replied. "Whoever had been in contact with Jaxton covered their tracks very well. You suspect one of the captains?

That would explain how our inside man got his hands on Level 4 clearance."

"Could be," Ziva said, looking around to see if the others were ready, "but it's more likely someone of lower rank trying to reroute the attention away from themselves. Start from the lowest possible position with Level 4 access and work your way up."

Adin nodded and shook her hand. "Please let me know if you all need any help. I know Saun too and I'm ready to do anything. *Anything*. Just say the word."

Ziva hesitated, her face grim, but finally nodded. "If I know Emeri, he kicked me off this case so he can look good for the Royal House and so he won't have the responsibility of cleaning up any messes I make. I'll contact you when we reach Sardonis and then you tell him exactly where we are and what we're doing and see if he's willing to send backup."

"I will."

Ziva clapped Aroska on the shoulder and put on her own helmet. "Let's get going."

The two of them walked over to where Skeet and Zinni waited with Marshay, Ryon, and the rest of Adin's team. "You're sure you've got everything you need?" the housekeeper asked in a motherly tone.

"If we don't, we'll survive without it," Ziva said, unconcerned. "You two—" she looked to Mari, Colin, and Mack as well "—*all* of you might want to lay low for a while. HSP won't be happy when they find out you've collaborated on a rogue mission."

She and Skeet and Zinni climbed into their cockpits and Aroska turned to shake Adin's hand. "Be careful," he warned as well. "Thanks for all your help."

"Glad to give it," Adin said as Aroska turned and headed for his own craft. "Hey, man, good luck."

· 34 ·
FRINGE SPACE
SARDON LOCAL TIME

Ziva loved traveling at FTL speed. She loved the momentum, she loved the dancing colors, but above all she loved the quiet. The steadiness and the low rumble of the ship's engine made her feel at peace. Sometimes she would nap during FTL trips, but not when she had a mission to take care of. Not like now. Now, the engine's hum and the gliding sensation helped her focus. She took a moment to study the tiny hologram of Dakiti that hovered on the control panel thanks to Zinni. If everything went according to plan, they would touch down on the roof of the compound's highest structure just before first light. They were equipped with suppressed projectile rifles rather than plasma rifles that would more easily be seen in the dark if fired. Ziva wasn't sure which she preferred—projectile weapons were more accurate and efficient, but plasma didn't leave nearly the mess, in a way making it just as useful.

She shook her head and checked the readings on her viewscreen. Two minutes to destination; after that, at least another twenty until they would reach Dakiti and be able to jump. Upon clearing the roof, they would rappel down an elevator shaft beside a maintenance ladder to gain access to lower levels of the building. It was still early enough that a fresh batch of guards wouldn't be on duty yet and late enough that the ones already on patrol might be getting lazy. In reality, their timing couldn't have been better.

Ziva looked at her readings again and adjusted the earpiece in her helmet. "All units stand by to cut FTL speed. On my mark."

She paused a moment, waiting until the last possible second. If Jayden was already at Dakiti, there was no time to waste. "Cut in sub-light engines."

Dropping out of FTL travel was always disappointing; it meant the time for relaxation and quiet reflection was over. But at the moment, she was pumped so full of adrenaline that she barely noticed. The dreary gray-brown world of Sardonis lay directly ahead, one half bathed in light as it rotated toward the sun and the other half cast in shadow. On the ground it was exactly how it looked from this view in space: cold and wet. Ziva had spent time on Sardonis on two occasions, but hadn't cared to stay long—after all, it had been the Sardons who were responsible for the explosion that killed her father during the War. It was a slimy, swampy mud hole in general, a fitting environment for the semi-amphibious Sardon scum who inhabited it. Above a certain elevation, however, there was next to no plant and animal life. Nothing but dirt and rocks. The H-26s would be safe there while the team was inside the facility.

"Zinni, do you have a reading on Jayden?" Ziva asked, veering toward the dark side of the planet.

The other three stealth fighters kept formation and followed. "Affirmative," Zinni replied. "It looks like our Tantali friends just arrived at the medical center."

"Hopefully they'll be able to fend for themselves until we can get to them," came Skeet's voice.

At the moment Ziva didn't really care what happened to Jayden and Bront, but knew Emeri would have her head if she defied orders to come here and then didn't get them out. She wasn't convinced Aroska's mind was right about this Saun Zaid woman, either. She would never abandon one of her own in a place like Dakiti, but something in her gut warned her to be cautious.

She switched comm channels. "Lieutenant Woro, come in. We've reached Sardonis."

There were several seconds of static, and then she heard Adin's voice. "Roger that. My team has the *Intrepid* and we're getting ready to leave the planet. I've got a captain back at Headquarters who's not very happy with me."

"Leave the planet?"

"We're not letting you four go in there on your own."

"Adin, no! If you come now you'll blow this entire mission."

He paused. "How about we wait just out-of-system in case you run into some trouble?"

There was no question of whether or not they would run into trouble. "Fine," Ziva said. "Just call the director. We're going silent for a while."

"I will. Be careful."

She cut the transmission and guided the H-26 a bit further into the planet's shadow. Sardonis was a smaller world than Haphez, but its lowlands were densely populated. Civilization was crammed into every livable crevice in the cities, but Dakiti was isolated, situated nearly one hundred kilometers from any populated area—another reason everything could potentially work to their advantage.

The four ships descended into Sardon airspace and pulled up just below the outer limits of the atmosphere. "Maintain thirty klicks," Ziva instructed. "Drop zone eight minutes and closing."

Looking down through the clouds outside the cockpit, Ziva could occasionally make out the faint lights from cities far below. They were flying higher than any major traffic lanes on the planet, though there was still the possibility of a smuggler's ship or something of the sort crossing paths with them. She turned her attention back to what was in front of her.

Skeet and Zinni had been chattering incessantly for most of the journey, telling jokes and reminiscing about old missions, but now the comm channel was silent as each agent mentally prepared themselves for the jump and whatever lay beyond. Ziva admired their abilities to balance business and fun—sometimes their jokes helped keep her sane, though she didn't dare admit it. Aroska hadn't said much since leaving Noro. She looked out to her left where his Scout lurked, invisible in the darkness and clouds. She hoped he was right about his friend Saun. She hated to think he'd been oblivious enough to not realize her true intentions.

Adjusting her earpiece again, she opened a direct transmission to his ship. "Are you with me?"

"I'm not against you if that's what you're asking," came the immediate reply.

Jumpy. Sharp. Even through the communicator she could hear the fear in his voice. He had less than three minutes to pull himself together.

"Are you afraid?" he asked after several seconds.

"No," Ziva replied. "Are you?"

No response.

She smirked. "The silence is very reassuring."

"What's your secret?"

"If I told you, I'd have to kill you," she said, hoping he'd think she was joking. She was confident in her own skills, but the underlying knowledge of her Nostia was what really made her fearless. But if anyone knew about it, she *would* have to kill them. She switched back to the four-way communicator. "Two minutes to destination. Setting VI pilot."

"Copy," three voices said simultaneously.

Ziva slid her visor down and locked it, then made sure the life support connection was secure. She flipped a small lever, transferring all control of the craft to the onboard virtual intelligence. After taking one last look out the front of the cockpit, she directed her full attention to the readings on the viewscreen. They were nearly on top of Dakiti.

"All right people, look alive. It's time." She took a deep breath and watched the screen. "Ejecting in five, four, three, two...punching out."

She mashed the button without another thought. The cockpit canopy over her head flew open and she felt herself shoot out into the darkness. Everything was still and quiet here in the clouds, though she could hear the faint hum of the other three ships as they zoomed by beneath her. Turning her body around, she flattened her hands to her sides and dove downward.

It was still too dark to pick up anything with the helmet's night optics, so Ziva kept her eyes on the altitude reading in the visor's heads-up display. The actual fall would take about four minutes plus a few seconds, and it was crucial that the parachutes were opened at the correct moment or the whole mission would be wasted.

Freefalling was a little like traveling at FTL speed in Ziva's opinion. Her jumpsuit did a good job of blocking out the freezing air at this altitude, but the sensation of the crushing wind still reached her skin and she found it relaxing. She hadn't had to HALO jump to reach a destination more than two or three times throughout her career, but there was something about the adrenaline rush that left her reenergized and ready to move upon landing.

Keeping her eyes on the altimeter and the time reading, Ziva waited a few moments and then leveled out and spread her arms, slowing a little. The numbers on the HUD continued scrolling as she descended. She counted in her mind, hoping the others were doing the same. *Now.* She yanked the release cord and felt the pack on her back open up as her chute deployed. For a split second, it felt as though she was traveling back upward as the lightweight material caught the air and harshly slowed her fall. Legs swinging, she reached into the darkness on either side of her and found the toggles, regaining control of her movements.

She could now see the structures of Dakiti through the helmet visor and steered herself closer to the landing zone. Skeet, Zinni, and Aroska were a bit further behind, but she could see that they too had successfully deployed their chutes and had control of the toggles. Phase one had gone smoothly enough, but they would certainly be taking things one step at a time. The next item on the list was the landing, which would require absolute precision and control. The initial fall had taken just over four minutes, as planned, and the remaining distance with the parachutes would be covered in another three. The roof on which they would land was large, but after falling from such a great height and at such a great speed, landing accurately on a surface of that size would be a challenge. It would take only the slightest error for one of them to miss the roof and either be detected by someone in the building or become stranded on the ground. Aroska was good, but her team was more experienced, and Ziva hoped he would be able to keep up.

The numbers on the altimeter continued scrolling, quickly approaching the building's height. Nearly all of the surrounding structures were visible now, and two narrow pillars of black smoke billowed up from unseen vents on the other side of the building. From this point, Ziva could make out two armed sentries walking along the low wall that lined the roof of the main med center. The roof access hatch was precisely where Zinni's calculations had said it would be. It would be best to do their work without taking out the guards, which would alert the entire compound if they failed to report at a set time or if someone found the bodies. It was rather foggy and still dark enough that her team could most likely get inside undetected.

Fifty meters to the roof's surface. Ziva kept the toggles steady and positioned herself directly over the center of the building. The guards were carrying what appeared to be high powered spotting scopes, which struck her as being somewhat ineffective in this weather. Twenty meters. Ten meters.

Ziva took a deep breath of the rich oxygen in her suit and let go of the toggles. She pulled the cable to close her chute and it retracted quickly and silently into the pack on her shoulders. She fell the remaining couple of meters, landing softly on the balls of her feet, and crouched low with her rifle up and ready. With the night optics in her helmet, she saw that neither of the guards had broken stride and that both of them were still pacing nonchalantly.

She heard the other three land behind her and rose to her feet, taking cover behind one of several large ventilation units that ran along the roof's surface. If the guards were carrying spotting scopes, they were probably focused on what was down on the ground rather than what was right in front of them, but she kept her eyes glued to them nonetheless. She slinked toward the access hatch in the center of the roof, pausing every few seconds to listen and study the guards' movements. When she was sure it was safe, she beckoned for the others to follow.

Zinni moved ahead and pulled out her little scanner, checking the area below the hatch for activity. She nodded to Ziva that things were all clear, and then pressed the controls to open it. She jumped down into the semi-darkness below while Ziva remained focused on the guards. Both of them had their backs turned, their attention directed toward the rest of the compound. As soon as Skeet and Aroska had passed through the opening, she stepped back and carefully let herself down the ladder, closing the cover behind her.

The floor upon which the four of them stood could most accurately be described as a wide catwalk that followed the same path as the ill-lit hallway directly below it. Dark pipes and cables lined the walls, setting a gloomy tone, and a couple of deactivated maintenance bots rested lifelessly in the corner. It was hot and muggy, and Ziva flipped her helmet visor open to get some air. Directly behind them were the ladder and the hatch through which they had just come. To the right, a rusty set of steps leading down to the next floor. Ahead lay the maintenance entrance to the elevator, their ticket to the restricted levels Saun Zaid had mentioned.

Ziva slung her rifle over her shoulder and removed her helmet, checking to make sure her earpiece was still snug in her ear. The others did the same. "We can stash our stuff in the top of the elevator shaft," she said, sliding the parachute case from her shoulders. "There's no need for it anymore."

They strode to the elevator door and Skeet removed a tool from his belt, jamming it through the crack where the door met the wall. "I wasn't sure if we were going to get past those sentries," he said. The device split into two claw-like halves and pulled the door open several centimeters, enabling him to slip his hand through and force it open the rest of the way.

"I'm just glad we didn't have to take lethal action," Aroska said. "Wouldn't want the whole place to know we're here before we even set foot in the building."

Pleased they were on the same page, Ziva stepped forward and peered down the shaft. Cold, stale air drifted up and dried the thin layer of sweat that had formed on her face. There was a maintenance ladder against the wall to their left that descended into the darkness, and she could hear the elevator car moving about somewhere far below.

A narrow lip directly above the door kept the elevator from crushing the power cables on the ceiling, and Ziva tossed her helmet and parachute up onto it. Unraveling her grappling cable, she leaped out across the shaft to the ladder and secured it to a sturdy pipe. "Let's go," she said, removing a glow stick from her belt and lowering herself a couple of meters. "We've got a lot of ground to cover and not a lot of time."

The other three repeated her actions and they descended together, four abreast, following the ladder. The walls were greasy and the shaft smelled as if this part of the building had probably been around for a long time. Most of the Dakiti compound had existed long before the Fringe War, but much had been added on since then. Although she'd been to Sardonis, she had never been to Dakiti, and now she was finally inside the famed facility...climbing covertly down an elevator shaft.

"This is a fifty-story building," Zinni said, "and we want to get to the bottom two levels?" This was a question directed at Aroska.

"Saun said they weren't letting anybody into the underground levels. She was on Level Three when we talked, but she could be anywhere by now."

"Bottom two, then," Zinni confirmed. She looked down into the abyss below them. "What have we gotten into?" she chuckled.

Ziva felt the message indicator on her communicator vibrate and switched her earpiece to a private channel. "Lieutenant Woro! What the.... What did the director say?"

"He's refusing to send any support. Said something about not wanting to take responsibility for any damage you cause while defying orders."

"I told you."

"Is it too late to get out?"

Ziva looked back up the shaft and then down toward their destination. "Just a little. We don't quit, Lieutenant. We never have, and we're certainly not going to start now."

He sighed. "Right. Alpha field ops standing by."

She switched back to the community channel the rest of the team was using and then continued descending. "HSP's not sending backup," she announced after several seconds of silence.

Nobody said anything for a while. Ziva truthfully hadn't been expecting any HSP support; part of her didn't blame Emeri for wanting to stay out of this, as any involvement with an unsanctioned mission could get him in trouble with the higher-ups in the capital. Then again, as head of the agency, he should have at least been willing to take *some* responsibility. She sighed and continued descending, reminding herself to focus on the task at hand.

After a few more seconds, her cable jerked and she came to a sudden stop. Using the faint light from the glow stick, she saw she had reached the end of the twenty-meter line. She looked to the others, who had also run out of cable. "Okay," she breathed, establishing a firm grip on one of the large pipes, "release on my mark. Three, two, one, now."

She flipped a tiny switch on the side of the cable spool and deactivated the powerful magnet that had been attached at the top of the shaft. The line retracted quickly and she caught the magnet, reattaching it to the pipe she currently held. They continued downward, releasing and reattaching every twenty meters. It was a slow process—*too* slow—but it was their best shot at reaching Jayden, Enrik, and Saun, assuming they weren't already dead.

"Are we all clear on the procedure once we reach the bottom?" she asked. "Aroska and I will go in first. We'll go as far as the old bunker and then split up to search for Zaid and the governor. Skeet, Zinni, you'll take the lower of the two levels and look for Jayden and the other Tantalis—they've undoubtedly been captured. We'll meet up at the south sewer access."

"If we go in for Bront and the other guards, we won't have enough transportation to get them out of here," Skeet said.

"Adin is waiting with the *Intrepid* just out-of-system," Ziva replied, bothered again that he would think she didn't have a plan. "We'll get everyone out."

"Elevator!" Zinni exclaimed.

The walls began to shake and Ziva let go of her cable, pressing herself as flat as she could against the crusty wall. The elevator car roared by in a gust of wind half a meter behind them and sped into the darkness above. All that could be heard for the next several seconds was the faint whistle of air swirling through the shaft and the four of them breathing heavily.

Cautiously, silently, Ziva let herself move away from the wall and carried on. "We're almost there," she said, glancing downward. She wasn't sure if she could actually see the bottom of the shaft from this point or whether her mind was just playing tricks on her.

"Yeah," Zinni confirmed. "This next one is it. Level 1B."

They all stopped and locked their lines. Ziva and Aroska swung across the shaft and clung to the cables that ran parallel to the door. Skeet followed with his tools.

"Zinni, scanner," Ziva said, extending her hand.

Zinni tossed her the handheld gadget and she held it up to the door. Nothing.

"We're all clear." She lobbed it back and nodded at Skeet. "Let's go."

He once again wedged the device into the door and forced it open. A long, sparkling clean hallway that smelled of chemicals stretched ahead.

"Keep as silent as possible," Ziva said, indicating her earpiece. "Again, meet at the south sewer entrance. Good luck, you two."

She and Aroska jumped out into the hallway.

· 35 ·

SUBLEVELS
DAKITI MEDICAL RESEARCH CENTER
SARDONIS

S keet waited a few seconds after the door closed before he put his
tools away and swung back across the shaft to where Zinni waited
with her own glow stick activated.

"Let's do this, sister," he said, unlocking his cable. They dropped
smoothly to the identical door on the next level, where all still seemed
quiet. Skeet took a deep breath and reached down to release his line, but
Zinni's hand on his arm stopped him.

"Wait." Her attention was directed downward.

He watched as she let the glow stick fall down into the darkness.
Instead of hitting the ground, it continued falling, illuminating the outline
of one last door before finding the bottom of the shaft. Unsure what exactly
he was seeing, he activated his own glow stick and held it down as far as
he could reach. Sure enough, there was one last level still to come. The
architecture around the door looked recent, by no means new, but
definitely not as old as the rest of the shaft.

Skeet looked back to Zinni, who watched him with bright eyes and
that same mischievous grin she'd had when she found the overwritten
transmission. "Check it out?" she suggested, dropping down before he
could even answer.

He unraveled his line and caught up to her, taking a closer look at the
door. There was a small black pad built into it, which he carefully reached
out to touch. A three-dimensional keypad formed in front of him. The layout
was the same as any standard keypad, but the characters were all in Sardon.

"This didn't show up on the schematics," Zinni said.

"Security is high, a governor, his son, and a foreign agent are being held captive, and now we have an unknown level that doesn't show up on anybody's charts. Where would you stash your hostages in a place like this?"

"We need to get in there," was Zinni's reply.

Skeet put a finger to his earpiece. "Ziva, we've come across an unmarked level of the building and we have reason to believe searching it should take priority over the other restricted level."

"Copy that, Skeet," came Ziva's quiet voice. "Proceed with caution."

"How's your Sardon?" he asked Zinni. "Think you can open it?"

She gnawed on her lip and nodded slowly. "I can try. We just have to hope screwing up doesn't trigger some kind of alarm."

"It looks like this is designed so that when the elevator door opens, this door will still be shut. The code has to be entered in order to get out, and the same goes for coming into the elevator from the other side."

Zinni nodded and looked up. "Speaking of elevator, it's headed back this way."

"Don't worry. What are the chances it's coming all the way down here?" Skeet pried at the black pad with his fingers. "Maybe if we could get this thing off—"

"Skeet, the elevator."

"I hear it."

"Skeet!"

He looked up to see the elevator car barreling toward them and showing no signs of stopping at either of the two levels above. "Whoa!"

With pure reflex taking over, Skeet released his cable and fell the remaining meter to the bottom of the shaft, landing flat on his back—rifle and all—on a bed of wires beside Zinni's glow stick. He gasped for the air that had just been punched out of his lungs. Zinni arrived next to him a split second later with a grunt. The car was still coming.

She put her hands up to shield her face.

He closed his eyes.

Boom.

Gentle creaking. Silence.

Skeet looked up, momentarily unsure whether he was still alive. The bottom of the car sat mere centimeters above his face, resting on a sort of shelf identical to the one at the top of the shaft. He could hear a series of key tones followed by the sound of the doors opening and hushed Sardon voices. Dim light seeped in through a crack between the car and the wall, and shadows crossed over his face as figures stepped from the hall into the elevator.

He rolled his head to the side to check on Zinni, who still had her eyes closed but had put her hands down to her sides. Her chest rose and fell steadily as she attempted to slow her breathing. She appeared to be listening.

The passage door and elevator door closed one after the other and the car took off up the shaft just as fast as it had come. Skeet watched it go until he could no longer see its outline in the light from the glow sticks and then scrambled to his feet. "That's one for the records," he said, dusting himself off and reaching down to help Zinni up. "You okay?"

"Fine," she replied, rubbing the back of her head and cracking her neck. She picked up the remaining length of her grappling cable, which had jammed, and wound it up manually. "How about yourself?"

Skeet nodded in response. "Did you get the code?"

"Do I hear doubt in your voice?" Zinni said, gathering up the glow sticks before pulling out her scanner again. She tapped her ear. "Of course I got it."

He laughed. "I just thought the fact that you were nearly crushed by an elevator might have affected your ability to retain that information."

Zinni held the scanner up to the door. The device beeped and she checked the reading. "I've got nothing for at least a hundred meters." She looked to Skeet, waiting for an order.

"Tunnel, maybe?"

"Find out?"

He nodded. "Open it."

Zinni re-activated the keypad and entered the digits to match the key tones they had heard a moment before, humming them to herself as she did so. The hologram glowed green and the door slid open.

Before them lay a long, straight tunnel with raw, earthen walls. Dim lights placed every few meters bathed the walkway in an eerie yellow hue. Another door lay at the far end, possibly another elevator.

A foul stench reached them as they climbed up into the tunnel and began walking. It smelled hot—it was already strangely hot and muggy down here—and it made Skeet's stomach churn. He took another whiff; it was a mixture of overcooked meat and something rotten.

"Smell that?"

Zinni nodded. "Disgusting. I don't even want to know where it's coming from."

"It's probably the source of that smoke we saw on the way down. That stuff was being vented from somewhere down here."

They made their way cautiously down the tunnel. There were no doors or other passages, only the occasional pipe running up the wall into the floor above. It reminded Skeet of a prison they had infiltrated once. There it had reeked as well, but of sweaty bodies and fecal matter. The smell here was neither of these. It wasn't coming from the walls or the pipes, but was growing stronger as they neared the door at the end. It made the hair on the back of his neck stand on end, as if he were an animal sensing a predator close by.

"I don't like this at all," Zinni murmured, glancing back down the tunnel. "There's something awful going on around here."

"Mmhmm," Skeet replied. He ran his tongue over his lips, which had suddenly become very dry, and raised his rifle toward the door. Whatever was behind it was a threat in one way or another; he could feel it. Beads of perspiration accumulated on his forehead, both because of the heat and because of nerves. He couldn't breathe.

Skeet blinked and they were at the door, or at least that's what it felt like. There was a little black touchpad built into the control panel identical to the one they'd just used, though upon closer examination this no longer appeared to be another elevator. He put his ear up to the door, listening, and Zinni held her scanner up, searching.

"Nothing," they said simultaneously, each taking a step back.

Skeet took a deep breath and waved toward the touchpad. "Try the same code. Let's get in there."

Zinni repeated the pattern of key tones and the door slid open. A massive heat wave hit them as they rushed in, weapons up.

Skeet froze.

· 36 ·
HOLDING ROOM
DAKITI MEDICAL RESEARCH CENTER
SARDONIS

The hood was yanked off Jayden's head and he cringed against the sudden brightness of the room around him. He sat in a chair with his wrists secured to the armrests, facing two figures. The first was a tall Sardon whom he assumed to be Dane Bothum. The second was a Haphezian woman who bore a striking resemblance to Ziva, but her eyes were sunken in and her face was ashen. She looked ill.

"Now Jayden—I hope you don't mind if I call you Jayden—see how easy this was?" Bothum strode over to him, hands clasped behind his back. "If you would have just come to visit me in the first place, this could have been over a long time ago and it would have saved you all the trouble with the Haphezians."

Jayden glanced at the woman, who watched him intently with cold purplish-pink eyes. He wondered who she was and whether she had been the mole at HSP responsible for this whole mess. He raised his eyebrows and shifted his attention back to Bothum. "I'd also be dead by now if I'd done that."

Bothum grinned, revealing a typical set of incisor-like Sardon teeth. "Yes, yes you probably would."

"I won't do it, Bothum. I know what you want from me. Even if I do delete that transmission, it's too late. HSP knows exactly where you are."

"I am well aware of that," the Sardon replied, "but do they know where *you* are?"

Jayden hesitated, mouth slightly open. He'd left in such a hurry without telling Ziva and the others of his plans. Would they be able to guess where he had gone? Would they even try to come get him out? He was beginning to wish they hadn't parted on such negative terms.

"Ah," Bothum chuckled again. "They have no idea, do they?"

"That's not true," Jayden replied quickly. "There's a squadron on the way here now." If there was indeed anyone coming for him, he doubted it would be any more than Ziva's spec ops team. Emeri Arion hadn't been happy when Jayden and Bront had informed him of the incident at her house, and he had threatened to have her thrown off the case. He hoped that wouldn't stop her from coming anyway.

"You're not very good at bluffing," Bothum said, clicking his tongue.

"Where's my father?" Jayden demanded, changing the subject. "If you've hurt him—"

"Never mind that, boy," Bothum snapped, his tone changing abruptly from smooth to threatening. "Is HSP coming or not?"

"Damn it, Dane, just kill him now," the Haphezian woman spoke for the first time, stepping forward with a newly-drawn pistol in her hand.

Bothum put his hand out to stop her and stood over her in a menacing manner. "Patience, Saun. I told you I'm not going to be killing anybody until we've confirmed that Tarbic and Payvan are on site."

"What?" Jayden murmured. If he'd just understood correctly, this was hardly about him anymore. This was a trap for Ziva and Aroska and he was the bait. Now part of him hoped they wouldn't come looking for him at all. "What are you going to do to them?"

Bothum and the woman stopped and stared at him thoughtfully for a moment and then glanced at each other. With a flustered sigh, she moved around to the back of Jayden's chair. He turned to find her just as a needle was jabbed into his throat. He gasped for a breath and then fell asleep.

· 37 ·
SUBLEVELS
DAKITI MEDICAL RESEARCH CENTER
SARDONIS

Z iva slipped cautiously behind the short wall that bordered the balcony with Aroska hot on her heels. She glanced back down the hall from which they had come, wondering if they were attracting attention yet. They'd already had an inevitable run-in with a couple of Sardons in medical attire who had mercifully continued studying their data pads without giving the intruders a second glance. Just a moment earlier, a doctor had come through with a man carrying an expensive, secure-looking case. The two had nodded in acknowledgement but had passed without a word. The thought occurred to Ziva that she and Aroska probably looked like a pair of security detail—if there was a Solaris cell here, it probably wasn't uncommon to see the odd Haphezian every so often. It now seemed that the doctors and other medical personnel wouldn't be a problem; it was the real guards that worried her.

They peered down over the edge of the balcony and scanned the huge floor below. It was vacant except for a Sardon man in a military get-up who paced back and forth in front of a large platform. A massive viewscreen rose up behind him, no doubt used for some sort of presentation. The man was clearly waiting for something, and Ziva found herself wanting to know what it was. The way she saw it, they were one step behind since the discovery of the additional level of the building that hadn't appeared on Zinni's schematics. Dakiti, one. Alpha team, nothing.

She directed her attention to a vast door that began to rise on the far side of the assembly area. She could see a row of boots lined up side by side, waiting to enter. The boots grew into legs, which eventually grew into Sardon bodies wearing identical uniforms and toting rifles. They marched in to the center of the floor, ten rows, six across. The man who had been waiting began barking orders, which they carried out in perfect synchronization. Jayden's words eased into her memory: *"Military stuff— the building of an army. They were calling it 'Shelora Boeta'."*

"What is going on around here?" she muttered.

"A whole lot more than we knew, that's for sure," Aroska replied, shifting his weight a little as he too stole a peek behind them. "We shut these guys down after the War over twenty years ago. What are they doing back in business?"

"I'm not so sure it's the same business. Look."

Ziva pointed down to the floor, studying the group of soldiers again. Sardons weren't known to be overly tall creatures—these were. In fact, they were all precisely the same height, and everything else about their physical appearance was the same. They were built like Sardons, strong and wiry, and had the classic leathery gray skin, but they had...hair. Yes, each of their heads was covered in a thin layer of fuzzy, light brown hair. Sardons never had hair of any kind.

"What are they up to now?"

She shook her head. "I think we need to find out."

There was a squeak of leather boots behind her and she picked up something black in her peripherals. She stood up and pivoted with her rifle raised, but lowered it slowly when she got a look at the man who had appeared. He was the same height as she was, clad in a black and gray uniform similar to the jumpsuits she and Aroska wore. It was clear that he was—or at least *had been*—Haphezian.

"What are you two nimrods doing?" he demanded.

Judging by his demeanor and the way he spoke, Ziva could tell he wasn't quite with it. His eyes were a brilliant green, though one was rather cloudy and kept drifting lazily in different directions. She wondered if it was even functional. His hair was black and close-cropped, with no stripes that she could see. One side of his face, the side with the lazy eye, drooped a bit. He was standing with his knees slightly bent and favored one leg as if he were in pain. She looked to where he clutched a rifle of his own and did a double-take. Each hand had a thumb but only three fingers.

"Get back to work before I report you," he growled, though his voice was a bit unsteady. "You're supposed to be making sure nobody gets through here without authorization."

Ziva glanced at Aroska and then back to the man, who appeared to be a captain judging by the symbols on his sleeve. She made eye contact, unsure for a moment which eye to look at. "And why is that again? We got this assignment late and missed the briefing. Nobody will tell us what's going on."

"I'm surrounded by idiots," he muttered. "Bothum's got the governor and now the son just showed up. You two are supposed to be keeping an eye out for HSP. Now be glad I'm not reporting you for missing a briefing."

"Sorry sir," Aroska said, catching on to Ziva's charade. "It won't happen again."

"It better not," the man said, turning to go. He waved his hand at their facial tattoos. "And wipe that paint off your faces before Bothum catches you. You know the rules." He glared at them for a moment and then hobbled away down the hall.

The two of them stood there in stunned silence for several seconds, mulling things over. The presence of this Haphezian—or whatever he was—and the fact that he had passed them—*Haphezians*—off as security detail told Ziva they were *not* safe here, for reasons other than wanting to rescue the Tantalis or find Solaris. The guard and the soldiers in the assembly area were a product of something unnatural, and she dreaded to think of what it was.

"What just happened?" Aroska said, staring in the direction the man had gone.

Ziva took him by the arm and dragged him down the hall according to plan. "That confirms that both Jayden and the governor are here," she said, glancing through the open door of a med room as they went by. "I doubt this guard act will last forever, but if we can pass off as security until we find them and your friend—"

"Start checking all these rooms then." Aroska went to the nearest room and opened the door, poked his head inside, and continued down the hall. "You check everything on that side."

They worked their way quickly in the direction they had originally mapped out, ducking into rooms and ducking back out, slowing to a more casual pace whenever a doctor or nurse came through. So they continued until they came to a T-intersection where one hall contained more rooms and the other hit a dead end and was lined with unused equipment.

Aroska went to the first door and found it to be locked. There were two more doors beside it, apparently identical small rooms, maybe for examination. He tried the others—the third was open. "You'd better come look at this."

She glanced up and down the hall before crossing to the open door. They were running short on time. She leaned in and took a quick glance around, but what she saw held her there. She took a step inside. The room was perhaps three meters wide and four meters long, and it was pure white. It was unusually cold, more so than the rest of the med center. An extremely bright light shone down on a long, metal examination table in the center of the room. At one end, there were two clasps meant to secure someone's ankles, with an identical pair near the center for the wrists. Two thick straps dangled off the edge, positioned so that they probably crossed over a person's chest and forehead. The table glistened as though it had been recently wiped clean and it smelled of disinfectant.

The only other structures in the room were a large monitor, currently powered off, and a large slanted table stocked with various sizes of syringes, all full of different colored liquids. The sight of those items along with what she had already seen in the facility made Ziva shudder.

Aroska moved over to study the collection of syringes and picked one up to examine it. "Axonyte," he said, "just like the one that Sardon used on Jayden." He carefully placed it back on the shelf and took a look at the others. "I couldn't begin to tell you what the rest of this stuff is."

"There are no surgical tools in here," Ziva observed. She reached out to touch a string of sensors connected to the monitor that appeared to stretch over to the table. She took note of the labels on some of the buttons and switches on the machine. "This is just for monitoring general wellness and vitals."

"Then what's with all of this?" Aroska scoffed, taking a closer look at one of the smaller syringes.

"And what's with the restraints?"

He turned and began fingering one of the straps. It was adjustable both in length and in position along the table. He sniffed it. His eyes grew wide and he held it out to Ziva. "Smell that?"

Ziva took a whiff. The smell was unmistakable. "Cha'sen."

· 38 ·

MEANWHILE...
DAKITI MEDICAL RESEARCH CENTER
SARDONIS

Skeet was worried. Zinni knew thanks to the telltale crease that had formed across the center of his forehead, the same crease that always appeared when he was nervous or had a bad feeling in his gut. Something wasn't right about this place—she could sense it too—but the fact that Skeet was anxious enough for that crease to appear made her feel worse.

Now, having opened the mysterious door at the end of the hallway, Zinni found herself standing in a room that made her feel very small. It wasn't that it was an overly large room—in fact, it wasn't that big at all. The heat and the stench they had picked up earlier were so overpowering that she wanted nothing more than to curl up on the floor with her arms over her head.

At first, she wasn't exactly sure what she was seeing, except for a wide-eyed Skeet and the barrel of her rifle as she swept it around the room. There was a large trap door in the ceiling, some sort of chute that connected to a steep, slick ramp. At the bottom of the ramp, a wide conveyor belt ran on a circuit toward a massive furnace from which flames protruded at intervals. Two pipes rose from the top of the furnace and ran up the far wall, no doubt the source of the smoke outside.

When she'd finally managed to take everything in, Zinni wanted to vomit. Moving along the conveyor belt, limp like rags, were bodies—five cold, shriveled, naked bodies of Haphezian men and women. The belt stopped as each of them reached the furnace. They fell in one at a time, incinerated instantly by the raging flames. Remaining ashes were dumped through an opening in the bottom of the furnace and onto a smaller conveyor that ran out of the room.

Three things hit her at the same time: anger at what she was seeing, the fact that they still had a job to do, and also the question of whether they had been led here on purpose and had walked straight into a trap. Jayden had left Haphez in such a foul mood—would he really betray them and work with Bothum to lure them in? Zinni dismissed the thought as absurd. The young man may have been angry, but it didn't take a genius to realize he had principles. She was losing her focus and letting her mind jump to conclusions. Still, something told her they had been led here just as much as they had come of their own volition.

"Z, you will not believe what we just found," Skeet said, covering his nose as another body fell into the furnace.

"We've made an interesting discovery ourselves," Ziva's voice came over the comm channel. "Let's hear your story."

"We've got bodies."

"Lots of them," Zinni added as three more slid down the chute. "Haphezian bodies, Ziva."

She could hear both Ziva and Aroska curse and begin speaking to one another, but she also heard a gentle *clink*, like a small metallic object colliding with a larger piece of metal. She directed her attention to a wide grate under the furnace's trap door. The ashes sifted through it onto the small conveyor belt while larger remains, bone fragments and such, were caught on the grate. Something glinted in the light of the fire as another batch of ashes was dumped.

"Skeet, look at this," Zinni whispered, cautiously moving down beside the furnace. She reached in slowly, careful not to touch the scorching metal, and brushed away the ashes. The object was still warm in her hand as she pulled it out and turned it over. It was the all-too-familiar round tag, complete with the thin chain, that she had seen so many people wearing every day back home. Shocked, she squatted down and moved as close to the grate as the intense heat would allow.

Even with the rest of the disgusting clutter that had accumulated, she could count at least seven other Haphezian military IDs, charred and softened from their trip through the furnace.

Fighting the tremble that threatened to take control of her hands, she reached in again and took hold of the two nearest tags. "I recognize these names," she said, scratching some of the black crust from them. "They're on the Grand Army's killed-in-action list, but their bodies were never found."

"Okay Ziva, looks like some of these people are...*were* GA and presumed dead," Skeet reported. "I mean, now they *are* dead, but—"

Zinni could tell he was trying hard to stay focused. "They were presumed KIA, but it looks like they've been here the whole time," she finished for him. "Are we dealing with some sort of cover up?"

"Think the director will have a change of heart now?" Skeet said, wiping the sweat from his forehead.

"I'm not sure," Ziva replied. "Even if he doesn't send reinforcements, it's a safe bet the GA will. The military won't take kindly to their people being held in a place like this. Brief Adin. Have him contact the base on Na and coordinate a ground assault with whoever's in charge over there. Looks like our plans have changed a bit."

"What about Jayden and the governor?"

"We have confirmation that they're both here. We've also been passed off as guards. I'm not sure if I even *want* to know how—maybe we just look like Solaris insurgents from home— but if it makes the extraction any easier, I'll live with it. I assume they'll catch on at some point so we have to work fast. It would be good to be walking out of here before the military arrives. Now get out of there. I think I'm starting to get an idea of what's going on around here and it sounds like down there is the last place you want to be."

Zinni didn't need to be told. "Copy that," she said, pocketing the three tags she held. Too eager to get out, she took Skeet by the arm and headed for the access staircase that came down beside the chute. "Let's do this, brother."

· 39 ·
Holding Room
Dakiti Medical Research Center
Sardonis

Saun studied the tip of her finger, or more accurately, the tiny transmitter on her fingertip that she had just found embedded in Jayden Saiffe's scalp. This was the little device that would lead Aroska to her so she could follow through on her promise to Bothum and get a new life. It hurt to breathe even now as she sat waiting for the young man to wake up. Bothum had disappeared to prepare for the "guests," leaving her to babysit. She was almost glad to stay—the pain in her chest was becoming so severe that any exertion at all was almost unbearable.

The door opened and Saun gasped, feeling like she'd just inhaled a rock. Captain Atu burst in, glancing at her with his eerie lazy eye. "Bothum wanted to see me," he stuttered, studying Jayden curiously.

"He's not here," Saun replied. In all honesty, she felt sorry for these rejects that made up part of Dakiti's security population. It wasn't their fault that they were the way they were. Bothum had realized this and had mercifully agreed to give them positions in the staff so they would feel like they belonged in the world. "He said to give you this." She handed Atu the data pad Bothum had left with her.

The captain took it and looked at the two images displayed on the screen. One was Aroska's HSP identification photo, and the other was a still of Ziva Payvan that had been transmitted by Solaris's stolen drone before it had been destroyed the day before.

"Spread those around to the rest of security. Bothum wants to know the second they arrive."

Atu's eyebrows were furrowed, giving Saun the impression he was thinking as hard as he was capable of. "They're already here," he said, much too matter-of-factly.

"What?"

"I saw them, maybe ten minutes ago."

Saun leaped to her feet, hands curled into fists. "You didn't tell anyone?"

"I thought they were ours!" Atu protested. "Look at *me*! Look at *you*! How do you expect me to tell the difference?"

Trying to control her breathing, Saun studied Jayden for a moment. Satisfied that he wouldn't be going anywhere, she turned to the door, shooting Atu an accusatory glare. "Come with me," she ordered.

· 40 ·
SUBLEVELS
DAKITI MEDICAL RESEARCH CENTER
SARDONIS

Aroska and Ziva made their way down another hallway as briskly as possible without outright running. She was against the opposite wall and several strides ahead of him. He dared not question her lead, but all he could think about was finding Saun and the fact that they had very little time. Try as he might, somehow he couldn't bring himself to believe looking for her was even in Ziva's agenda. The way she'd talked about Saun earlier had got him thinking. *"For all we know, she could be the Solaris informant."* He didn't want to believe she had anything to do with this, but even if she did, he wasn't going to just leave her here.

"It's nearly time to split up," Ziva said, almost in a whisper.

Aroska made no move to respond. His mind was on Saun and how he was going to go about rescuing her once he was on his own. It felt wrong to just call her a friend; whatever the two of them shared, it surpassed even his longtime friendship with Adin. She was different than any woman he'd ever been with—which was saying something—and he found himself wondering if what he felt could be considered love at this point. Regardless, he cared about her more than anything and was ready to do whatever it took to get her out.

"You afraid?" Ziva said, the same question he'd asked her during the flight.

He smirked and parroted the response she'd given him. "No. You?"

She might have chuckled—he couldn't tell.

They arrived at the entrance to the old bunker, where the hallway turned into yet another T-intersection. That's what the underground levels of the building seemed to consist of: a maze of intersecting corridors, identical corners, and closed doors, all built around the bunker that had been part of the original Dakiti military base. A person could get lost far too easily.

Ziva stopped and took a look in either direction down the hallway. "This is it. You go right, I'll go left. If you find anything, let me know so we're not running in circles. You get in there and get back to the sewer entrance as soon as possible."

She turned abruptly and strode away, holding her rifle a bit higher and a bit tighter than she had been. In a way, Aroska felt empowered knowing that the seemingly-invincible Ziva Payvan was even having some reservations about this mission, but it also made him feel more uneasy than he otherwise would have been.

He began to walk in the opposite direction, listening both in front and behind him for any sign of danger. They'd ended up passing two other pairs of guards, neither of which had paid any special attention to them and both of which also had eerily-Haphezian characteristics. He may have looked like them at first glance, but he doubted the "face paint" was going to fly much longer. He brushed his fingers across the dotted *gesh punti* on his cheek and brow, wondering if he should find some way to cover them up.

Hushed voices could be heard ahead and to his left where yet another hallway ran perpendicular to the one in which he now stood. He slowed his pace and listened. The language was clearly Sardon, but one of the voices sounded uncannily familiar. He rounded the corner, glancing briefly to his right, and found himself face-to-face with Saun. She stood maybe three meters in front of him, speaking to the strange Haphezian man with the lazy eye he and Ziva had encountered earlier.

He found his finger had moved unconsciously to the trigger of his rifle. "Saun?"

The realization that something was wrong hit him just as something hard and heavy struck the back of his head.

· 41 ·
MILITARY BUNKER
DAKITI MEDICAL RESEARCH CENTER
SARDONIS

As far as Ziva could tell, she was moving in a very wide and very deformed circle back toward the balcony from which they had observed the soldiers drilling. Dakiti's underground levels, perhaps with the exception of the one Skeet and Zinni had stumbled upon, were far more extensive than the tall structure above them and stretched throughout the majority of the compound. They had a general idea of Jayden's location—he was somewhere under the main building, but Zinni could only track him to within eight meters. It would be difficult to even tell which floor he was on, let alone what room he was in. With an eight meter radius, his signal could be picked up from up to three floors away. She hoped that wherever he was, the governor was with him, allowing them to knock out two birds with one stone.

"Got anything, Zinni?" she spoke into her earpiece as she passed a nurses' station. Several Sardon women sat there monitoring a vast array of screens. They all glanced up as she came by, though one in particular seemed to take more interest than the others. She picked up her pace.

"I've got a strong signal," Zinni replied after several seconds of silence that made Ziva's skin crawl. "We're right below you now. He must be down here somewhere."

"When you find something—"

"—you'll be the first to know."

The hallway widened significantly ahead and gave way to a set of clear double doors bordered by black and yellow stripes and blinking orange lights. Beyond them, the room or hall—whatever it was—was dark, lit only with columns of phosphorescent blue light. There was an identification scanner outside the doors, restricting further access, but a doctor in a long, white lab coat approached from within. Ziva slowed to a more casual pace and began going through her uniform as if searching for her access key. Immersed in his data pad, the doctor scanned his own key and came through, nodding her way as he passed. She slipped through the open door.

Upon closer examination, she saw that the blue columns were in fact narrow, cylindrical tanks positioned about a meter apart, each of which held a limp, motionless body suspended in clear fluid. They all looked slightly different; some appeared to be identical to the soldiers in the assembly area, while others were deformed like the Haphezian captain. Each wore gender-appropriate coverings and a mask over their mouth and nose that connected to a tube running up from the base of the tank.

The hall stretched into the darkness further than Ziva could see from where she stood. The tanks lined the wall on either side until they faded into an undefined blue line. The floor beneath them slanted down into a trough in the center where a long drain ran the length of the room.

Satisfied that nobody seemed to be nearby, she stopped to take a closer look at each body. Some were more—*immature* was the first word that came to mind—than others, with oversized heads and short arms and legs. Some had underdeveloped skin through which tangles of nerves and blood vessels were visible. Several of the tanks had even been turned off; their occupants were slumped grotesquely against the inside of the glass. These were severely deformed, perhaps the reason for their abortion. One had an extra leg. One had no legs at all. Ziva grimaced; the man in front of her at the moment had two heads.

She heard voices approaching and ducked behind the deactivated tank just as a group of medical staff strolled through the double doors from which she had come. They all appeared to be pure Sardon, with the exception of one. The hybrid—the only thing that made sense to call it—stood a head taller than the others and pushed a gurney that hovered above the ground.

Ziva watched from the shadows as the five of them stopped in front of one of the tanks she had passed and began going over the readings on the control panel. One of the men deactivated the tank and held out his hand to receive a tool from his associate.

"We want to get her up to one of the operating rooms, stat," he said. Ziva recognized him as the doctor she had passed just before coming in. "We're supposed to prep her for surgery but Bothum says to wait until he gives the word to operate."

The physician took the tool and loosened something at the base of the tank. A steady stream of fluid shot from a previously-unseen tube and splattered onto the floor, where it flowed down the slanted surface and disappeared into the drain. The woman inside slowly crumpled into a heap at the bottom of the tank as the liquid drained out.

Satisfied that the last of the fluid had drained, the doctor played with the controls and the front panel of the tank hissed open as the airlock released. Two of the technicians stepped forward to catch the body as it fell forward. The leader tenderly held the back of her head as they moved her over and laid her out on the gurney. Ziva leaned as close as she could without being spotted—if she wasn't mistaken, the woman they'd just removed from the tank was Saun Zaid.

"Tarbic," she whispered, one finger to her earpiece. "I think I found your friend."

No response.

"Tarbic!"

"Let's get her breathing on her own," the doctor said as he carefully removed the mask and tubing from her face. The hybrid handed him a manual resuscitator, which he promptly placed over her mouth and nose and began pumping. "Come on, sweetheart." He tried a few chest compressions and continued. "Breathe!"

Ziva could hear the air rush into the woman's lungs even from her hiding spot. She began to writhe about, though her eyes were still closed. Her skin was wrinkled and pale from being submerged for such a long period, and her whole body was sickeningly thin.

"There we go, that's a good girl," the doctor praised. "Now that, gentlemen, is the sound of the healthiest set of lungs on this side of the galaxy. Let's move her and get her covered before her temperature drops."

Ziva looked up when the doors opened again, as did the others. A squad of guards— mismatched species in mismatched attire—stormed through and immediately began to spread out and search the room. Ziva peered as far as she could see in the other direction. There didn't appear to be another way out.

"Is anyone else in here?" a guard barked at the startled group of techs.

"Not to my knowledge," the head doctor stammered. "We're trying to move a patient here so if you don't mind…"

The guard grudgingly stepped aside and turned to his colleagues. "She's in here somewhere. Station 64 said she was headed this way."

So the nurses *had* caught on to her. Ziva shrank back as far as she could against the wall. At this point, escape wasn't an option, but neither was killing the guards and leaving a mess that would alert the entire facility to her presence. The thought occurred to her that, if she played her cards right, allowing herself to be captured would most likely get her closer to where she needed to go, especially if her cover had been compromised.

Sighing because she knew what she had to do and also because she didn't want to do it, she stepped out from her hiding spot and made a beeline for the tanks against the opposite wall. This drew surprised shouts from her pursuers, who rushed toward her with weapons raised.

Ziva let her rifle clatter to the floor and held up her hands. "Morning, gents," she spoke in Sardon. "Just passing through. Don't mind me."

They didn't appear impressed. One of them slapped a pair of cuffs over her wrists and two others held her arms. The next thing Ziva knew, she had a hood over her head and was being led out of the room.

· 42 ·
HOLDING ROOM
DAKITI MEDICAL RESEARCH CENTER
SARDONIS

At first the scraping sound was only in Jayden's dream. He was back in the clearing, standing motionless in the heart of the battle between his people and the Haphezian insurgents. He realized that although he was being pelted with plasma bolts, he felt no pain and could only stare straight ahead. The shuttle, the same one that had taken his father, had touched down in the clearing, only now he was seeing Lieutenant Payvan being dragged up the boarding ramp rather than the governor. A combination of blood and mud had rendered her face nearly unrecognizable. Her boots scraped against the metal as the ship swallowed her and she disappeared from sight.

Jayden tried to cry out, to go to her, but his feet were like lead and anchored him hopelessly to the ground. He began looking wildly about for Lieutenant Tarbic, Gavin Bront, *anyone* who could save him. To his horror, all the Tantalis who'd been with him had already been struck down, their faces bloodied in the same manner as Ziva's. The Solaris attackers were closing in on him, towering over him and increasing in number as they grew closer. A leathery, salty arm grabbed him from behind, but when he turned to face his assailant he found the Haphezian woman who had been with Bothum. Her fuchsia eyes had been replaced with wide yellow Sardon eyes.

"Don't worry Jayden. I'm coming for you," she said.

Through her voice he heard the scraping again, but now it jarred him awake. Well, maybe not *awake*. His head hung down at an awkward angle, causing a crick in his neck and upper back. His eyelids wouldn't budge from their closed position, so he rerouted all his energy to his ears. The scraping was somewhere above and behind him, not coming from the next floor but from within the ceiling. It was moving.

"Jayden?"

The voice from the dream! This was certainly not the fuchsia-eyed Haphezian woman. Jayden remained motionless.

The scraping was no longer moving, but was hovering over one particular place and was accompanied by another sound. Something metal was being loosened. The grill from a ventilation shaft? He could tell the exact moment it separated from the ceiling.

Soft material rubbed against metal. A pair of boots gently hit the floor. Jayden could almost *hear* the stealth and skill of the individual as the soft footsteps came up behind him. He finally managed to raise his head.

"Shhh," the person whispered as gentle hands began to work at loosening the clasps on his wrists.

Jayden obeyed, not feeling at all threatened by this visitor. He forced his eyes open just long enough to catch a glimpse of a black head with cerulean highlights passing in front of him as the person began freeing his feet.

"Officer Vax?"

"Shhh," she said again. "We're getting you out of here."

"How did you find me?" Jayden summoned all of his strength and stood up, but the blood immediately drained from his head and his knees gave out.

Zinni caught him under the arms and stood him back up on his feet. "Slow down there, kid." She left him teetering for a moment and bent down to pick something up from the floor. "We were tracking you with this. Not to mention this was the only locked door in this hallway. And—" she tapped her nose "—we picked up your scent once we got closer."

Jayden could hardly see the tiny transmitter on her fingertip. He shook his head and tried to rub some of the spots out of his eyes. Zinni was dressed in some sort of tactical jumpsuit and was covered in a fine layer of dust. He turned and looked up at the vent through which she had come. "Do you know how long I've been under?"

"No idea. Do you remember anything that might be of use to us?"

"Bothum was in here questioning me about whether or not you people were going to show up," he replied. "There was a woman, too. She was definitely Haphezian, with pink eyes."

Zinni stopped cold. "Fuchsia?"

"You could call it that, yes."

"That's Saun!" she exclaimed. "Was she okay? Did he take her somewhere?"

"You don't understand. She was *with* him. She's Solaris. She's the one who put me out."

Zinni wiped her hand across her mouth and muttered something that sounded like a Haphezian curse. "Okay. We've got to get out of here." She went to the door and put her ear up to it, then manipulated the controls to unlock it. When it opened, they found Skeet waiting outside, looking agitated. There was another open vent above him where it appeared he had lifted Zinni into the duct. He handed Zinni her rifle and fell into stride with them as they turned and hurried down the hall.

"Where's Ziva?" Jayden asked, suddenly flashing back to his dream as he stumbled along in an attempt to keep up with their long strides.

"She and Tarbic split up to look for your father and a captive HSP agent," Skeet replied. "We're going to the rendezvous now."

"About that," Zinni said. "If Mr. Saiffe here is right, Saun Zaid is no captive agent. She's working closely with Bothum, if not his right-hand man."

Skeet groaned. "You sure, kid?"

"Positive." He pulled his shirt collar aside to show them the puncture from the large syringe. "She knocked me out. I told you!"

They stopped where two hallways intersected and Zinni checked the screen on a small handheld device she carried. "Do you know where your people are being held?" she asked, leading them to the left.

"They're not. They're all dead, wiped out the second we got here."

"Oh."

"That's all you have to say? 'Oh'?"

"I'm sorry for your loss, but that *does* make our job a little easier," Skeet said.

Jayden wanted to protest about the way they were treating him but thought better of it. He had wanted a second chance. Now he had it, and this time there wouldn't be anyone else to save him if he blew it. It seemed now that they needed his help just as much as he needed theirs. Perhaps it was time for him to redeem himself.

Skeet and Zinni were speaking quickly and quietly to each other in Haphezian, discussing the situation. Jayden couldn't catch everything but thought he heard something about "cover being blown" and "being in trouble." Their tones were both abrupt and their bodies were rigid as they walked.

"Give me a weapon," Jayden instructed, unsure whether his request was even relevant to the conversation. "I'm good with a gun. I can help."

Zinni appeared hesitant, but when she locked her eyes with his, she saw he was serious. She reached down and removed a tiny sub-compact pistol from the side of her boot and handed it to him. "Ziva, we've got Jayden and we're heading to the rendezvous," she said into her comm unit. "The other Tantalis are no longer a factor."

Skeet was listening in through his own earpiece. "Copy that, Z?"

All that could be heard for the next few moments was the soft sound of their boots on the tile floor. "I've got nothing," Zinni said, the anxiety apparent in her voice.

"That Haphezian woman, Saun, she wanted to just kill me," Jayden explained, "but Bothum told her nobody was going to die until Ziva and Aroska got here. They wanted you people to come, and they were ready for you."

Jayden had admired Skeet and Zinni's abilities to remain focused so far despite the barrage of bad news, but this information stopped them dead in their tracks. For several seconds that felt like an eternity, they just stood, listening, their faces distant. Jayden, feeling nearly as on-edge as they were, glanced back and forth down the hall, waiting to hear the shouts of surprised guards who had discovered he was missing.

Heaving an unsteady sigh, Zinni turned to Skeet. "Your orders, Sergeant?"

Skeet only hesitated for a moment before he took hold of Jayden's arm with a large gloved hand and began walking again. "We carry on," he replied. "If they've been captured, they *will* find a way out and they'll want us to stick to the plan. If we go in after them, we risk losing Jayden again."

Zinni uttered another doubtful sigh and studied her tiny screen again. "We're almost to the sewer hatch. The trick is to get there without running into any trouble."

No sooner were the words out of her mouth than a squadron of Sardon guards appeared out of one of the corridors ahead. They didn't seem to pay the group any mind, at least until they noticed Jayden. However, rather than charge at them with rifles ablaze, one broke off from the group and approached them warily. "Where are you taking him?" he asked, waving his gun at them.

Skeet maintained a firm grip on Jayden, who instinctively held his hands behind his back as if bound. "Bothum wanted him moved before HSP could find him," he growled in response. "Just our luck, they'll catch up to us while you've got us held up here."

The man kept a suspicious eye on them as he held up a data pad. "You seen her?" he asked, indicating the grainy photo of Ziva on the screen. "There's word that she's here but nobody's been able to find her. She was posing as one of us."

"If we *do* see her, we'll report it immediately," Zinni answered.

"Good. Now if you don't mind, we'll handle things from here." He reached out to grab Jayden.

"Be my guest," Skeet muttered.

Jayden took a hesitant step forward and fingered the tiny pistol tucked into his pants at the small of his back. Five soldiers versus himself and two well-armed, unhappy Haphezian operatives—the odds of winning this fight seemed to be very good, even if he somehow screwed up.

The instant the man touched his shoulder, Jayden whipped the little gun out in front of him and fired a well-placed round into his throat. With a war-like shout, he swung his elbow around, cracking the Sardon's jaw and sending him to the floor for good. Skeet and Zinni's suppressed rifles discharged behind him and bullets whizzed past his head on either side, dropping the other four guards in a matter of seconds.

Before the last of them had even settled to the ground, Skeet was down on one knee, gathering their communicators and hurling them as hard as he could back in the direction from which they had come. Zinni joined him in collecting as many of their fallen weapons as they could carry and the next thing Jayden knew they were running.

"It won't take long for someone to find those guys," Skeet panted. "We need to be long gone by then."

·43·
MILITARY PRISON CELL
DAKITI MEDICAL RESEARCH CENTER
SARDONIS

The door slid shut with an echoing *bang*, leaving the room cast in almost total darkness. The only light seeped in through a narrow observation slit in the door, and it seemed blinding in comparison. Ziva looked up to where her arms were pinned to the wall on either side of her head. They were obscured by the blackness around her, but she could feel the cold metal clasps securing her wrists. Primitive.

Her captors had stripped her of her flight suit and weapons, leaving her with only her boots and the lightweight clothing she'd worn underneath. The wall against her back was cold and slimy and the moisture soaked through her shirt, making her shiver. The dampness of the room told her she was still underground, but it was difficult to tell where—the Sardons had led her on a strenuous detour that could have put her on the opposite end of the compound. All she'd been able to see through the hood were shadows.

Judging by her distance from the door, Ziva guessed the room was maybe three meters wide but she couldn't see into the darkness to tell how long it was. There were two or three centimeters of standing water on the floor that splashed and rippled when she moved her feet. It was dripping from somewhere.

The room smelled worse than anything she could remember smelling. It was a mixture of cha'sen—maybe a little of her own, she couldn't tell—and rotting flesh. She wondered how many prisoners had died in the very position she was in now. Out of curiosity, she yanked at the clasps. They were firmly fixed to the stone with long bolts, immovable.

The light coming in shone straight into her eyes and she blinked against it. Anyone who looked in would be able to see her and only her. She looked down at the water. There was a dim reflection there, and she could see the rippling rings in the light.

Just then another set of rings joined the ones she had created. They were wide and deteriorating, having travelled from the void on the other end of the prison. She strained to see. There was someone—or some*thing*—else present.

The water splashed. Chains jingled. A groan followed, along with low noises that sounded like an attempt to speak. Ziva wound up the muscles in her legs, ready to defend as best she could against anything that came at her. She tried to lean away from the light.

"Ziva Payvan," a weak voice said.

She didn't move.

More quiet splashing. The sound of something sliding through mud. "Ziva?" the voice said again, clearer this time. "Is that you?"

It couldn't be. There was no way. She'd seen the remains of the building where Aroska's team had died. This was impossible, but she'd recognize Jole Imetsi's husky voice anywhere.

"Jole?" she ventured.

A sigh of relief penetrated the darkness. "I remember your scent," he mumbled. "After being in here, you have no idea...how amazing you smell...right now."

His words were slurred as if he were just waking up from a drugged state. Ziva could barely make out his shape moving around as her eyes finally started to adjust. "Where's Tate?" she asked.

"I knew someone would come."

"Jole! Where's Tate?"

"Tate...not sure...maybe...here."

She pulled at the restraints again, harder this time. The sharp metal edges pressed against her skin. If there was some way to pick the locks....

"I knew somebody would come," Jole said again.

Ziva was dying to ask him how it was possible that he was still alive, but figured it could wait until after she got him out to the rendezvous. "Do you know where we are?"

"I think this is...the first time I've really been awake...for three months."

She took that as a no. She had to get to him, help him. Watching the observation slit for a moment and listening for approaching footsteps, she kicked her legs up over her head and hung there upside down, suspended by her wrists. The cuffs cut into her skin as she reached into her boot and felt around for the narrow pocket sewn into the lining inside. Her fingers brushed over a tiny throwing knife before finding the set of three delicate picks that had come in handy for picking old locks in the past. Unsure if any of them would even work, she let her legs back down and began probing the clasp for any form of key hole, wincing at the pain that shot through her hands and forearms.

"Jole, what did they do to you?"

His only response was a groan. After seeing and hearing of so many disturbing things in this place, Ziva was puzzled as to how he could have survived. The tool fell into the key hole and she worked it carefully until the clasps sprung open with a pop that echoed through the chamber.

Restraining herself from simply leaping across the room, she cautiously felt her way through the darkness and muck on the floor. So far, there had been no other sounds or indication that someone other than Jole was present, but judging by the smell, she guessed there *were* others and that they had long since expired. If Tate was there, the chances that he was still alive were slim.

Her foot hit something hard enough to be a body and soft enough that she didn't have to guess whether it was rotten. She bent down to a crouching position and probed the space in front of her. Her fingers found a face—a nose, a mouth, even some remaining hair. She felt into the void beyond the body and, finding nothing else in the immediate vicinity, gingerly stepped over it.

"Jole," she whispered, hoping to get a better idea of where exactly he was. If he would just make some more noise....

Ziva's hand found a foot, an ankle with a metal clasp that felt like one that had been around her wrist only moments before. The toes twitched when she touched them and Jole moaned. "Ziva," he mumbled.

She immediately began prodding at the clasp with her lock pick, all the while listening for anyone who might be coming to check up on her. "Are you going to be able to walk once we get out of here?" she asked, finishing with one ankle and moving to the next. She had a good idea of what the answer would be, but she wanted to keep him talking, coherent.

"Don't...count on it," he replied. He moved his arms and the sound of more chains could be heard. "Wrists, too."

The remaining clasps came open easily enough, and she returned the pick to her boot. There were moments where she thought she could smell Tate, though the general stench in the room was so over-whelming she could never say for sure. If he was alive, if there was any way he could be saved, she would do it, and even if it was too late she didn't want to just leave the body to suffer the same fiery fate as the ones Skeet and Zinni had seen. Either way, she wouldn't be able to transport both him and Jole at the same time. She hated the thought of having to make two trips, but it would most likely have to be done.

"Okay, let's get you out of here," she said, taking a look back at the door before slipping her hands under Jole's arms. Carefully, not wanting to make excess noise, she began to drag him through the water and slime. He came along startlingly easy, weighing significantly less than she'd expected. She could feel his ribs, and the bones jutting from his shoulders were so sharp it almost hurt to touch them.

Ziva set him down long enough to take a look through the observation slit in the door. To her delight, a hybrid sentry, bearing similarities to the captain they'd crossed paths with earlier, was walking sluggishly toward her. He too had a slight limp, but it appeared his hands had the correct number of digits. Even from a distance, however, she could see he was severely cross-eyed.

She ducked away from the opening and envisioned the sturdy deadbolt that held the door shut from the outside. If she was careful and timed it right, she could use her Nostia to slide the bolt away, open the door, and grab the guard as he passed. She took a deep breath and listened to the approaching footsteps, tugging at the bolt with her mind just as she might if she were using her hand. After spending so much time in deep concentration during the flight to Sardonis, she found that her Nosti abilities came about with much less effort; she felt the familiar surge of energy course through her, and her head didn't hurt yet. She looked over to where she'd left Jole on the floor. Even if he was lucid enough to see her, he would still have no inkling as to what she was doing.

The lock was normally disengaged by scanning an access card, so it took a bit of doing to move the bolt manually. As near as Ziva could tell, the lock was about halfway open when the bolt stopped sliding altogether. She winced and pulled harder, shuddering when she heard the scrape and squeal of rusty metal. The footsteps outside stopped. *Sheyss.*

A shadow passed in front of the slit as the guard moved up to examine the lock. He began muttering to himself and waved his access key over the scanner, pulling the bolt out the rest of the way.

The moment Ziva heard the locking mechanism release, she yanked the door open, seized the man by the shoulders, and pulled him inside. He flailed at her, tried to reach for his weapon, but she drove her knee into the base of his spine and caught his head in her hands as he collapsed. She wrenched it to the side, twisting up and to the right, and with a grotesque *pop* the man fell still.

"It was nothing personal," she muttered as she heaved him up and locked his arms into the clasps that had held her. She removed his supply belt and put it on herself then took up the plasma rifle he'd dropped and strapped it over her shoulder. His key had fallen just inside the door and she picked it up as well, wiping it off on her pants before finding a convenient place for it on the belt.

Eyes on the door, Ziva took Jole under the armpits again and dragged him out into the light of the hallway. After hearing his voice and feeling his weak frame, she'd formed a picture in her head to prepare herself for this exact moment, but what she'd seen in her mind hardly compared to what she saw now. This was not the Jole Imetsi she'd known since her early days at HSP, the bright-eyed, handsome, and ever-smiling young man who had partnered with her a few times during hand-to-hand sparring sessions. What she saw now could hardly even be described as a person. This creature lying there in front of her was a mere skeleton with a thin and sagging layer of skin stretched over it. The closed eyes had sunk deep into their sockets, and the cheek and jaw bones protruded grotesquely from a face that had once been so full of life. The arms and legs were so thin and frail that they looked like they would simply snap like twigs if they moved at all. Ziva could count the individual ribs as Jole's chest rose and fell with each labored breath. Bony hips could be seen just above the waistband of a ragged excuse for a pair of pants that might have been white a very long time ago. In all, the man was completely unrecognizable. The only thing that told her this was indeed her old HSP acquaintance was the elaborate tattoo across the back of his shoulders and the familiar pattern of dark blue *gesh punti* around his left eye.

His condition couldn't possibly be the result of torture and imprisonment alone. It was almost as if all the energy had been drained from him—then replenished, then drained, again and again and again. After all, he was still alive after being in this place for three months, meaning he had to have received some form of nutrients and care during that time. What had they been using him for, blood transfusion, organ donation?

Realization hit Ziva as if Jole himself had landed a perfect headshot during training years before. The captive Haphezians, the disposal of the bodies Skeet and Zinni had witnessed, the hybrid soldiers, the mutant guards.... The scientists at Dakiti had always been known for their genetic experiments, and now they had gone so far as to try to create a Sardon-Haphezian cross-breed. The captive military and HSP personnel were tested, experimented upon, tortured, kept alive for the sole purpose of providing their genetic information. When too weak to contribute any longer, they were thrown in these prisons to rot and then they were discarded like trash into the furnace.

The individuals in the blue tanks were the products of the experiments. Defective ones were killed off, capable ones were kept alive and given jobs and duties here where they were created—the only place they would ever belong—and the successful ones went on to be trained and drilled in military procedure. Dane Bothum was using them to create an army of super soldiers. For what, Ziva dreaded to find out.

Mind racing, she grabbed Jole's arms and hefted his feeble body up onto her back. There were several other cell doors in this hallway, and judging by the room numbers they were one floor below and a little to the west of where she had been taken. It would still be a bit of a trek to the sewer entrance, especially if they ran into anybody unwilling to let them through, but she had a good idea of their exact destination and quickly went over a route in her head. Taking a deep breath, she took off as fast as she could with Jole on her back.

· 44 ·
PREP ROOM
DAKITI MEDICAL RESEARCH CENTER
SARDONIS

"**N**o, I want him awake," said a woman's voice.

Aroska's eyelids fluttered open and he squinted against the blinding light positioned directly above his face. He was lying on a cold metal table to which his wrists and ankles were securely fastened. Two straps stretched across his chest and forehead, rendering him almost completely immobile. His surroundings, or what he could see of them, were pure white, with the exception of a rusty old   medical bot that hovered over him with a massive syringe. Whoever had spoken was standing just shy of the reaches of his peripheral vision.

When he and Ziva had first discovered the white room with the table and collection of syringes, he'd pictured poor individuals being held, tortured, interrogated, and maybe even killed there. Now that he recognized that he was in that very position, there were only two things on his mind: first, he *was* still alive, and second, there was plenty of time left for something unpleasant to happen.

"Maybe I was wrong when I encouraged you to join that spec ops task force," the woman said. "You've always been a good agent Aroska, but this? This is pathetic."

He closed his eyes in disbelief and swallowed past the sickening knot that had formed in his throat. All along, his gut had been telling the truth, and he had refused to believe it. Ziva had been right—even when he thought she was wrong—just as Skeet had warned. His mind drifted back to the conversation with Vinny Jaxton.

"Who is the Solaris agent working inside HSP?"

"You don't want to know."

When he opened his eyes again, Saun stood where the bot had been, watching him with the same sincere look that she always had, only now it was unsettling. He'd always told her that her eyes reminded him of the brilliant rujuba flowers that grew out in the jungle, but at the moment they had that same hateful quality Ziva's often did. They were also welling up with tears.

"You're like a stupid animal that walked straight into the trap without even knowing it," she said through her teeth.

"All I cared about was the bait, I guess," he muttered, straining to see the door or any other means of escape.

"As you should have." She crossed her arms and took a step away from him as if she were uncomfortable with the situation.

Aroska had to give her credit for being an incredible actress, and he took some comfort in knowing he wasn't the only one she'd played. "How long have you been working for them?" he asked, afraid of what the answer might be.

"The whole time. You know you were supposed to be inside that building when it blew?"

"Why do you want me dead?"

"You don't understand, Aroska. *This* is exactly where I've wanted you all along. Trust me, you *will* die, but for now this is precisely where you're supposed to be."

He closed his eyes again, and then thought better of it. He was already completely defenseless, but he wasn't about to be caught off guard any more than he already had. "I *did* trust you," he said. So far, nothing Saun had told him made much sense. His thoughts shifted to Ziva and the others—he wondered how long it would take them to realize he was missing, and he prayed they were better off than he was. He hoped his lack of a comm signal would alert them to the situation.

With a gloved hand, Saun selected a syringe from the case against the wall and held it up to check the dosage. "This will...*sting* a little," she said. Her face had a greenish tint as if she were about to be sick. "After that, you shouldn't be able to feel anything for a while." She eased the needle into the skin of his left arm, and Aroska immediately felt searing pain spread up into his shoulders and chest. His blood vessels—his heart—were on fire and he suddenly felt as though his entire body was going to shut down. He forced his eyes to stay open.

"They wanted the ones who were naturally strong," Saun said. Her voice was firm but tears streamed down her cheeks. She stifled a cough. "They watched, they waited, they picked the ones with desirable characteristics. It was like they were just shopping in a market. Sooner or later though, they started to run out of the good ones. The only ones left were too hard to get, so they started grabbing any they could get their hands on. Some of them, the ones who would be missed, were set up to look like they were killed in such a way that nobody would ever bother looking for any remains." She paused and made a sound that was either a chuckle or another cough—Aroska couldn't tell. "But none of them have ever come willingly."

"Saun, what are you talking about?" Aroska demanded. The words had been loud and enunciated in his head but they came out in the form of a slurred croak. He couldn't feel his legs.

Saun had leaned down over him, but her face was blurry despite its close proximity. "Where's Payvan?" she hissed.

"She was right about you," Aroska replied. "She was right all along, and I didn't believe her."

"She sounds like an intelligent woman." Saun's hand closed around his throat and she pressed down, steadily increasing the pressure. "Where is she?"

Aroska felt as though his eyes were being sucked from their sockets as he desperately gasped for the air that was unable to enter his lungs. He tried to yank on his arms, tried to fight her off, but the clasps over his wrists were a solid reminder that he could not.

"She's not here," he wheezed, suddenly feeling overwhelmed with anger. The woman he'd come to trust and care for had not only betrayed him but now appeared to be more than willing to kill him.

"Liar!" she screamed, pressing down so hard Aroska was afraid she'd somehow break his neck. She was nearly sobbing when she finally let go and stepped back, hands on top of her head.

Aroska opened his mouth as far as he could, letting the sweet oxygen fill his lungs. "What?" he gasped. "You don't think I'm capable of coming here on my own?"

"I think you're protecting her."

"Emeri kicked her off the case for what happened to Jayden the other night. I can assume you had something to do with that." That much was true.

Saun, silent but still crying, turned and looked over the syringes again. She took a deep, raspy breath and rubbed her throat briefly before returning her hand to her side as if nothing had happened. "You're a good man, Aroska. I liked you...a lot. I wish it didn't have to end this way."

Aroska wiggled his fingers, tried to move his arms, or at least he thought he did—they didn't budge. "No kidding," he replied. His jaw felt like it was starting to lock up and it was becoming increasingly difficult to breathe, even without her hands on his neck. "Tell me something though—why are *you* doing this? What force in the galaxy could possibly make you betray everything and everyone you've ever known for *this*? Tell me it's not about money, Saun. Is this about money? It's not too late to take everything back. I can talk to Emeri, work out some kind of deal. We can *help* you, Saun."

"You can't help me, and even if you could, I wouldn't want you to," she growled.

He watched her for a moment, straining to see out of the corners of his eyes. She wasn't looking at him, but was staring vacantly at the monitor against the wall. He wasn't sure if it was due to the revelation of her true identity, but something seemed oddly different in the way she spoke and the way she carried herself. It wasn't just in his mind— it was something real, something on the outside, something physical.

"You're sick, aren't you. Dying."

Saun forced a bit of a sad smile and wiped the tears out of one eye with the back of her hand.

"How long do you have?"

She shook her head quickly but maintained that hint of a smile; paired with her furrowed brows, it looked almost maniacal. "No, you're wrong. I'm not dying, not anymore." The smile vanished. "I get to live, you have to die. Think of it this way, Aroska. You're giving your life to save a friend."

· 45 ·

SUBLEVEL SEWER SYSTEM
DAKITI MEDICAL RESEARCH CENTER
SARDONIS

I t smelled like what it was—a sewer full of unpleasant and unidentifiable refuse from the med center and all of its occupants. On top of that it was pitch dark, leaving Skeet only able to imagine what sort of nasty, slimy things lurked around him and in the water that flowed past him at knee-level. He longed to activate one of the glow sticks and take a look around, but Zinni had suggested they save them until they began moving.

He kept his eyes on the thin halo of light surrounding the access hatch through which they had come. It didn't cast enough light into the tunnel for him to see Zinni and Jayden, but it would be sufficient enough to see the shadows of anyone coming in from above. All three of them remained silent, compensating for lack of sight by devoting all their energy to listening to the sounds around them. The tunnel was clear as far as Skeet could tell—all they needed now was to wait for Ziva and Aroska.

The water pressure and flow around his legs changed and Skeet could sense Zinni moving toward him through the darkness. She sidled up to him and reached out to find him, her small hand meeting his chest at mid-breastbone.

"Where are they, Skeet?" she spoke softly in Haphezian. She brought her head to rest against his shoulder and held on to his arm.

He put his arm around her shoulders and held her gently for a moment, straining to see Jayden in the darkness. "You know they'll be here," he replied in Standard so the young man could hear. As of this moment, Skeet was in charge of a mission without communication and without any idea what was going on around them, and the last thing he needed was for Jayden to think things were anything but under control.

He still couldn't see the young human, but he did catch sight of the shadow as it passed over the crevice surrounding the access hatch. He alerted Zinni with a quick shove and moved across the tunnel to secure Jayden, rifle raised.

The hatch cover cracked open with an echoing groan that thankfully hadn't seemed nearly as loud from the maintenance closet above. Light poured down into the tunnel and Skeet flattened himself against both Jayden and the wall, waiting with bated breath for either Aroska or Ziva to appear. What he saw instead were a pair of bare feet lowering themselves through the opening, followed by grimy legs, some form of tattered clothing, and a bare torso. The strong stench that accompanied this person added to the already-foul atmosphere and Skeet nearly gagged. Jayden did.

"Help me with him!" Ziva's firm voice commanded from above. Skeet could now see her hands supporting the man under his arms.

Zinni switched on a glow stick and the two of them stepped forward to gingerly bring the man down into the tunnel. He was grotesquely skinny but clearly Haphezian. Skeet tilted his head back into the light as Ziva dropped down into the water and shut the cover behind her.

The *gesh punti* were unmistakable. "I don't understand how this is possible," he said, looking up at Ziva.

"There's still a lot I haven't figured out either," she replied. "Tate's here too. From what we've found, it's clear that they've been experimented on and would have most likely wound up in that furnace you two discovered." She shifted in the water. "How are you holding up, kid?"

"Fine," Jayden replied.

"Where's Aroska?" Zinni asked.

The water seemed to stop flowing for a moment as Ziva tensed and looked around. "You mean he's not with you?"

Skeet felt the nervousness creep back toward him like some slimy creature in the water. "We thought you were together," he said, exhaling a sigh through his nose.

Ziva placed one hand on a hip and ran the other over the top of her head. She sighed as well, taking a few seconds to stare into the darkness of the tunnel before sweeping her gaze over the three of them. "You go without me," she said. "Take Jayden and Jole to the end of the sewer and wait. I'm going back for Tate and Aroska."

"What?" Skeet cried. "Ziva, I can't let you go back up there by yourself."

"The last time I checked, *Sergeant*, I was your commanding officer," she snarled. "I don't think it's your place to tell me what I'm not going to do. Now, get these two out of here. I don't want you under here when the Grand Army unleashes hell on this place. Besides, me going back alone is going to attract a lot less attention than all of us caravanning through."

Zinni crossed her arms, successfully pulling off a threatening look despite the size difference between her and her superior. "We can only assume Tate is in the same shape as Jole, if not worse, and who knows where Aroska is and how much trouble he's in."

"And Solaris is after you," Jayden put in quietly.

The tunnel fell silent and all heads turned toward the young human, who was lingering in the shadows at the edge of the halo of light cast by the glow stick.

"Excuse me?" Ziva said.

"That's what I was telling you," he said to Skeet and Zinni before shifting his focus back to Ziva. "That woman and Bothum were questioning me, asking whether or not you were coming. I didn't tell them anything because I didn't know. They knew it was too late for me to do anything about that transmission I intercepted—as far as I could tell, they were using me to bait you. They said something like, 'Nobody dies until Tarbic and Payvan get here'."

Zinni swore. "Would it have killed you to elaborate earlier?"

"I'm sorry!" Jayden cried. "I didn't realize it was relevant, and then we were trying to get out and—"

"Just stop," Ziva ordered, holding her hand up for silence. She was quiet for a moment, staring into the cloudy water flowing around her legs.

"We're running out of time," Skeet murmured.

"I know." Ziva swallowed, then looked over each of them in turn. "They've got Tarbic. I'm going back for him, and then we're going back for Tate. You three take Jole and proceed to the end of the tunnel like I said."

"Here, then," Zinni said, removing her earpiece. "You should take this."

Skeet watched as Ziva nodded her thanks and inserted the device into her own ear. "What happens if you can't handle both of them?" he asked. "What if you need help?"

"That's what the military is coming for," she replied. "Now go, Skeet. Get Jayden out of here. That's an order."

She opened the hatch and disappeared.

· 46 ·
PREP ROOM
DAKITI MEDICAL RESEARCH CENTER
SARDONIS

Aroska was fading, becoming incoherent. It would be difficult to extract any useful information from him before long. Saun couldn't imagine that he would have come here without Payvan, and Atu *had* claimed to have seen the two of them together. The woman was around the facility somewhere, and they would find her with or without Aroska's help.

Saun watched as the medical bot administered a small dose of a substance she wasn't familiar with. This initial prep procedure was tedious and time-consuming, but once they were able to begin the cloning process, the subject could basically be harvested at will until there was nothing left. She almost hated to see such a thing happen to the man she had truly come to care about, but her own clone was currently being prepped for surgery and Bothum had made it quite clear that he wanted both Tarbic and Payvan incapacitated before she was rewarded in any way.

The door hissed open and Atu burst in as wide-eyed as he was capable of. "My men found the woman," he exclaimed.

At last. All too eager to get on with things, Saun took a quick look at Aroska's monitor and then fell into stride behind the captain as he led her out the door and down the corridor. "Do you have her in custody?" she wheezed, trying to control her breathing despite the sudden excitement.

"They found her before the photos had completely circulated so she hasn't been taken to Bothum yet," he replied. "One of the nurses reported a suspicious person and they found her in the extraction chamber. She's in one of the holding cells downstairs."

They descended a stairwell to the second underground level, where a squad of guards met up with them from another hallway. "We put her in cell D24," one of them informed Atu, sliding a stun pistol from his holster.

The holding cells were dark and reeked of death and decay, but they were reinforced with War-era nitamite, an alloy developed by the Biasi that the Sardons had paid an outrageous sum of money to install. The cells had been put to good use over the years and were virtually indestructible. Saun had spent time in one while Bothum tested her intentions when she'd first volunteered her services nearly a year prior. If Payvan was in one, she was certainly secure.

"She was wearing some kind of flight suit when we found her," the sentry said. "We confiscated it and all of her personal effects."

"That's what Tarbic was wearing too. Could they have flown in here? Are there more of them that we don't know about?"

A different guard, one who appeared to be full-blooded Sardon, spoke up. "We checked up on that. No ships without clearance have been picked up on radar. Honestly, we don't know how they got in. As for there being others, that's unclear. There was a whole squadron of security personnel shot to death in the east hallway on this level, but it's difficult to say who the shooters were. They've done a good job at avoiding surveillance."

Saun was grateful to finally be speaking to a competent person who had facts. "What about the boy? Is Jayden Saiffe secure?"

"Pardon me for asking ma'am, but what good is it to keep him here?"

"He's a witness," Saun answered. "If we let him go at this point, he'll just go back to Tantal and launch a counterstrike. That's the last thing we need to worry about right now. Send someone up to check on him."

"Right away."

They reached the cell block and proceeded to D24, one of the larger and older rooms on the floor. A member of the medical staff waited there with a response kit; he removed a syringe of Axonyte from it as they neared, passing it to Saun and stepping back with a respectful dip of his head.

Saun removed the protective cover from the needle with her teeth and held the instrument up to the light. Satisfied that the dose would be enough to neutralize Payvan but not render her completely numb just yet, she cleared her throat and nodded toward the door. "Open it."

The bolt slid away with a swipe of someone's access key and the door eased open. The guards rushed in, illuminating the shadowy chamber with the lights mounted on their weapons. Saun directed her gaze into the room and focused on the figure who hung limply from the clasps attached to the wall. To her horror, it was not Payvan, not even a woman, not even a Haphezian. The person suspended there was one of Bothum's men, a cross-breed, stripped of his weapon and supply belt. His head leaned severely to one side, his neck broken.

Saun stared, speechless, as the guards swept over the rest of the cell. The syringe slipped from her fingers and clattered to the floor, partly out of resignation and partly because she began to cough so violently that she was forced to step away. Each breath felt like fire eating away at her lungs. She tasted blood as she regained composure and wiped her hand across her mouth. When she brought it away, her fingers were stained crimson; she quickly wiped them on her pants before turning her attention back to the cell.

Atu was just emerging from the darkness with his communicator to his mouth. "What have you found?" he demanded.

"The Saiffe boy is gone," replied the voice of the guard who had been sent off to investigate. "His restraints have been released and the ventilation shaft is open."

Saun summoned all the breath she had, allowing anger to numb most of the pain. "Find Payvan and Saiffe, *now!*" she screamed.

· 47 ·
INTREPID
FRINGE SPACE

S hades of bright blue and silver swirled by outside as the *Intrepid* surged forward at FTL speed, closing in on the swampy world of Sardonis. Adin sighed and crossed his arms, watching the space out the front viewport as Mari and Colin piloted the craft. Using a limited amount of portable equipment en route and assistance from Mack Markel, they'd been able to narrow down the Solaris mole to someone inside the SCU. That left twenty possibilities, excluding Aroska and Mack, but Adin couldn't shake the feeling that Saun was somehow involved. He hadn't personally spent a lot of time around her as of late, but after making some calls and obtaining any information Mack had, he could conclude that she had at least been up to something unrelated to any ongoing HSP investigations.

Somewhere out in the swirling colors, a sizable chunk of the Grand Army's fleet zoomed along with them. Adin had briefed the colonel and his captains on all the information he had, which wasn't much considering he'd lost communication with Ziva and hadn't heard anything since Skeet had instructed him to bring the military into play. Unsure what exactly they would find upon reaching Dakiti, Adin had left the majority of the tactical decision-making to the military men, feeling content to provide what little HSP support he and his team could.

Mack appeared in the cockpit beside him, studying Dakiti's schematics on a small data pad. Adin was grateful for his help on such short notice. He'd never met Markel before the previous evening, but any friend of Aroska's was a friend of his.

"I just filled the director in on our progress," Mack reported. "Now he at least knows what's going on, even if he's still refusing to send any HSP support. He wants updates from both you and Colonel Sheen every half hour."

Adin nodded and stroked his chin but said nothing. Emeri was being a coward, and if they were too late to help Ziva and her team, Adin would hold him personally responsible. He didn't doubt their abilities by any means, but judging by what little Skeet had told him when he'd called, it was quite possible that they were in way over their heads. He was determined to prove the director wrong, whatever that meant.

"Agent Woro," came Sheen's voice over the comm system. "We're all set up for a full ground assault, but we'd like a twenty on your people before we proceed."

Adin picked up the receiver. "We haven't been able to make contact for nearly an hour. You'll be the first to know if we hear anything."

"Copy that. ETA, thirty minutes."

· 48 ·

SUBLEVELS

DAKITI MEDICAL RESEARCH CENTER

SARDONIS

S aun lifted her face from her knees when she sensed someone standing in front of her. It was the Sardon who had spoken so intelligently to her earlier, towering over her as she sat on the floor with her arms around her legs. He studied a data pad and shifted his gaze over to meet hers when she looked up.

"One of the prisoners is missing," he informed her.

Saun held her breath to postpone the pain and scrambled to her feet. "Out of here?" she scoffed. "The crop in this cell block has already been harvested. They're useless now, if not dead. Ready for the oven. If Payvan was here, why would she bother taking one of them with her?"

The guard shook his head and gestured back at the data pad. "The missing prisoner is Imetsi, Jole, one of Tarbic's former team members. Final harvest took place yesterday—he's still alive."

Saun took the data pad from him and looked over it herself. She remembered the day they'd brought Jole in like it was yesterday, though it had been nearly three months earlier. He'd fought hard, stayed alive longer than many of the others. It was almost as if his body had started becoming immune to the continuous drugs and medications administered during the harvesting prep, so they'd had to stop before he became too much to handle. His partner Tate had been a fighter too, though they had started his harvesting process a few weeks later. Between the two of them, the facility had been able to generate over twenty successful products, all of whom had immediately been selected to begin military training.

"What's Luver's status?" she asked.

"Still here," he replied. "Alive, but barely."

The back door had just been opened. "If she took the time to take Imetsi, she'll more than likely be back for Luver," Saun said, handing the data pad back. "Station someone here to wait for her, and have security monitoring Tarbic's prep process in case she finds him. No one rests until she is found, understood?"

· 49 ·

SUBLEVELS
DAKITI MEDICAL RESEARCH CENTER
SARDONIS

I f Dakiti's restricted levels had been quiet before, Ziva might as well have been deaf now. Quite suddenly, in her opinion, there wasn't a soul to be found nor a sound to be heard, making the hairs on her arms and neck stand up as if they too were searching, listening. What disturbed her most was the lack of medical personnel who had been so abundant earlier, telling her they had been alerted to her presence and ordered to withdraw. The occasional nurse or doctor still scurried by, ducking into rooms to continue their work from behind locked doors. She doubted it had taken long for someone to find the unfortunate sentry she'd killed in the prison cell. His missing access key would be a sure giveaway.

Ziva had opted to search for Aroska first, hoping he would be in better shape than Tate and therefore more capable of backing her up during any form of escape attempt. She came to a stairwell that would take her up to the floor the two of them had come in on and stopped to listen. Finally, her ears picked up the sound of faint Sardon voices. She began to climb, silently placing one foot in front of the other until she reached the landing. The voices were at the top of the stairs and to her left, at the place where she and Aroska had split up as far as she could tell. Yes, she remembered passing this stairwell—the examination room where they'd smelled the cha'sen would be to her right.

She stopped at the top of the stairs and stole a peek out into the corridor. There were four guards, all apparently full-blooded Sardons, standing at the T-intersection and equipped with rifles and headsets. As she watched, one of them signaled for silence and listened to his earpiece. Simultaneously, they all turned toward her hiding place, sending a violent tingle down her spine. She refrained from moving just yet, however—they'd showed no signs of actually seeing her. They were listening too. Whoever was on the opposite end of that transmission was talking about this very stairwell. *Is there some way they could know...?*

A faint hum reached Ziva's ears and she turned her attention away from the guards to find a small surveillance bot hovering at eye level about two meters away. She froze and it froze, its lens moving delicately in and out as it focused. The camera was no doubt transmitting her image directly to Bothum or whoever was controlling the guards, who were now on the move.

She raised her stolen rifle and blasted the tiny bot back against the wall before leaping down to the landing. More shouts came from the bottom of the stairs as another squad of guards quickly approached.

"Skeet!" she shouted in Haphezian through her earpiece, hoping the Sardons wouldn't understand. She turned back up the stairs and darted down the hall to her right just as the two squads collided in a confused jumble at the top of the stairwell. "I've been made. Go! Just get out, do you hear me? Advise Adin—"

Something small and sharp latched onto the back of her left thigh, clinging to her flesh with the most violent pinch she'd ever felt. A second barb attached itself to her other leg and she fell, finding herself at the end of the long cables connected to the weapons from which they had been fired.

"Go Skeet!" she hollered again, crawling on her hands and knees as an electric current began pulsing into her legs. She felt her whole body cramp up and collapsed onto her stomach, clawing at the slippery floor with sweaty hands as she was slowly dragged backwards.

She rolled onto her back, tangling the thick cables around her legs. The guards were reeling her in with their hands now, and those not pulling had plasma pistols aimed for her. Taking advantage of the last few seconds before they grabbed her, she ripped her earpiece out and slammed it as hard a she could against the cold floor, successfully destroying it and any way they would be able to trace Skeet's location if they tried.

Several sets of rough hands hauled her to her feet and the barbs were torn out of her skin with a grotesque ripping sound. She immediately felt the blood soaking through her clothes. Her legs felt as though they were on the verge of giving out.

Cuffs connected by a thin but sturdy chain were slapped over Ziva's wrists and two different guards wrenched her arms back and held them fast. Another took hold of her hair and pulled her head back, forcing her to look up as a tall Sardon man emerged from another hallway and began moving toward them, wearing a smug grin.

"Easy, men," he said smoothly. "Don't damage her. We need her in prime condition."

Bothum. Ziva yanked at her captors' firm grips, but they only tightened their hold. She watched as the man picked up the rifle she'd dropped and removed the power cell, checking its charge level before fitting it back into the weapon.

"Agent Payvan," he chuckled. "I was beginning to wonder if I would ever have the pleasure of meeting you in person. I'm glad I didn't have to kill you first."

Ziva said nothing. She watched him, tried to move her head. He was tall for a Sardon, nearly her height, but was still slender and wiry like the creatures typically were. She could feel the guards holding her tense up in his presence, though he didn't seem nearly as threatening as she'd imagined.

Bothum held the rifle out to her head with one arm, his bicep bulging. With the barrel he gently tipped her chin back further than it already was and ran his eyes from her forehead down to her feet, then back up again. "I must tell you what a delight it was when I first heard you might be paying me a visit," he said. "You are a fine specimen indeed." His reptilian eyes lingered on her for a few seconds more, and then he pivoted and beckoned. "Gentlemen, please escort Agent Payvan to my office."

He turned and strode down the hall and the guards gave Ziva a rough shove, urging her forward. She went without trouble, curious as to whether she could gain any information, or better yet, find Aroska and the governor. If Adin had called in the military exactly when Skeet had instructed him to, she would have approximately twenty minutes to get out again. It would be enough time—it would *have* to be.

A short walk through the facility brought the group back past the balcony where Ziva had encountered the first hybrid captain. The vast floor below was empty again with the exception of the drill instructor and the large presentation screen. Bothum led them around the corner from which the cross-bred captain had come and the hallway opened up into a foyer that served as a lounge for the medical staff. Several rooms branched off of it, one of which Bothum opened.

The office was already illuminated and two more armed guards turned to look when they walked in. With a wave of Bothum's hand they parted, revealing a male human bound to the seat that belonged at Bothum's desk. He made eye contact with Ziva when he saw her and ran his tongue over his dry, bloodstained lips. A stream of red dribbled from his slightly-displaced nose. One eye was nearly swollen shut, and splotches of purple and blue bruising covered the left side of his face.

"You shouldn't have come," he croaked.

Ziva's eyes grew wide. The man's face may have been nearly unrecognizable, but his clothes were unmistakable. This was Enrik Saiffe, still alive after two days.

The guards sat Ziva down in a chair opposite the governor, holding her hair back again to ensure that she maintained eye contact. Bothum gave Enrik a firm pat on the shoulder, still toting Ziva's rifle in his other hand. "I told you I was a man of my word, Governor."

"Look," Saiffe panted, addressing Ziva, "I don't know who exactly you are, but I want to thank you and your people for anything you've done to help me or my son. I'm sorry you had to be involved in—" He stopped and winced when Bothum pressed the rifle barrel against the back of his neck.

"That will be all, Governor. You see, Agent Payvan, I made a strict promise to my friend here that neither he nor his son would have to die until I had possession of both you and Agent Tarbic. I guess you could say that you're the one who killed him just by coming here." He leaned down over Enrik and moved the barrel of the rifle up to the back of his head. "Do you hear that, Governor? The deal is off now. Blame Agent Payvan for what's about to happen to you."

Ziva straightened in the chair and pulled her arms forward, but the chain held them fast. Enrik stared straight forward, a sorrowful look visible in his eyes just before he closed them.

Bothum pulled the trigger.

· 50 ·
INTREPID
FRINGE SPACE

T he hologram of Colonel Sheen waited patiently on the *Intrepid's* communication pad, patched into the conversation between Adin and Skeet. Just the sound of the sergeant's voice took a sort of burden off of Adin that he couldn't describe. Jayden had been rescued and Jole and Tate had miraculously been found—that would sit well with the director. He listened to Skeet's garbled voice over the comm system, trying to decide whether the remaining news would help or hinder the operation.

"My best guess is that she wanted me to tell you we've still got people in there," Skeet said after relaying Ziva's final words. His voice echoed as though he were in a cave. "With the strong Haphezian presence we've discovered at this point, proceeding with a full-scale attack would cause massive collateral damage."

That was the hard part. The easiest solution would be for Ziva to either apprehend or kill Bothum, therefore crippling Dakiti's operations and allowing them to conduct a rescue on their own terms. Cut the head off the snake and the body dies, so to speak. According to Sheen, the capital hadn't exactly given this mission a green light, but thankfully he and the men he'd assembled were all willing to take whatever heat resulted from saving their own people from such a sickening place. Adin's own head was on the chopping block, and the last thing he wanted was to be responsible for causing another war between Haphez and Sardonis. In a sense, whether or not that happened depended entirely upon what Ziva accomplished in the next eighteen minutes.

"What do you propose we do, Skeet?" Adin asked, rubbing his eyes.

For a moment, the only reply was static and other unidentifiable sounds. Mari leaned over the control panel and checked the connection, signaling to Adin that they were still live.

Sheen's hologram shifted in its place. "Awaiting your orders, Sergeant. Time is of the essence."

"Proceed with the attack," Skeet replied. "If you can help it, refrain from utilizing destructive force until we've confirmed that Ziva, Tarbic, and any other survivors are out of there. Also, we'll be needing support waiting at the south end of the sewer system. The coordinates are..."

· 51 ·

SUBLEVELS

DAKITI MEDICAL RESEARCH CENTER

SARDONIS

S aun stormed into the lounge, too worked up to care about the steadily-increasing pain in her chest. Bothum had failed to inform her he'd had Ziva Payvan in custody for nearly ten minutes. Her life depended on the fact that the two lieutenants had been secured, and she was not going to let him treat her like this after all the time and work she'd put in to ensure his plans succeeded.

She burst past the two guards and into Bothum's office. The Sardon rested on the edge of his desk facing Payvan, who sat in a chair with the chain on her cuffs strung through the slats. Saun sent a malicious glare her way and then looked to Enrik Saiffe, who was slumped over in his own seat with a smoldering hole in the back of his head. So, Bothum had kept his "promise" to the governor but had yet to follow through on his agreement with her.

Flustered, she crossed her arms and swallowed, still able to taste a little blood from her most recent coughing fit. "When are you going to hold up your end of the deal?" she demanded, stealing another glance at Payvan.

"Patience, Saun," Bothum chided. "You'll get your reward soon enough. The surgeons have orders to not make a move until I give the word, so you'd better behave yourself."

If he told her to be patient one more time, she'd kill him herself. He was a confusing man, Bothum. Why he hadn't just done away with Saiffe and the boy in the first place, she would never understand.

"Have you started Lieutenant Tarbic's harvest prep yet?" the Sardon asked, examining his weapon.

"Yes," Saun replied. "It's taking a while for the procedure to stabilize, but I've got a bot working on him now." Her eyes once again wandered toward Payvan, and when she caught the woman in her sight she immediately felt an irrational combination of anger and jealousy welling up inside of her. "What is *she* doing here?" she finally muttered.

"Agent Payvan is keeping me company until one of the other two prep rooms becomes available. I must admit she's not a very lively guest."

When Saun looked at Payvan again, the lieutenant was staring back at her with those piercing red eyes. She began to sweat. There were mere hours left before one or both of her lungs collapsed, dooming her to a slow and painful death. She had no idea what Bothum was waiting for, but she thought she'd hurry it along.

"You've caused a lot of problems for me in the last couple of days," Saun said, addressing Payvan. She moved her hands down to rest on her hips. "You killed my men time after time, got me in trouble with my boss, and if it weren't for you, I would be able to breathe right now."

The woman smirked and shook her head. "You're the traitor, Saun," she said, voice low. "You're the one who turned your back on everything you know and love, and for what? I know you're sick. I saw your clone, the one whose only purpose in its short, miserable life is to provide you with a new set of lungs. You came here because you thought you could live, but you've had to know all along that you're just going to die. Either we'll kill you for treason, or they will because they don't need you anymore."

Saun wasn't buying it. She knew exactly what Payvan was doing; this was a last-ditch attempt to pit her and Bothum against each other by making him sound like the enemy. He was the one saving her life here. She'd come too far and done too many things she regretted to let anyone tell her otherwise.

"You're wrong," she replied. "They're taking better care of me here than any of you people ever could."

"You and I both know that isn't true," Payvan said, remaining infuriatingly calm. "I never knew you Saun, but it sounds to me like there were a lot of people who trusted you. Think of Aroska. It's clear to me how much he cared about you, and you turned around and broke his heart. Now you're going to kill him."

Saun felt burning tears welling up in her eyes. "*Shouka!*" she screamed, drawing her pistol and taking aim for that mouth that wouldn't shut up. "You don't know anything!"

A sizzling white bolt came out of nowhere, striking the gun and throwing it from Saun's grip. Out of the corner of her eye, she saw Bothum's rifle extended toward her. She lowered her head in submission and shrank away from Payvan, aware that her hands were shaking. Such an emotional outburst had been a mistake. If the lieutenant was right about Bothum's true intentions in any way, behavior like this would cause him to lose faith in her all the more quickly.

Without looking up, Saun could feel penetrating stares coming from both Bothum and Payvan. Each of them was waiting for her to make some form of decision, but the Sardon had the gun, making the choice easy. With a sigh, Saun raked the loose hair from her face and recovered her pistol, though it had probably been rendered useless. "My apologies," she murmured.

· 52 ·

SUBLEVELS
DAKITI MEDICAL RESEARCH CENTER
SARDONIS

Bothum's personal office was neat and uncluttered, and everything in it had a cold, metallic look to it. His desktop was nearly empty, occupied only by his keyboard, comm system, and a deactivated data pad. Information flowed steadily across his transparent viewscreen, though he didn't seem to be paying it any mind. The only wall coverings were a good-sized monitor, no doubt for video conferencing, and a large window behind the desk that looked down over the training floor. Against the far wall were a floor-to-ceiling safe, a shelf with more data pads arranged in alphabetical order, and a small wet bar. The chairs in which Ziva and the governor's corpse were seated made up the rest of the room's furnishings.

The chain on the cuffs was long enough that she could still move her arms a bit, albeit not far enough to grab onto anything or defend herself. Her legs, on the other hand, had been allowed to remain free, an interesting choice on Bothum's part. He needed her alive and well if she was going to undergo this "harvesting" process, so surely he wouldn't actually kill her if she tried anything. However, something told her Saun would be delighted to put her down if she even looked like she was going to move, so she settled for staying still at least until the woman was otherwise occupied.

It was obvious that Ziva had struck a chord somewhere in Saun's mind, judging by the sudden aggression incited by the mention of Aroska's name. This was a broken individual who had been manipulated and brainwashed to the point that she had no perception of how conflicted she even was. She was exactly the type of person Bothum would not hesitate to kill when he had no further use for her.

The two of them stood by the window now, watching a new batch of troops in session and discussing various matters regarding the medical center. Saun had settled down considerably, though she still stole occasional, spiteful glances in Ziva's direction. Ziva couldn't quite bring herself to feel sorry for her. While it was true that there was nothing left for her in this place, convincing her of that would be next to impossible. She *was* most likely going to die, and it would be her own fault.

Keeping an eye on her captors, Ziva fiddled with the chain behind her back, running her fingers over the slats on the chair. While the seat and the armrests were made of some form of metal, the back was fashioned out of a sturdy plastic. With enough force, she would probably be able to shatter it, or at least break the two center slats through which the chain was strung. She turned and checked the distance between herself and the wall. The chair was somewhat bulky and awkward, but with a running start, smashing it against the wall would most likely work. Time was running out, though. The military would be arriving any minute and she still needed to devise some sort of distraction for Saun.

"So tell me, which one of you is paying for the damage to my house?" she called.

Both Bothum and Saun spun around, startled by the sound of her voice. The Sardon stared at her for a moment, processing the strange question, then he smirked, flashing his disgusting yellow teeth. "What are you doing, Payvan?"

"I've got a broken window, a demolished HSP car, and a string of bullet holes up my wall. I'll admit you caught us off guard with that drone. But we dealt with it, just like we dealt with your Sardon dogs, and just like we dealt with the Solaris insurgents." She paused and shrugged. "You've lost every time, Bothum. What's to say you won't lose now? I'm not sure what you think you're trying to accomplish here."

He took a step toward her and crossed his arms. "Oh, Agent Payvan," he said, clicking his tongue. "All of this is to ensure that we will *never* lose again."

"Dane," Saun protested.

"Quiet, Saun!" Bothum roared. In an instant, his rifle was up and he'd fired another shot. Saun dropped to her knees, teeth gritted, clutching her left shoulder.

Ziva tensed, ready to make her move while the woman was down, but the hateful look in Bothum's eyes held her back. His flaring temper made him unpredictable; as long as he was armed, he was a threat. *Come on, come on. Put the gun down.*

The Sardon kept a menacing eye on Saun for a moment before turning his attention back to Ziva. "I'm sure you remember the Fringe War," he began nonchalantly. "You must have only been a child. It was a fine contest between our two civilizations to be sure, but your people prevailed before we could get what we came for."

She scoffed and shook her head. "You can't seriously tell me this is still about the caura extract."

"You left us no choice but to take it by force. When retrieving a lizard ourselves didn't work, we saw no other way to accomplish our goal than to occupy your planet."

"We offered you a contract you refused to agree to. You could have had a sample of the extract for a fair price."

"You're missing the point, Agent Payvan. Such a rare and unobtainable substance is invaluable. Does the power to heal come with a price? If anything, your people should be willing to use that power for the good of the entire galaxy and not just yourselves."

"Don't try to tell me this is for the good of the people, Bothum. You want that extract because you want the money that will come from everyone who travels across the galaxy to get it. You'll have a monopoly over all the other medical centers in the Fringe, shut them down. You'll be at the top of the food chain."

Bothum chuckled. "Now you're getting it. However, while my people are quite capable, yours far outclass us in both size and strength."

"Which is why you kidnapped them and used them in your sick experiments. You created the perfect combination between the two species, but loyal to you to help even the odds."

"You're a smart woman, Agent Payvan," Bothum praised. "We began developing our own cloning technology long before the War even began, and we first incorporated it to replace troops lost during battle. We've been at this for a while, you see, and I can promise you it's going to do more than just 'even the odds' this time. We are currently producing enough troops to eventually match both your military and HSP in numbers, and thanks to Saun here we know exactly what those numbers are. Now you know our little secret, compliments of Jayden Saiffe and his imprudent snooping. You and Tarbic are both going to die though, and that secret will die with you." He strode over to her and leaned down into her space. "And don't worry. We'll find the boy and anyone else who's here with you."

Ziva merely shook her head. "It's not going to work."

Bothum stood back up and took a step backward. "And why exactly is that?"

The timing couldn't have possibly been better. A distant explosion rocked the building, followed by a frantic jumble of transmissions coming through the comm system.

Bothum looked from his desk to Ziva and then to Saun. "Find Atu," he ordered. "Tell me what's going on." Then he added, "Lock the door behind you."

Ziva watched as Saun scrambled to the door, still holding her shoulder, and went out. Two guards were posted directly outside, speaking into their headsets in response to the noise. They would need to be dealt with as well.

Another explosion shook the floor, closer this time. When she looked back up, Bothum was at his desk, trying to make sense of the chaotic voices coming through the speaker. A red indicator light blinked steadily, signifying an incoming message from a communicator outside of the building's system. He pressed the button.

"This is Colonel Kevyn Sheen, Grand Army of Haphez," a man announced. "To whom am I speaking?"

Ziva could read the genuine fear and shock in Bothum's face as he listened. He looked up at her, brows furrowed, then swallowed. "My name is Dane Bothum. I run this facility."

"Mr. Bothum, it has come to my attention that you are unlawfully holding two of our agents in your compound and that you've been responsible for abducting numerous Haphezian military personnel for use in creating an army. In doing so, you are out of compliance with the agreement that was made with your civilization following the Fringe War, giving us the right to retaliate with destructive force. We are, however, willing to negotiate new terms of surrender if you so choose. You have fifteen minutes to let our people out unharmed, but be assured that if you make any form of aggressive advances we will respond accordingly. Now Mr. Bothum, do you understand what I've told you?"

Ziva didn't see Bothum rub his eyes. She didn't see him run his hand over the top of his bald head. What she saw was his arm as he slowly reached over to his desk and set the rifle down. The time was now.

Not giving it any more thought, she leaped up, holding the chair by the arm rests, and hurled herself as hard as she could against the wall. She heard the satisfying sound of plastic cracking, but Bothum had reacted quickly and recovered the rifle. Ziva dove to the floor, taking the chair down with her and using his desk for cover. She gave the cuff chain a good yank, successfully snapping the damaged slats and freeing herself.

As Bothum came around the corner of the desk, she swung her legs at him as hard as she could, sweeping his feet out from under him. He fell beside her and the rifle clattered to the floor by her head. Arms still behind her back, she kicked him hard in the stomach and wriggled toward the weapon, nudging it out of his reach with her shoulder.

Taking a few precious seconds, she folded her legs up and tucked them through the loop created by her arms and the chain. With her hands in front of her at last, she scrambled to her feet just as Bothum did the same. His fists came at her with incredible speed and power, but she deftly ducked around them, keeping her weight forward and her chained hands up. With the cuffs still on, her greatest weapon would be her elbows, and she made good use of them with back-to-back blows to Bothum's face. He responded with a shot of his own and she stepped back to steady herself, catching his next swing with the chain.

"I must admit, Payvan, you had me fooled," Bothum sneered, taking hold of one of her cuffed wrists, "but you're not leaving this place alive."

Ziva set her jaw and lifted their tangled arms up above her head. He was strong, holding her just as tightly as she held him. The cuffs were proving to be a disadvantage, as it took both of her hands to do what he could with one. Bothum leaned forward, pushing her down, down, down, eyeing the elusive rifle as he did so.

Knees only centimeters from the floor, Ziva stopped struggling and dropped suddenly. The change in resistance forced Bothum to take a staggering step and she pulled him down with her, rolling his body over her back and hooking his neck with the chain.

Before he could regain his bearings, she jerked back onto the floor, pulling him by the throat with her knees against his back so his flailing arms could not reach her. Bothum grabbed at the air behind him, swatting at her face with one hand while tugging desperately at the chain with the other. He kicked wildly at anything and everything, dislodging the governor's body from the chair. The limp corpse toppled and fell on top of him.

Ziva looped the remaining chain around each hand and pulled all the harder, looking toward the door as she leaned back out of his reach. It was still locked, but she could hear the guards hollering outside and knew they would eventually get in.

Blood dribbled from Bothum's mouth onto her arms and he sputtered, choking on fluid. He no longer fought with his arms but his boots were still squeaking, leaving black marks on the floor as he searched for traction. Gradually he stopped making noise, and little by little he stopped moving. Ziva didn't let go of the chain until he twitched one final time and his arms sagged to the floor.

Taking a deep breath, she pulled the chain out from where it had embedded itself in his neck and pushed him off. Her own wrists were already sore from her escape from the prison cell, but the cuffs had left them raw and bleeding. With the amount of adrenaline surging through her, she barely noticed the pain as she removed Bothum's sidearm from his holster and rolled away. The instant her back hit the wall, the door opened and the two guards from outside rushed in, looking wildly about for the threat. Ziva dropped them before they even saw her and immediately reached into her boot, selecting the smallest of the three picks. She carefully unlocked the cuffs and removed each bracelet from her mangled wrists.

Taking up Bothum's communicator, she darted for the door and found her stolen supply belt and access key waiting in a chair just outside the office. She secured the belt to her waist and opened a transmission to Adin as she began to run. If she was correct, she had about twelve minutes.

· 53 ·
SUBLEVEL SEWER SYSTEM
DAKITI MEDICAL RESEARCH CENTER
SARDONIS

L ight was visible at the end of the sewer now, filling Zinni with the most relief she'd felt in a long time. Having just rounded a bend, they had perhaps a hundred meters to go before they reached fresh air and freedom. She looked to her right at Jole, Jayden, and Skeet, all of whom were looking ahead with the glimmer of light reflected in their eyes.

"See that, Jole?" she said, feeling a great urge to smile. "We're almost there."

"Quiet, Zinni!" Skeet snapped. His voice possessed the same uneasy tone it had outside the "furnace room," as they had come to call it.

She stopped, momentarily shocked that he would speak to her that way, but then she picked up the sound of voices at the end of the tunnel. She and Jayden backed up against the slimy wall with Jole's frail body supported between them. Skeet moved back into the shadows on the opposite side, rifle raised and ready to fire at anything that moved.

Squinting into the light, Zinni could make out two dark figures leaning against either side of the tunnel entrance. It was difficult to discern what they were wearing, but they were clearly armed.

"Hello!" one of them called, waving his arm. "Friendly! Friendly!"

Zinni heard Skeet shift his weight, unsure whether to proceed. She kept her eyes on the figures. They were watching and waiting as well, unmoving.

"Sergeant Duvo? Officer Vax? Friendly forces!" This time it was spoken in clear Haphezian.

"Here!" she shouted back. The four of them quickly began moving again with Skeet a few steps ahead, his rifle still up.

The two men proceeded into the sewer, followed by three others. Glow sticks were activated, illuminating the tunnel in shades of green, yellow, and orange. The men surrounded them, relieving Zinni and Jayden of Jole and helping them along with gentle hands. "I'm Sergeant Major Anden Fay," said the one who had first spoken. "Ground forces, twenty-second platoon. Are you all right?"

"We're fine," Zinni replied, shrugging him off as they stepped into the gray light outside. It was cloudy and the air was wet and salty, but she paused for a moment and took it in anyway, grateful to be safe and out of the dark.

Fay ordered immediate medical attention for Jole and led them up the bank past four dead Sardons who had no doubt been responsible for guarding this entrance. Zinni studied them for a moment and then turned her eyes to the sky just as three fighters made a flyover mere meters above the top of some nearby trees. At least three flagships were visible at a higher altitude, and several gunships were preparing to touch down in the vicinity. GA ground marines ushered clusters of Sardon prisoners back and forth along the river, and explosions rumbled somewhere on the other side of the compound.

"How many of our people do you reckon they've got in there?" Fay asked, squinting up at Dakiti's enormous structures with his arms folded across his chest.

"Realistically, we may never know," Zinni replied. She found the military tags she'd stashed and handed them over to him. "It's too late for many of them."

"They killed Tantali troops too," Jayden piped up. "Thirty members of the Tantali Royal Guard, executed without question."

Fay swallowed, his face contorted with anger. "If it were up to me, we'd already be in there exterminating them like the animals they are, but Sheen is giving them fifteen minutes to surrender. Far too generous, in my opinion." He stopped and glanced behind Zinni, wide-eyed. "Sergeant Duvo, where are you going?"

Zinni whirled just in time to see several soldiers surround Skeet as he was stepping back into the tunnel with a fresh rifle. "Skeet!" she hollered, sliding down the muddy bank after him.

"I'm going back for Ziva," he said, his features stone cold.

"And I can't let you do that, sir," Fay said, taking a stance between Skeet and the tunnel entrance. "We're going to level this place in less than fifteen minutes and you're not going to be in there when we do. Now, we received word from Lieutenant Woro just before you came out—Payvan contacted him from inside and she's on her way out. She wanted to pass the word along for you to personally oversee the recovery of your H-26s and escort Mr. Saiffe back to Haphez. She also wanted you to know that '*that's an order*'."

Skeet sighed. "Of course she did." He reluctantly relinquished the rifle to one of the soldiers and manipulated his communicator, summoning the Scouts via their onboard computers. "All right, I'm going to need two of your men and a fighter escort, at least until we clear Sardon airspace. Zinni, Jayden, come with me."

SUBLEVELS
DAKITI MEDICAL RESEARCH CENTER
SARDONIS

Z iva didn't even break stride as she downed two guards who had just appeared from around a corner. Thanks to a slip of the tongue on Bothum's part, she had a good idea of where Aroska was. They'd made it quite clear that he had begun his "harvesting prep"—whatever that meant—and that they were going to place her in one of the "other two" rooms when they became available. The first place that came to mind was the bank of three examination rooms they'd come across earlier. *That makes sense, doesn't it?* Was it just wishful thinking? There were hundreds of rooms in this building alone, most of which were exam rooms or something similar. Her mind was racing as fast as her legs were, and she convinced herself she knew what she was doing.

She paused where two hallways converged, attempting to re-gain her bearings. A large squad of approaching guards had already forced her to find a new route, as she didn't have adequate firepower to take them on single-handedly. She once again felt as though she was running in circles through the eternal labyrinth of white corridors and nearly identical rooms.

The formerly quiet building had come alive once the military had arrived. The medical personnel were rushing wildly about, shouting frantically to each other in Sardon. Teams of hybrid soldiers mingled with them, most of whom didn't pay Ziva any mind. She was able to take down the ones who *did* easily enough. Luckily they had more important things to focus on than a single intruder who could be disregarded without too much fuss.

After jogging a little further and studying the numbers on each room she passed, Ziva realized where she was and veered to the right at another intersection. The stairwell where she had been discovered by the probe dropped away from the floor directly ahead. Coming from this direction, the three examination rooms would be on the left this time. She checked the pistol's diminishing plasma charge and hoped she wouldn't run into too many more guards.

She stepped around the corner without hesitation and took aim for one of the three sentries who waited outside the prep rooms. She recognized the other two as part of the group who had captured her only a little over twenty minutes ago. They reacted slowly, distracted by the chaos and noise around them. She shot them both, as well as another security officer who had been hurrying by and had drawn his weapon upon seeing her.

This particular hallway fell silent except for a high-pitched alarm that had begun screeching a few minutes earlier. Ziva could hear the rumble of ships passing overhead as she moved cautiously toward the nearest of the three doors, stepping over the dead guards as she went. The other two had been locked earlier, telling her they were probably the ones that had been occupied. She took the access key from her belt and paused a moment before waving it over the scanner. If Aroska wasn't in here, she had no idea where to go, and there wasn't time to be running all over the building.

He was there—dressed in a new version of Jole's white pants, wrists and ankles clasped to the table, head and chest strapped down. The sensors from the monitor were adhered to his upper body in no particular pattern, and an IV ran from a bag hooked to the machine into his left arm.

The IV and a medical bot that had seen better days were the only things new to the scene, with the exception of the man himself. His boots, clothes, and flight suit were tucked neatly into the corner of the room, ready to be put back to use. The rifle he had arrived with was nowhere to be found.

Ziva fired a round into the bot's face and it toppled over, dropping the dose of whatever drug it was about to administer. She stepped inside and pressed her fingers to Aroska's neck, checking for a pulse. He was alive and breathing slowly, but his jaw was slack and his eyelids were fluttering.

"Aroska," she said, shaking him. She undid the straps from his head and chest. "Tarbic, come on."

She grabbed the IV line and yanked it from his arm, then did the same with the little sensors. The monitor began wailing and flashing red alert messages, so she fired another bolt at it and then tossed the dead pistol aside.

"Come on, Aroska," she said a little louder, shaking him harder. His mouth had moved a bit and his eyes had stopped twitching. He seemed to be growing cognizant, albeit slowly. Too slowly.

Becoming impatient, she slapped him hard in the face. His eyes opened wide and he coughed and sputtered for a moment, blinking. Taking in a deep breath, he groaned and moved his head from side to side until his squinting eyes settled on her.

"Ziva?" he murmured.

"Wake up. We need to get out of here."

Aroska coughed again. "You came back for me?"

"Of course I came back, you idiot," she muttered, going to work on the clasps.

She freed his arms and moved on to his feet. His skin was slick with sweat but was cold and clammy to the touch. It had also taken on a sickly pale gray tone, much like how she had found Jole. His toes wiggled when she touched his feet.

"I don't think I can feel my legs," he said, his voice barely audible.

"Well, you're moving them," Ziva responded, releasing the final clasp. She picked up each of his legs in turn and lifted them over the edge of the table. "Can you sit up?"

He took the hand she offered and hefted himself into a sitting position with her help. His body quivered and his eyelids drooped. Most of his previously-neat hair had come loose from his ponytail and was plastered to the sides of his face with sweat.

Ziva took hold of his head and forced him to look her in the eye. "Look. We have a very limited amount of time to get out of here, and we still have to find Tate."

"Tate?" Aroska repeated, more of an airy sound than actual word.

"He's alive. He and Jole both are, but he won't be much longer if we don't go now."

Aroska said something unintelligible and held her for support as he slid off the table. She put her arm around his shoulders to help him stand up, but his legs immediately gave out and he fell, his weight bringing both of them down against the case of syringes.

She cursed and scrambled to her feet, rushing outside long enough to grab a pistol from one of the dead guards. She readied herself for an onslaught of soldiers, but nobody seemed to have paid their commotion any mind. Aside from distant shouting and the howling alarm, all remained quiet.

She returned to the room and rolled Aroska onto his back, dragging him over to the wall beside his personal effects. He probably weighed a good fifteen kilos more than she did, and his head bobbed limply from side to side as she propped him up. He was in no condition to be going anywhere.

Frustrated, Ziva leaped back across the room and returned to the hallway, catching a panicked doctor by the collar of his jacket just as he ran by. She spun him around and threw him against the wall. "Be quiet and listen to me," she shouted in Sardon, pinning him there with her pistol to his forehead. "I need epinephrine, and you're going to get me some."

He whined something she couldn't understand, so she covered his mouth and leaned down closer. "I've got no reason to kill you unless you give me one. Get me what I need and I'll let you go. Understand?"

Beads of sweat glistened on his forehead and he managed a nod. She released him, keeping the gun aimed for his head, and followed him down the hall. He led her to a small supply room around the corner, one of the many she and Aroska had investigated while searching for Jayden. The shelves were thoroughly stocked with spare equipment and medical apparatus, and an emergency response station, devoid of all its weaponry and gear, was positioned against the near wall. A large cabinet containing more syringes and vials of medication stood before them.

With trembling hands, the Sardon used his access key to unlock the case. He reached in as gingerly as possible and selected a vial from which he then filled one of the empty syringes. He handed it over to Ziva, an uncertain look in his eyes.

"Now get out of here," she ordered, taking it from him. She left him standing there and tore back to the exam room, wondering how much time was left before the building collapsed on top of them. Aroska remained exactly as she'd left him, against the wall, head sagging.

Not wanting to waste any more precious moments than they already had, she immediately dove down to him and jabbed the needle into his chest. The plunger let out a faint squeal as she injected the adrenaline and then tossed the syringe away. "Come on, Tarbic!" she shouted, rubbing the injection site with one hand while shaking him with the other.

Within a few seconds, he sat bolt upright and gasped for air. He glanced around for a moment, disoriented, but upon seeing her he seemed to remember everything that was going on and quickly reached for his boots. "I don't understand," he said tugging them over his bare feet. "How can my team be alive?"

"If we don't get moving, we'll die before we find out," she replied, helping him stand.

Aroska teetered for a moment until he found his balance, then he bent down and took up his shirt and the tool belt from the flight suit, both of which he put on. "Can I assume the military showed up after all?"

Ziva nodded and collected more weapons from the dead guards as they exited the room. "If I've counted correctly, we have about seven minutes to find Tate and get out before we get buried under this place." She handed Aroska a pistol.

They began to run.

· 55 ·
HSP HEADQUARTERS
NORO, HAPHEZ

Emeri Arion stopped pacing the second the transmission came through. In his haste to accept the call, he knocked a small sculpture from his desk. It fell to the floor, shattering upon impact. He swore, bent down to clean it up, decided it could wait, swore again, and finally managed to press the right button.

"Yes!" he answered, nearly shouting.

The voice that came through belonged to Kevyn Sheen. "Director, my men found Sergeant Duvo and Officer Vax, as well as Jayden Saiffe and another HSP agent. They are preparing to return to you per orders from Lieutenant Payvan."

Ziva. Emeri wasn't sure what sort of title she would hold when he was done with her—certainly not lieutenant. "Is she there? Let me talk to her now!"

"She's not here, sir," Sheen replied. "She's still inside."

"Still inside!"

"Lieutenant Tarbic was captured and she's attempting to extract him as we speak. We haven't heard anything since she ordered Duvo and Vax to leave, and we haven't been able to re-establish contact."

Emeri leaned down over his desk and rubbed his face. "Do you have men inside the facility?"

"Yes sir. I'm with a squad inside overseeing the collection of some of our captured troops. We'll be evacuating shortly."

"Keep an eye out for Payvan and Tarbic. If you find them, put them through directly to this office. I want to talk to them *yesterday*."

"Understood, sir," Sheen said. "I'll inform you when we begin the attack."

· 56 ·
SUBLEVELS
DAKITI MEDICAL RESEARCH CENTER
SARDONIS

T he number of people in the hallways had diminished significantly, Aroska observed as he pushed his weak legs to keep up with Ziva. Everyone had either surrendered already or had tried to escape, and all available security personnel had been called to deal with the impending attack. The alarm still blared, grating on his nerves and aggravating the headache he already had.

Ziva seemed to know where she was going. Without a word, she had led him to the next level down and had begun working her way into an older area of the building, judging by the deteriorating condition of the walls and floor. Aroska couldn't fathom that Tate and Jole were still alive, and wondered if he was still somehow sedated and it was all part of a dream. However, the injection site in his chest was a throbbing reminder that Ziva had just saved his life and that if he didn't move fast, all of her work would be crushed as Dakiti fell in a matter of minutes.

The two of them presently came to a set of secure double doors that seemed to lead into a separate wing of the facility. "The holding cells are just up here," Ziva said, breathing hard as she reached to her belt for the access key.

The beep of the scanner and the sound of the doors hissing open were drowned out by the thunder of footsteps and sudden Haphezian shouts behind them. Aroska instinctively raised his arms in surrender and turned to find a squad of angry GA marines arranged in a tight semi-circle around them, fingers only a twitch away from pulling the triggers on their weapons.

"Turn around, hands in the air!" one of them, apparently the man in charge, ordered.

"Friendly! HSP!" Ziva screamed back, hands out in front of her but poised to draw her pistol at a moment's notice. "Don't shoot!"

"Lieutenants Payvan and Tarbic?"

"Yes!"

The man signaled for his men to lower their rifles, which they did immediately. "Colonel Sheen, Grand Army," he introduced. "Are you all right?"

"Never been better," Ziva quipped.

Sheen removed two earpieces from his pocket and handed each of them one. "I have instructions from your director to give you these. It's a direct line to his office. Now, I'm going to have to ask both of you to come with us—we're the last group to evacuate, and we have to leave *now*."

"No," Aroska said. "I'm not leaving without Tate."

Ziva nodded in agreement and turned to continue through the doors, which had been standing open for the duration of the conversation. "There's still time for us to get out, but the longer we stand here, the more we waste."

Sheen's gaze shifted between them for a moment, but he finally sighed and dipped his head in respect. "I'll see if I can buy you a couple of extra minutes. Lieutenant Woro left your ship waiting on the north landing platform."

Aroska waved his thanks and turned to find Ziva already hurrying away. He sprinted after her and caught up just as she made a right turn into a narrower corridor lined with old-fashioned prison cell doors. One of them had been left ajar and she angled for it, pistol ready. She paused for only a split second before pushing it open the rest of the way and rushing inside, quickly concealing herself in the shadows from anyone who might be waiting in the darkness for them to return.

After hearing no gunfire or surprised shouts, Aroska ventured a few steps into the cell. His boots sank a bit into the muck and water on the floor, and when he tried to lift his feet he nearly slipped. The crushing stench of the room almost forced him back out the door, but Ziva's hand beat it to the task.

"I'll get him," she said. "You make sure we don't end up with company."

He obediently returned to the hallway, wondering how much help he could be anyway in his weakened state. As much as he hated the thought of constantly bowing to Ziva's wishes, he felt that in this particular situation they would both benefit if he let her take center stage.

A noise in one of the other cells grabbed his attention and he took several cautious steps toward it. After listening further and hearing nothing else, he disregarded it and turned back around to where heavy footsteps were approaching.

"That was fast," he said, ready to follow Ziva out of the building and to safety.

His body went rigid and his eyes widened. He couldn't even raise his arm to aim his weapon at Saun, who had come up behind him and now stood between him and the open cell door. With a trembling right hand, she extended a pistol toward him; her left arm dangled limply at her side, a nasty plasma wound marring her shoulder. Her face was green and her skin and clothes were soaked through with sweat. She was panting, taking in deep, raspy breaths, and her eyes burned with hatred.

Aroska regained his composure and shifted his weight, however refraining from raising his weapon. Saun wouldn't kill him, not now. The only way she could win now was to give herself up and get out with them, and he would try to help her work out a deal when they got back to Haphez. The choice would have to be hers, though, and judging by her twisted facial expression, convincing her of anything wasn't going to be easy.

"Last chance, Saun," he said flatly.

She gritted her teeth and took in another breath that almost sounded like a growl. This was not the woman he had shared the past three months of his life with. The creature standing before him now was a confused, terrified monster who'd had everything taken away from her by those she thought were her allies. Worse yet, despite the current turn of events, her cold eyes were still looking on him as the enemy when in fact Aroska believed he was the only one left capable of saving her.

"This place was all I had left," she said, almost a whisper, "and you just helped destroy it. You killed me, Aroska, and you're going to die too for what you did to me."

The quivering in her arm stopped when her muscles tensed and Aroska knew she was going to pull the trigger. He raised his pistol to defend himself, or at least he thought he did. His arm was still at his side, suddenly paralyzed by the thought of having to kill this person he cared so dearly for. On the verge of panic, he willed it to move with all of his strength, and it finally sprang into action just as a shot echoed through the hall.

Saun fell, twisting one leg and collapsing onto her back as she hit the floor. Her gun bounced out of her grasp and clattered to a stop several centimeters shy of her hand. Her other hand clutched at the hole in her chest where the scorching plasma round had burned through her body. She lay there gasping, wheezing, writhing slowly.

Aroska shifted his attention to the cell door, where Ziva stood with her smoking pistol still aimed at the woman on the floor. She looked up to meet his gaze, breathing hard and supporting Tate's limp figure with one arm and one knee. The area fell silent except for Saun's rasping as she curled her fingers in a hopeless attempt at reaching her weapon. Blood pooled under her head where her skull had collided with the hard floor.

As he strode over to her, Aroska could feel the first signs of tears creeping into his eyes. However, as he looked down upon her twitching form, the sympathy and regret he'd expected to feel were trumped by anger and disappointment. *Why did you do this?* He shook his head, blinking back the stinging tears, then without another word or thought, he shot her in the head.

Saun's body bucked violently one last time and then went still. Aroska watched her for what seemed like a long time, though it was probably only a few seconds. Some bizarre compulsion urged him to nudge the gun away with his foot; he did so and watched as it slid across the floor. He was vaguely aware of Ziva coming around behind him, but was startled when he felt her hand give his shoulder a firm squeeze.

"We need to go."

· 57 ·
LANDING ZONE
DAKITI MEDICAL RESEARCH CENTER
SARDONIS

T he shuttle's boarding ramp hummed closed and Sheen held on to one of the grab rings as it lifted off the ground. He watched out the viewport as the landing pad where Lieutenant Payvan's ship sat grew smaller and smaller. It had been nearly five minutes since he'd met up with her and Tarbic, and he prayed they hadn't run into any delays. He didn't want to postpone the attack any longer than they needed to, but at the same time, the protector in him felt a great need to wait until he knew they'd made it out.

"Do we know where they are?" Adin Woro asked. He and the other three agents with him watched Sheen expectantly, eager for some good news.

Sheen nodded and braced himself as the shuttle banked and headed toward one of the bigger flagships. "We found them in the second sublevel prison wing," he answered. "They were going back for someone and refused to come out with us, but they should be on their way now."

"Can you delay the attack?"

"We're already running late as it is. I'm afraid we're going to have to proceed and hope they make it. I'll see what we can do about focusing the initial strike on something other than that main structure, at least until we hear from them."

The shuttle docked with the flagship with a hollow *thud*. Sheen exited, along with his squad and the HSP agents, and made his way through the ship to the bridge. The helmsmen and technicians stood when he entered, but he motioned for them to go about their business and went straight to the communications center where the holograms of his subordinate officers awaited instructions. He took a stance on the communication pad and faced them.

"Begin the attack procedure," he sighed.

· 58 ·

Main Level
Dakiti Medical Research Center
Sardonis

"Payvan!" the director screamed through the earpiece, followed by a string of colorful language that made even Ziva flinch. With the noise around her, the sound of her own breathing, and the static over the system, his voice was nothing but angry gibberish. Amid the chaos she caught, "What the hell do you think you're doing?"

Aroska loped along beside her as she carried Tate on her back in the same manner as she'd carried Jole. He was in worse shape than his comrade, if such a thing were possible, and his head and arms bounced and bumped against her as she ran.

"Sir, you have to understand that we came here with the best intentions," Aroska said in response to Emeri's demand.

"I'll handle this," Ziva snapped as the director went off on another rant. They rounded a corner and could see an exit at the end of the hall. "Sir, everything is under control."

"That's not what it sounds like to me!" he shouted. "I'm here trying to explain to the Royal General why some of his best men are following *my* people's lead on an operation that was never authorized by either organization. Are you *trying* to start another war with Sardonis?"

They burst through the doors and found themselves in a small patch of swampy jungle that probably concealed the entrance from the air. A wide path was carved before them, and the landing pad Colonel Sheen had described was visible through the trees a few hundred meters ahead.

"It's a long story, but I think we were on the brink of war anyway and we didn't even know it. I'll explain everything when we get back."

"I'm looking forward to it!"

Something exploded somewhere above them and struck the top of the massive building, telling Ziva the attacks had begun. The blast wave shook the ground, causing her to stumble, but she caught herself and kept running, clutching Tate's legs to keep from dropping his slippery, fragile body. She turned briefly and looked up to where a bright orange fireball billowed from the side of the building. Debris rained down behind them, crashing through the foliage.

From this point, Ziva could see that the landing pad was in fact part of some ancient structure, with only the foundation and six magnificent columns remaining. The *Intrepid* waited for them on the far side, landing ramp already down.

Emeri was hollering again, but Ziva was too busy listening to the droning hum above to pay him any mind. A fighter belonging to one of the GA's airborne squadrons plummeted toward them, billowing with jet-black smoke. It crashed into the trees with a loud crack and fell through, it seemed, just above their heads.

"Go, go!" she shouted at Aroska, pushing him along as best she could while supporting Tate. "Move!"

The fighter struck the ground behind them and erupted in a fiery cloud. Ziva fell forward, throwing the unconscious man from her shoulders as she landed in the mud and wet leaves. Aroska came down several steps ahead of her and rolled, scrambling back to his feet with surprising quickness considering what he'd just been through. He began to run again but pulled up when he realized she wasn't following.

"Ziva?"

She remained where she had fallen, clutching the long chunk of metal shrapnel that had impaled her left leg just below the hip. "Take Tate to the ship," she ordered through clenched teeth.

He came back and dropped to one knee, leaning over her to get a look. "Let me help you," he said, reaching for the piece of metal.

She kicked him away with her good leg. "I said go! I'll be right behind you."

Aroska blinked and hesitantly rose to his feet. He gathered Tate up and stumbled up onto the landing pad, the edge of which was only a few meters away from where she'd fallen. She watched to make sure he obeyed, then turned her attention back to the metal embedded in her leg.

It had entered at such an angle that it hadn't penetrated very deep, but rather had slid in horizontally like a splinter under several layers of skin. With a deep breath, she established a firm grip and pulled. For a moment it seemed to be caught, but ever so slowly it began to ease out, blood dribbling with it. Once it was most of the way out, she gritted her teeth to keep from crying out and gave it a final yank, cringing in response to disgustingly-moist sound it made as it slid free.

Panting and in pain, she managed to get her legs under her and stand, only to be knocked back down when something on the edge of the landing pad erupted in another explosion. She covered her head with her arms as small chunks of stone showered down around her. Aroska lay on the landing pad, having been on his way back across to assist her. For a split second, she was afraid he was either dead or had been knocked out, but then she saw him rub his head.

What she also saw was one of the ivy-adorned columns begin to topple, its shadow crossing directly over where Aroska had fallen—and he was making no effort to move.

Before Ziva knew it, she was running, pumping her legs as fast as the nasty wound would allow. "Tarbic! Get out of the way!"

Even from that distance, she could see his eyes widen as he finally realized what was happening. He flipped onto his side to get up, but it was clear he wasn't going to make it. Within another two strides Ziva was there, diving, sliding across the landing pad on her back. Aroska was almost to his feet. She put her arms up.

Oh please, oh please, oh please.

The gigantic column actually rested in the palms of her hands for a fraction of a second before it shot back up into the air, propelled by a wave of Nostia she'd felt building inside of her for the past several minutes. She struggled against its weight for a moment, using all of her body strength plus all the power she was capable of. The structure quivered unsteadily in the air, rolling and bucking in her invisible grasp before it finally began to float away. As soon as it was out of range, she scooted backward and let it fall. It came down with a monstrous *crack.*

The explosions around her, the ships passing by overhead, even the director's voice in her ear demanding to know what was happening—all of it was drowned out by the sound of Ziva's own heart thumping mercilessly inside her chest. She worked her way into a standing position, feeling weak and drained of energy. Her stomach churned as she turned to find Aroska standing on the ship's boarding ramp, watching her with an expression that read of awe, fear, and anger simultaneously. His mouth hung open, but he held still and remained completely silent.

For a long time they both did. Eyes locked. Heads spinning. The *thump thump thump* was almost deafening in Ziva's ears as she waited for him to show any form of reaction and as she herself tried to process what exactly she had just done.

Aroska ran his tongue over his dry lips, though the rest of his body remained still. "You're a Nosti," he murmured in disbelief.

In that instant, the heartbeat died away and everything around her returned to the front of her mind. She heard Emeri ordering either of them to respond, asking for a repeat of Aroska's last statement. She saw Tarbic still staring at her, confused, one hand to his ear as he listened to the director.

"That's it. Lieutenant Tarbic, arrest her!"

In a flash, both of them had their pistols out and aimed at each other. Ziva stared him down over the barrel, contemplating whether or not to just shoot him on the spot. She thought back to the old man she'd killed in the alley as a teen. It had been necessary; she'd had to make sure he couldn't tell anyone what he'd seen, and she'd taken every precaution since then to make sure no one ever saw her again.

This time was different. This time, Aroska had not only witnessed it, but the director of HSP—a man who was already unhappy with her— had heard about it directly. Killing Aroska would do her no good at this point, Ziva knew, being as half the Haphezian government had probably heard the news by now. She still had the option of taking him out anyway and then making a run for it. HSP had trained her to do exactly that, after all. She knew how to disappear, to be invisible.

An image crept into Ziva's mind as she stood there with her mind racing. She saw herself dangling from the cliff outside her house, nothing but Aroska's hand stopping her from plunging to her death.

That was his choice. He could have just let you fall. You owe him nothing.

She didn't move. *He saved you because he's a good person. He doesn't deserve to die.*

But this is what you do! Pull the damn trigger!

No matter what her brain said, she couldn't make herself put the gun down, nor could she fire it. She did reach up and dig the communicator out of her ear, glad to be rid of Emeri's incessant shouting. She dropped the device on the ground and crushed it under her boot.

He's a threat. Treat him the same way you've treated every other threat in your life. This was the professional killer talking. *Put him down. It's necessary.*

But you know what else was necessary? The Nostia, she realized. Using the Nostia had been necessary. But it hadn't been to save herself like it always was in the past. She'd done it to save someone else—a man who hated her, of all people. *Why would you do that?* Confusion gripped Ziva's mind, rendering her speechless and immobile. It dawned on her that if she hadn't pulled the trigger by now, she probably wasn't going to.

The silence between them was broken when Aroska fired his weapon. Ziva had just enough time to inhale a short breath before the searing plasma bolt struck her in the right knee. Almost by reflex, she transferred all her weight to her left leg—which was only slightly less painful—before she could fall. She saw Aroska's pistol shift slightly as he took aim for her other knee and realized what he was doing. He'd done what he was trained to do, the same thing she'd have done had she been on the opposite end of the situation. She wouldn't be able to outrun him now, and if she wasn't going to kill him then the only option was to surrender.

It was then that Ziva noticed she'd been holding her breath. She exhaled everything at once, and the decrease in pressure allowed her to drop her arm. Her blood felt like it was boiling under her skin, and her eyes and nose began to sting. Maintaining eye contact with Aroska, she threw her pistol aside and slowly dropped to the ground, keeping all of her weight on her good knee. She lowered herself onto her stomach and interlocked her fingers behind her head. Then she waited.

It seemed like a lifetime before Aroska moved down the ramp and took hold of one of her arms. She stood up as best she could on her own, though both of her legs were in so much pain that she allowed him to do most of the work. His movements were stiff, unsteady, telling her he was entirely uncomfortable with what he was doing. She let him shove her back into the ship without fuss, and he led her into the cargo hold and sat her down on the single bunk amid several supply boxes.

"I think it will be better for both of us if you don't say anything," Aroska muttered. He began rummaging through the boxes.

Ziva didn't look at him as he put a pair of cuffs over her wrist and fixed her to the bunk's metal frame. She thought of the picks that were still tucked into her boot, but there was really no point in using them. The only alternative was to lie down and be quiet. Fire shot through both of her legs, burning so fiercely that her entire lower half felt like it was going numb.

Aroska watched her a bit longer as if unsure whether she was going to stay put. He took in deep, hissing breaths through his noise, and when he finally cleared his throat it sounded like he might cry. He turned and stormed away into the cockpit.

The ship's engines roared to life and the ground shook as the explosions grew nearer. Ziva closed her eyes as she felt them began to lift away from the landing pad, part of her hoping they'd get shot down and the other part arguing that Aroska was doing exactly what she would do and there was still no reason for him to die. Seconds passed and they didn't get hit. Minutes passed and the sounds of the battle began to die away. When the ship eventually lurched forward at FTL speed, Ziva knew there was no turning back. She settled down and let her mind go blank.

· 59 ·
HSP HEADQUARTERS
NORO, HAPHEZ

The early morning sun cast a warm glow over the city, bathing the rooftops in pale yellow light and glinting off of the thousands of aircars that passed by HSP headquarters. A rectangular shaft of light, interrupted by Aroska's elongated shadow, penetrated the director's dark, cold office.

He squinted against the sun, looking at nothing in particular, and thought. That's what he'd spent the last day and a half doing—pondering, considering, mulling things over. Several times he'd thought there was nothing left to think about, but try as he might, he hadn't been able to stop. He'd thought the whole way home from Sardonis. He'd thought for the entire day he'd been held under observation at the med center. Now here he was again, thinking. His mind was exhausted, his body was exhausted, and he was ready to get this over with.

When the door opened and the lights flickered on, Aroska turned to find the director standing there, hand still hovering over the door controls. "Lieutenant," he said when he realized who was intruding in his office. He went to his desk and set down the data pads he'd been carrying. "They told me you wanted to see me first thing this morning, but I guess I wasn't expecting you quite this early. Shouldn't you still be at the med center?"

"I just had to ask the nurses nicely and they let me go," Aroska replied with a sheepish chuckle, immediately regretting it. What was he talking about? He was starting to lose focus, and he needed to hold himself together for a few more minutes, at least until he had accomplished what he had come to do. Emeri watched him with one eyebrow raised, so he added, "I'm fine. Any word on Tate and Jole?"

The director brought up the agents' information at his terminal. "They're both still at the Severe Cases Center in Haphor. From what they've seen so far, Sergeant Imetsi is already showing great signs of improvement and is expected to make a decent recovery. As for Agent Luver, we know he's going to live but the extent of his recovery is unclear at this point. He's in pretty bad shape, Lieutenant."

This he knew—after all, he'd helped rescue the man and even carried him part way. He was nothing but skin and bones, in the most literal sense of the phrase. "Do we know how either of them could still be alive in the first place?"

Emeri brought up several photos on the screen; Aroska immediately recognized the location as the explosion site where Tate and Jole had been presumed dead. "As soon as we received word that you found them, I sent a team out to take another look at ground zero. As it turns out, there was something there that we had originally overlooked being as we never thought they could have possibly survived. That particular building was a crucial hub for intel during the Fringe War and even before your time. It had an ingenious system of tunnels and passages running both through it and under it. It's possible that Solaris could have infiltrated the building while you were outside and smuggled them out through one of the tunnels. They knew that explosion would be enough to make everyone think your team was just vaporized along with that entire half of the structure."

"Saun was no doubt behind it," Aroska admitted. The thought of having ever trusted her made him want to kill himself.

Emeri gave him an understanding nod but said nothing. The entire office remained silent for several long seconds, making Aroska fidget. He looked down at his feet to stop his mind from wandering again.

The director opened the secure drawer of his desk and removed an antique bottle of some aged exotic liquor, then proceeded to pour himself a glass—odd for this time of day, Aroska noted. He obviously knew something was up.

"I know you're concerned about your team, Lieutenant," the man said, staring at the glass he'd just poured, "but something tells me that's not the reason you're here."

"You can't execute Ziva," Aroska said quickly. There. He'd said it.

Emeri lifted the drink to his lips, smelled it, then set it back down on the desk with a soft smile and a wag of his head. "And why is that?"

"Because she saved my life."

This time he actually took a sip from the glass. "Is that the best you've got?"

"She saved me twice—three times! She saved both Tate and Jole. Without her, Jayden and the rest of us would probably be dead and you know it."

"The GA saved *all* of you and *you* know it."

"That's not true!" Aroska exclaimed, slamming his palms down on the director's desk.

"Why are you suddenly defending her?"

"Why *aren't* you? You've said it yourself: she's the best agent in the history of this organization. You're never going to be able to replace her, do you understand? She's your best weapon and you're ready to just throw her away like a piece of garbage."

"She made a mistake," Emeri replied coldly.

"A mistake that didn't hurt anybody! A mistake that *protected* me from getting hurt! She knew she was putting her life on the line, but it was the only way she was going to save me and she chose to do it anyway."

"You're missing the point. I don't care what she meant by it—she broke a law punishable by death, and I'm not going to make any exceptions to that penalty, not even for Ziva. She knew the consequences, and she did it anyway."

Aroska sighed and rubbed a hand over his tired eyes. "Exactly."

Emeri downed the rest of his drink and glanced at the bottle as if he wanted more, but instead he put it back in the drawer. Aroska could tell the wheels were starting to turn inside his head, albeit slowly. "I don't know what you want me to do."

"How many people have you told?"

The director leaned over his desk, staring down at his hands, and didn't reply.

Aroska bent down to a closer proximity and asked again. "Who have you told?"

Emeri looked up at him and made eye contact from under his furrowed, gray eyebrows. "No one," he admitted gruffly. "If we go public with the story, the Federation will be out here running a witch hunt in a heartbeat. And the last thing we need around here is a bunch of people thinking they can recreate that sorcery just because Ziva did it."

Aroska blinked. "You haven't said anything?"

"All the government and the rest of the agency know is that she's scheduled for execution due to a severe—and highly classified—violation of agency protocol."

"That's it then! Just drop the charges and nobody will ever know."

Now the director took a seat and rubbed his face with his hands, which he then folded in front of his mouth with his elbows resting on the desktop. "A week ago, you stood right here ready to kill Ziva because of what she did to your brother. Now you're asking me to spare her. How much sense does that make?"

"Things have changed," Aroska replied. "I may not agree with how she operates, and I may not be happy that she killed Soren, but I learned some things during my time with her. She's done—and still *does*—some horrible things, but what she did on that landing pad wasn't one of them."

The director remained silent, hands still folded in front of his face. The golden sunlight reflected off of his eyes when he turned and looked out the window.

Aroska stepped back and crossed his arms, also stealing a glance out the window. "I felt like I at least needed to plead her case," he said quietly. "I owe her that much."

Emeri hung his head and ran his hands over his face again, letting them linger in his silvery-gray hair for a moment before bringing them down hard against the desk. "I've placed Ziva under house arrest until her execution this evening," he said, taking an empty data pad from a drawer and connecting it to his terminal. "It didn't make much sense to let her wander free until then—nobody would ever be able to catch her again. There are three squads of agents posted outside her home to make sure she doesn't try to leave, and all vehicles registered to that household have been confiscated."

Aroska's heart skipped a beat as he realized what the director was doing, but he said nothing as he watched the official pardon document transfer from the computer to the data pad.

"Show this to them and they will be relieved of their posts," Emeri explained, sliding the pad across the desk but maintaining a grip on it when Aroska reached hesitantly for it. "Lieutenant?"

A beat.

"No one is to ever know the truth, understood? Not Sergeant Duvo, not Officer Vax, not even the king himself. *No one.* I want you to forget why this ever happened. Now get out of here before I regret doing this."

It was difficult for Aroska to suppress a smile as he took up the data pad and nodded his respectful thanks. "Understood, sir."

He turned and walked out, feeling as though a massive burden had just been lifted from his shoulders—which it had.

· 60 ·
PAYVAN RESIDENCE
NORO, HAPHEZ

T he guards had been outside all night and the full previous day, pacing, speaking into their communicators in low voices, jumping to attention every time a door or window opened. So far though, they hadn't intruded except for a couple of routine checks inside the house. Sometimes they could be heard laughing and joking among themselves, a brief escape from the tedium of standing outside all day, but they had remained quiet for the most part.

When Marshay had responded to the gentle knock on the door and the single chime of the bell, she had expected to find one of the agents requesting another run-through of the house. At first, she'd been grateful they'd learned to quit pounding and be more polite, but the thought had occurred to her that something was different just as she'd opened the door.

Now, as she looked up into Aroska Tarbic's warm amber eyes, she realized she no longer heard the sounds of the agents outside. She stared past him and caught sight of the HSP cars just as they disappeared back into the city. It was clear their departure was directly related to Aroska's presence, but she wasn't sure how.

The lieutenant was a charming young man with a kind heart, excellent work ethic, and good intentions—Marshay had been able to tell all of this almost immediately upon meeting him several nights earlier. He was tall, strong, and handsome, the kind of man she would allow to court her daughter if she had one. However, Ziva, who was close enough to being a daughter, was scheduled for execution in less than twelve hours and this was the man responsible for it. No matter how much Marshay had liked him before, he was certainly not welcome now.

"What do you want?" she demanded, placing her hands on her wide hips and glaring up at him through narrowed violet eyes.

"Marshay, please," he said. His tone and posture were calm, almost apologetic. "I need to come in."

She put her thick arm across the doorway, blocking his entrance—not that it would do much good if he really tried to get in. "Not a chance. Do you know how much trouble and pain you have caused this house in the last two days?"

"Please Marshay!" Aroska repeated, more desperate this time. "I know, and I'm sorry for everything, but you need to let me in. I have to talk to Ziva right now."

"She's not here! Do you really think she's dumb enough to stick around just waiting to die? A few guards aren't going to stop her from going anywhere. She's long gone by now."

Marshay watched carefully to see how he might respond to that news. Her words had floored him; he stood motionless, eyes unblinking, mouth slightly open. Even if he had something else to say, the ability to speak eluded him. His knuckles were white as he clutched a small data pad in one hand. He uttered a small sound reminiscent of the word "no."

Satisfied by his reaction, Marshay felt herself relax. The arm that blocked the door slid back to her side and her other hand settled over her heart. She studied him for a moment, trying to see into his mind, figure out exactly what he was thinking. "Lieutenant, what's going on?" she asked warily.

The sound of her voice snapped him out of his dazed stupor and he looked down at the deactivated data pad. "So she's gone?"

Marshay neither confirmed nor denied.

"I needed to give her this," Aroska said, handing over the pad. The disappointment and dread were apparent in his face.

She took it from him, activated the holographic screen, and read over the first part of the document that came up. What she saw made her gasp. The document was an official pardon, authorized by Director Emeri Arion himself. Ziva was listed as the recipient.

Marshay looked back up at Aroska, who watched her hopefully with a remorseful look in his eyes. For a moment she thought she might cry, but she swallowed back the knot in her throat and stepped aside, inviting him in.

"You did this?" she asked as he came in and stood quietly in the living room.

The lieutenant nodded. "I did some careful thinking," he said, hands folded behind his back. "A very wise man told me Ziva is always right, even when I think she's wrong." He forced a short chuckle. "I realized *he* was right. I'm the one who's been wrong all along."

Marshay smiled. She'd heard Skeet explain that to many people, all of whom had eventually understood the merit of his words. In fact, she was one of them.

Aroska looked back at her. "Please, Marshay. If you have any way of contacting her, I need to know."

She sighed and took him by the arm. "Follow me."

·61·
PAYVAN RESIDENCE
NORO, HAPHEZ

Z iva listened to the conversation unfold from a place that had come to be known as "The Loft" over the years. It could most accurately be described as a storage space built into the support beams of her bedroom ceiling, but it was virtually invisible to someone who didn't know it was there and it wasn't used for simple storage anymore. Upon moving back into this house eight years before, Ziva had converted it into the ultimate hideout, complete with food, clothes, weapons, and any other survival necessities that would allow for a quick escape or enable her to hide there for up to several days. She'd spent the entire morning pacing back and forth across her room, but had climbed up into The Loft for a better vantage point when she'd heard Aroska's voice.

Aroska. The man was a fool for returning. She'd thought long and hard about their confrontation on the landing pad and now wished she would have simply shot him in the head when she'd had the chance. She had an escape plan in the works, but she'd also had a feeling he would come. It was the only reason she'd stayed put until now. She was ready for another shot, in every sense of the word.

At the moment she could hear him begging Marshay to let him inside. She turned and selected a suppressed projectile pistol from the meager weapons cache she kept in The Loft. If he even took one step into the house, she'd kill him.

She walked noiselessly over to the ventilation duct that allowed air to flow between the hidden room and the kitchen. Through the metal slats she could see Marshay standing at the front door holding what appeared to be a data pad, talking to Tarbic who remained outside and out of sight. What caught her attention was the housekeeper's facial expression, which read of suspicion and shock. When she stepped out the way to allow Aroska to come inside, Ziva gripped her pistol so tightly her whole hand turned white. She refrained from giving herself away just yet however, curious as to the reason behind Marshay's actions. She watched as Aroska came to a standstill beside the sofa, waiting to see what the housekeeper would say next.

"You did this?" the woman asked quietly, still staring at the data pad in disbelief.

Tarbic nodded in the affirmative and proceeded to go off on a spiel about realizing he was wrong, no doubt something he'd heard from Skeet. Ziva's inner leader and teammate urged her to listen to him and give him another chance. But the operative and killer were there too, warning her it was just another revenge trip, one last chance for Aroska to get close enough to finish her off himself.

When Marshay placed a hand on his arm and began leading him into the hallway, Ziva wound herself up even tighter, if it were possible. She moved back to the edge of The Loft where she had a clear view down to her bedroom floor four meters below. Her door was still shut, but they'd kept it unlocked to allow the agents to come and go without question.

The door slid open with a hiss and Aroska stepped into the room, holding the data pad Marshay had been looking at. He took several hesitant steps forward and stopped, taking a moment to look around. The room was large, bigger than the entire apartment Ziva and her team lived in while working on Aubin. Her bed and wardrobe, along with an ancient keyboard instrument that had been in the house since she was little, rested on a mezzanine two steps above the level of the rest of the room. The remainder of the room was occupied by her personal computers and communications grid, disassembled weapons and machinery, and not much else. Knick-knacks and mementos held little value for her—they only caused clutter and informed others of what she cared about, two things she did not want.

Aroska stood, taking all of it in, but made no move to search further or touch anything. He swung his head in a slow arc, probably listening more than looking. Thanks to Marshay, he knew she was there somewhere. "Ziva?" he said quietly.

Ziva remained motionless. If he happened to look up in exactly the right place, he might see her. But he didn't look up—his focus remained on the data pad. He was waiting for her to make the first move, letting things fall into place on her terms. Ziva was suddenly greatly curious as to what was so special about that data pad.

Aroska took one last look across the room and then turned to leave. As soon as he cleared the doorway, she let herself down from her hiding place, hanging from a beam for a moment before dropping silently to the floor on sore legs. She raised the pistol to the back of his head, but lowered her arm again just as he turned around, having sensed movement behind him.

They watched each other with unblinking eyes for what seemed like a long time. Tarbic didn't go for his weapon, and Ziva didn't remove hers from her side. She waited, muscles tense, for him to give her some explanation as to what was going on.

He finally stepped back into the room and shut the door behind him, moving over to place a foot on the bottom step up to the mezzanine. He didn't look around, didn't try to figure out where she had been; he kept his eyes glued to her until he stopped moving.

"You look like hell," he said.

She felt like it. She'd been awake since they'd left Sardonis, only worsening her state of exhaustion. She hadn't had much of an opportunity to clean up, either. There was still unidentifiable gunk on her skin and in her hair from her brief imprisonment. She sported a black eye from the fight with Bothum, and a good portion of her body was covered in other cuts and bruises. She'd managed to at least change clothes and apply caura treatment to her legs and lacerated wrists. Still, her whole body ached, her head throbbed, and she wanted nothing more than to go to sleep for about three days straight.

Aroska glanced down at the data pad and shifted his feet, clearly uncomfortable. "You know you have a very beautiful home. I meant to say something the other night. Marshay and Ryon seem great...." His voice trailed off.

Ziva set her face in stone, refusing to give him any clues as to the hundreds of thoughts spinning inside her head. Her finger remained poised over the trigger guard on her pistol, still itching to put a round through his forehead.

"But I suppose it's obvious that I'm not here to compliment you on your house," he continued after several awkward seconds of silence, forcing a bit of a nervous chuckle. More silence followed, and he finally took several stiff strides forward, set the data pad on the desk nearest Ziva, then retreated back to the steps.

Ziva took her eyes off of him long enough to look down at the small screen and take in the first few lines of text. After overhearing the conversation in the living room, she'd had a general idea of what it was, but she couldn't begin to understand the reason for it. She looked back up at him, her gaze drilling straight through him, probing his mind, testing his motives.

"Ziva Jai Payvan, you're free to go."

While that much was clear, he still wasn't giving her a sufficient explanation as to what force in the galaxy had caused the director to change his mind. A certain relief was fighting its way into her, but she refused to let it overtake her until she was completely certain this wasn't just an act on Aroska's part. She didn't believe he was lying to her, but then, she wasn't exactly sure *what* to believe after he'd turned her in for saving his miserable life. *Some thanks that was.*

"I talked to Emeri early this morning and convinced him to drop the charges. Lucky for you, he never told anyone because he was afraid more Nosti might show up and it would attract the Federation. As of this moment, the three of us are the only ones who know the truth. A story has been leaked to the public that there was a great misunderstanding and you were falsely accused of breaching protocol. Nobody knows I was involved." Aroska paused, watching her, arms folded across his chest. After another period of silence, he turned toward the door. "I just thought I'd let you know in person."

"Why'd you do it?"

The sound of her own voice startled Ziva as much as it startled Aroska. He whirled, having only made it a step or two from where he'd just been standing, and stared. She waited for an answer, significantly loosening the grip on her gun.

Aroska straightened and cleared his throat. "When you can trust your sworn enemy more than the woman you thought was your closest friend, it really puts things into perspective. I'll give it to you straight: you're not the person I thought you were. I'm honestly not sure if I'll ever be able to forgive you for killing Soren, but it hasn't been as easy to hate you as I thought it would be. You risk everything on a day-to-day basis, and for what? Jole and Tate are never going to be one hundred percent again, but you put your own life on the line to get both of them out. You came back for me when you could have just let me die—would have solved all your problems, right? To top it off, you trusted me enough to share your secret, and I turned my back on you."

Ziva wasn't sure if "trust" and "sharing her secret" had even been part of her thought process at the time. Using her Nostia to move the column had been more of a simple reflex than anything else. But she was glad Aroska was acknowledging the fact that she'd risked her life for nothing.

He sighed and raked his hand back over his hair, which was neatly pulled back into the short ponytail he'd worn before his capture. "You've got a heart, whether you want to admit it or not, and you don't deserve to die after everything you've done these past few days. That's why I did it—I'm giving you a second chance because you gave me one. It's the very least I could do."

For a while as she watched him stand there, breathless, Ziva wasn't sure if he was done. She saw his next words pile up on his tongue, but he shut his mouth before they could come out. He finally glanced away, his face red with embarrassment.

His little speech had successfully shut her down and she slowly set the pistol down beside the data pad. She raised her eyebrows and leaned back against the edge of the desk, arms crossed. "I'm not sure if I know what to say."

"A simple 'thank you' would suffice," he replied.

She shook her head and scoffed. "That wouldn't even begin to cover it."

"Say thank you and we'll call it even. I pulled you up off the cliff and bailed you out of this, and you got me out of Dakiti and kept that pillar from crushing my sorry ass."

The incident on the cliff seemed like a lifetime ago, but she could picture it perfectly as the memory flashed through her mind again. She smirked. "I believe you still owe me one for taking Saun out before she could blow your head off. However, under the current circumstances, we *can* call it even." She rose to a standing position and placed her hands on her hips with a slight tip of her head. "Thank you, Lieutenant, for everything."

Aroska beamed and moved toward her, closing the gap between them to less than a meter. "Let's start over, shall we?" He offered his hand. "Hello, Lieutenant Payvan. My name is Aroska Tarbic, and I think I'd like to be your friend."

She returned the handshake and crossed her arms again. "What would you think of a permanent position in special ops?"

He stared, dumbfounded, and stammered for a moment. "Is that okay with you? What would the director have to say about it?"

"That's not what I asked."

He thought for a few more seconds, then shook his head. "Honestly, I don't feel it's my place. If you don't mind, I think I'll stay and oversee the disbandment of Solaris, then we'll see where things go from there."

Ziva gave him a respectful nod. "I understand. Let me know if there's anything that Skeet, Zinni, or I can do to help."

She limped through the door and led him out into the living room, the first time she'd left her bedroom in almost two days. Marshay was busy in the kitchen but politely vanished to give the two of them some privacy. They stopped at the front door and Ziva let it stand open, smelling the cool mid-morning air.

"You hungry?" Aroska asked, pausing with one foot inside and the other out on the front step. "We could go get something to eat, maybe grab a drink, talk things over. I'm buying."

Ziva felt her stomach growling even as she shook her head. She stepped forward, forcing him the rest of the way out the door. "I think you've caused enough trouble for now. However, I might take you up on that some other time."

Aroska shrugged and turned to leave, but spun back around quickly as if overcome by a sudden thought. "You don't have one of those retractable swords, do you?"

Ziva couldn't help but smirk as she reached for the door controls. "Goodbye, Aroska."

The door slid shut.

DAKITI

SPECIAL THANKS...

...to Phil and Nick – without you guys, this story and these characters might never have existed.

...to Tanni, for putting up with my procrastination and providing such wonderful feedback over the past couple of years. Your support has been invaluable.

...to Nola, Amanda, and Jameson, for being fantastic beta readers. Never underestimate the value of a few extra sets of eyes.

...to the rest of my family and friends who have listened to my brainstorming rants, acted as a human thesaurus, referred me to a resource, and helped me out in any other ways. The little things do count and your contributions and support mean a lot.

The craft ricocheted off of an enormous tree branch, throwing her into the back seat. They were descending head first at one moment, but the next collision with a tree flipped the aircar onto its side and propelled it off in a new direction. Before Ziva knew it, they were upside down—her head snapped back as she hit the car's ceiling. Indicator lights sparkled throughout the vehicle and emergency alarms wailed as branches tore at the exterior and ripped through the windshield. Dizzy and disoriented, she braced her arms and legs against the wall just as the craft finally met the ground.

Upon impact, her body bounced against the ceiling with a dull *thump*. She lay there for several long seconds with her head pounding, listening to the gentle creaking in the car's frame and the alarms that had all morphed into a single multi-toned screech. She blinked several times as her vision began to right itself and wiped away a trickle of blood that oozed toward her eye. Her neck ached as she twisted her head to look out the window, but she found that it was so cracked and plastered with mud that her view of anything outside was completely obscured.

Coughing, she worked her body around to face the front of the battered craft. She could feel more blood seeping into her hair thanks to a cut somewhere on her scalp, and a pounding ache rendered her left shoulder and elbow numb. In the grand scheme of things, she remained relatively unscathed, and after testing the mobility of her legs, she was reasonably sure she could walk or even run. By the looks of it, however, the other two passengers hadn't been so lucky. She wormed her way between the two front seats to get a better look.

The pilot was crumpled against the ground, his full body weight bearing down on a neck that was quite obviously broken. She checked for a pulse anyway, and, finding none, turned her attention to Spence. The other agent was in a similar position, though further on his side.

He stared out through the open space where the windshield had been, eyes frantic, taking in raspy breaths through the bloody saliva that filled his mouth. His chest was stained a dark crimson where a long shard of glass had embedded itself in his flesh.

She eased herself back into the back seat, this time facing the opposite direction, and began to deliver powerful kicks to one of the windows. Pain pulsed through her ankle as her foot broke through, separating the entire pane of reinforced glass from the frame of the car. Cool, clean air rushed in and she gladly accepted it, allowing herself the luxury of a couple deep breaths before wriggling out into the leaves and mud.

It was no longer raining, but a damp mist rose from the drenched earth and underbrush. She couldn't see anyone around, but she could hear the occasional vehicle pass by on the service road a short distance away. The crash had carried them far enough that they were safely out of sight of anyone traveling by, but she doubted it would take long for someone to come looking for them. A good chunk of their fifteen minutes had already been spent, and who knew what sort of distress signal could have been automatically sent out during the crash.

Ziva worked her way to her feet and staggered around to the front of the aircar, forcing her sore ankle to bear her body weight. She knelt down and examined the windshield. It was almost entirely broken out, and she could see Spence inside; he appeared to be watching her, but his eyes were out of focus.

"Hang in there," she said, wondering if he was even coherent enough to hear her. She got down on her stomach and crawled under the nose of the craft that jutted out over the windshield frame, clearing as much of the broken glass out of the way as possible. Her head and shoulders entered the vehicle, and she pulled her arms along until they were in front of her.

She gritted her teeth against the pain in her shoulder as she reached in and slid her hands under Spence's arms. Digging into the mud with her knees and feet, she began to tug him out centimeter by centimeter. He squeezed his eyes shut and assisted her by pushing against the seat with his legs.

Once the upper half of his body had cleared the window, she slid out from under the nose and regained her footing, then pulled Spence the rest of the way out from a standing position. She dragged him across the ground and propped him up against a nearby tree where she took a moment to survey his wounds. The shard of glass had by far caused the most damage, but it appeared he would remain stable at least until someone found him.

He stared up at her, struggling to focus, and clutched at his chest with an unsteady hand. He closed his other one around her forearm. "Y-y-you..."

Ziva pried his fingers off and placed his hand firmly in his lap. "Hold on, agent," she said, rising. "Just hold on, and know that I didn't do whatever they said I did."

She paused for a moment and listened as a flood of garbled transmissions came through on the aircar's damaged comm system. Someone somewhere had no doubt seen the craft go down and reported it, or worse yet, they'd been picked up on HSP's scanners and a squad of agents was already closing in.

Taking one last look around, Ziva stooped down and gathered up Spence's pistol and communicator. She tucked the gun into her pants at the small of her back and jogged over to the bushes on the edge of the service road, chucking the comm unit into the back of a shipping rig as it rattled by. Hoping the mobile comm signal might distract the agency for at least a few minutes, she moved back into the trees and took off as fast as she could back in the direction of Noro.

Like what you read? Tell someone about it!
Taking the time to leave an honest review is immeasurably helpful
for any author, new or established. Your opinion helps other
people make informed decisions about their reading options and
allows the book to reach its target audience.

Your ratings and reviews are greatly appreciated!

ABOUT THE AUTHOR

EJ Fisch is a long-time fan of the science fiction genre. She'll readily admit that she has a vivid imagination, which can be both a blessing and a curse. She has been writing as a hobby since junior high and began publishing in the spring of 2014.

When she's not busy writing, she enjoys listening to music, working on concept art, gaming, and spending time with her animals. She currently resides in southern Oregon with her family.

Dakiti is her first novel.

Find EJ Fisch on your favorite social media site!

Keep up with news, catch sneak peeks, and more at:
www.ejfisch.com

Questions? Comments? Use the resources above or email at:
ej@ejfisch.com

Your thoughts about the characters and storylines are always welcome and appreciated!

CPSIA information can be obtained
at www.ICGtesting.com
Printed in the USA
LVHW092210021219
639228LV00003B/973/P

9 780692 230954